CEDAR POINT

SHAUN MCGREGOR

In Memory of Tina Davidson.

April 1 1957

March 26 1973

"Cedar Point"

"Growing Cold" Book 1.

First published October 2024 by Shaun McGregor.
Second Edition December 2024
Copyright 2024 © by Shaun McGregor.
The right of Shaun McGregor to be identified as the Author of the Work has been asserted by him in accordance with the Copyright, Designs and Patents Act 1988.

Proofread by Joshua Pfleger and Carrie McGregor.

Authors Note

"A huge thank you to my family, who has been there through my best times and through my worst times. Thank you to all the people who purchased this book and read it when I had no business writing a book. Thank you to everyone who purchased the first Edition, which was full of errors. You could have demanded a refund but instead you gave me praise and encouragement. Thank you to the people who listened to my podcast when I had no business investigating anything, let alone an unsolved murder and making a podcast out of it. Not only did you listen, but you shared it. It turned a young girl's murder that had been mostly forgotten into something that people talked about around the world. I still hold out hope that one day it will be solved. Thank you to everyone who supported my dream of becoming a Private Investigator. It wasn't easy, but it was fun. Most importantly, thank you Quinn and Asher, my beautiful children. Everything I do is for both of you. Dad loves you."

-Shaun McGregor

CHAPTER 1

"The Mannequin"

The leaves dance across the sidewalk. Orange, red, and yellow figures twirl among the stray strands of toilet paper, skirting over the broken eggshells. Judging by the carnage on this street alone, the kids in town enjoyed themselves on Devil's Night last night.

"Hopefully, this garbage gets cleaned up before trick or treating tonight," Nancy Peters said to her grandson, Jake, as she pushed him along in his stroller. He just cooed as babies do. She had lived in Cedar Point for all 64 years of her life and the night before Halloween was always the same. The local teenagers run amok and terrorize the entire town. They dress all in black, buy up all the eggs and toilet paper from the Harvest Market, and then go and vandalize everything. Windshields pelted with eggs. Tree branches wrapped with toilet paper. Paper bags filled with dog feces set on fire on doormats. It was criminal, and she wished the sheriff would do something about it.

She had to zig-zag the stroller to avoid getting egg or toilet paper stuck to the wheels. She was hopeful that the punk teenagers at least left the playground alone so she could spend some quality time with her grandson.

It was still early, and the sun barely peeked above Mount Hood in the distance. She turned left onto 17th St and into Davidson Memorial Park. She could see Halloween decorations thrown onto the wood chips at the playground. Pieces of pumpkins littered the grass surrounding the play area, and plastic skeletons hung from the swing set.

Over on the slide, she saw a white shape towards the end. Her eyes grew into angry slits as she saw a human form lying on it with the legs splayed openly. How rude of someone to take a mannequin, strip the clothes off, and pose it in such an obscene manner that children could see it. What a terrible prank.

She pulled her scarf tight as she got closer and felt a chill run down her spine. She would lay the mannequin in a decent position off to the side of the park and cover it with some sticks. Then, when she got home, she would phone the sheriff and have him dispose of it. At least that way, no children would see it if they came to play at the park today.

As she got closer, she stopped and noticed blood- all the blood. There was brown rust color streaked and splattered all over the playground, covering the slide and wood chips underneath. What she thought was a mannequin was the nude body of a young girl. Her pale skin had what must have been almost one hundred stab wounds. Her brown eyes stared blankly up at Nancy.

In shock and panic, she almost ran off without taking her grandson, who was bundled up, warm and happy in his stroller. She stopped, spun him around, and ran off towards the sheriff's office not caring this time if she ran over eggshells or toilet paper. She saw a cruiser driving up as she approached the sheriff's office and frantically waved her arms while screaming for him to stop. The deputy rolled down his window as he pulled up alongside the hysterical woman.

"Help! There is a girl! At the park. On the slide. I think she's dead!"

The deputy instructed Nancy to wait where she was, and he drove off down to Davidson Memorial Park. She was far too scared to go back there anyway. Nancy scooped Jake from his stroller and hugged him close. She would never go back down 17th Street again and never go to another park again as long as she lived.

When the deputy approached the gruesome scene, he didn't bother to check for a pulse or any signs of life. Based upon the number of stab wounds around the neck and chest area, the blood, and the state of the pale, stiff, nude body in this cold northwestern climate, it was apparent that the girl was no longer living. He returned to his cruiser and grabbed his radio.

"sheriff, you're gonna wanna get down to Davidson Memorial Park, pronto!"

The sheriff's gruff voice crackled across the radio a few seconds later.

"What do you want Dougie? I'm still drinking my coffee."

"There's a girl down here, George. It looks like she's been stabbed to death. Damn near cut her head off. Sweet Jesus there's so much blood!"

Within minutes, the sheriff had arrived along with the remaining deputies. As they taped off the playground area, the sheriff removed his hat and shook his head in disbelief.

"That's the Fields girl."

"Who's that sheriff?" Asked the deputy.

"Lisa Fields. I served with her daddy, Otto. We were stationed together back in 1960 at Hickam Air Force Base in Honolulu. That's where he met Lisa's mom, Kelly."

"Isn't he the one who died last year when his truck hit that tree?"

"Same one. Poor family. How am I going to tell Kelly her daughter is dead? I don't even think she turned 17 yet." The sheriff rubbed his eyes, dreading the duty he would soon have to perform.

The coroner, Doctor Cunningham, arrived at the scene and carefully approached the sheriff.

"What do we have here, George?" he asked as he knelt beside the body.

"Looks like she was stripped, stabbed, and posed."

As the coroner looked over the young girl's body, he casually spoke out loud, more so to make mental notes for himself but also to show off his medical and investigative skills in front of the deputies.

"Female appears to be young, between the ages of fifteen and seventeen. Short and slender. Brown eyes with significant hemorrhaging in her right eye; most likely due to blunt force trauma with a heavy object. Said force probably left the young girl immobilized; if not unconscious.
It appears the girl's dark brown hair has been crudely cut, perhaps with the same instrument used to stab her. I'll have to clean her up to see how many stab wounds we have here, but I'm going to estimate between 60 and 80. Most are centralized around the throat, neck, and chest area. She has a cut along her left cheek with no self-defense wounds on her hands or arms."

"So I'm going to venture to guess that she was unconscious or unable to put up a struggle as she was stabbed." Cunningham continued. "She does appear to have scrapes and abrasions on her body. She has gravel and wood chips inside the wounds on her back and rear. Along with the trail of blood, it's pretty apparent she was dragged over here. Based on the stab marks all being on the front of her body, she was dead before she was posed up on the slide like this. The killer must have sat with her for some time to keep her legs open like this. Jesus, what kind of monster could have done this, George?"

The coroner looked off towards the sky as he pulled off his latex gloves. He was not expecting an answer to his rhetorical question. The sheriff could only look off in wonder as well.

As officers documented the scene, taking photos and searching for the girl's clothes, the sheriff drove over to Field's small two-bedroom house on Cary Street, a small dead-end road with less than a dozen tiny homes.

By this point it was getting late in the day, and the sun was setting off over the woods surrounding the town. Mrs. Fields had just returned home from work at the Harvest Market. She was checking on a roast in the oven for dinner when she heard a knock at the door. She wiped her hands on her apron and went to see who it was.

"sheriff? What can I do for you, George?"

"Evening Kelly, how have you been?" asked the sheriff, removing his hat and holding it with both hands down by his beltline while trying to muster the fortitude to relay the bad news.

"Oh, you know, trying to make ends meet. Things have been pretty tough since Otto passed."

Passed. She uses that word as if he died in his sleep of a heart attack and not driving head-on into a tree while driving too fast for the snowy conditions last Christmas Eve. While Kelly was still coherent, George tried to get as much information about Lisa's last whereabouts as possible. He knew once he told her, she would be a mess.

"When's the last time you saw your daughter?"

"Oh, around supper time last night. She said she would go sleep over at Deena Fox's house. Those two didn't go and get themselves in trouble again, did they? I swear that Fox girl is a bad influence on my Lisa."

"Can you tell me what she was wearing? Did she tell you if she and Deena had any plans?"

"What was she wearing? Oh, yes, I remember. She was wearing one of her dad's old olive green service jackets. She was wearing this new white blouse I got her with some brown pants and those dirty old boots she loves. Lisa said she was going to spend the night at Deena's because they were going to work on their costumes for Halloween. I am expecting her back very soon since she knows what time dinner is."

She looks over her shoulder towards the kitchen and hears the buzzer on the stove go off, alerting her that the roast is finished. "I need to grab the roast from the oven. Can I fix you a plate, sheriff? You can wait for Lisa if you'd like."

"Um, no, thank you, Mrs. Fields, I hate to have to do this. Kelly, I'm sorry to tell you. We found your daughter. She's dead."

The color drains from her face as shock takes over. The smell of the roast starting to burn fills the room. "What? No! What happened? Was it a car accident?"

"No," the sheriff takes a long, deep breath. "We believe she was murdered. Mrs. Peters found her down by the playground this morning. It looks bad."

That image of her daughter, her baby, dead and murdered causes her to collapse onto her knees and let out a guttural scream. She holds her hands to her face as she sobs.

"No! No! No! Not my Lisa! Not my baby!"

Smoke begins to trickle from the kitchen as sheriff George Dalton crouches down beside Kelly Fields and does his best to comfort her.

CHAPTER 2

"The Last Boy Scout"

"On next week's episode, we'll explore who Lisa Fields was and what happened the night she was murdered. Devils Night, October 30th 1977. If you knew Lisa or have any tips you'd like to leave, find me on Facebook and send me a message. I'll gladly include you on the podcast. This has been the Growing Cold podcast, and I'm your host, Sadie Koop. Until next week, thank you for listening!"

The upbeat female voice fades into the outro music, and Nathan Taylor looks at his phone and hits the stop button on his podcast app. The first episode of the podcast described in detail how a young girl's body was found murdered in this very town back in 1977, and the killer (or killers) were never identified. Cedar Point is a relatively small coastal town with a population of only 20,000, and he had never heard of it. He was the only Private Investigator not located in Portland and had never been asked to investigate it. This was all the same to him since only suspicious spouses usually hired him.

They would pay him hundreds of dollars to drive 40 minutes over to Portland, sit in his car, and wait for their husband or wife to go out and see if they were cheating. It was the easiest money he had ever made in his life.

He was sitting in his White 1981 GMC Sierra Grande 2500 Pickup with a fake contractor logo magnet on the side doors. The windows were tinted, and you couldn't see him casually reclining in the driver's seat with a pair of Sunagor 30-160x70 Mega Zoom BCF Binoculars. He was on assignment, and he had to take a leak. At only four hours into a twelve-hour assignment, he was so bored he listened to a podcast since there weren't any good radio stations in this part of the State.

He brings his binoculars to his eyes and watches the blonde woman standing in her driveway by the garage door. She has her daughter strapped into a stroller, and it doesn't look like her daughter is happy. The woman is playing on her cell phone and casually moving the stroller back and forth, back and forth, as she swipes on her phone. Finally, she lets out an exasperated sigh, adjusts her large fake breasts underneath her low-cut black shirt, stuffs her phone between said large fake breasts, and walks the stroller down to the end of the driveway. She looks down the road both ways, then leans her head back, muttering something to her daughter that Nathan can't hear.

She pulls her phone out from between those large fake breasts, taps it once, smiles, and stuffs it back into her bosom. She must have been checking the time because she quickly moved onto the street and out in front of her house. She then turns and makes it look like she's almost returning home from a long walk. If he were just a random guy driving by, he would have thought this was a young, pretty mother who just got done taking her young daughter on a nice long walk.

Right on time at 8 am, Nathan's client pulls up in his oversized red Hummer; he parks and slides out. He unstraps his daughter from the stroller, lifts her high in the air, and gives her a giant hug. He might drive a douchebag SUV, but he seems like he's a good Dad. The client owns a mold and water renovation company on the south side of Portland. Nathan assumes the guy must make good money because he bought his soon-to-be ex-wife a fancy 3-level salon in the heart of downtown Portland. Of course, he also bought her implants. Mr. Hummer made sure to point that out numerous times during the consultation with Nathan, including showing him multiple before and after photos, clothed and fully naked. Nathan didn't know how he felt about that besides being uncomfortable.

While Mrs. Implants ran her salon, she also embezzled hundreds of thousands of dollars. Eventually, the stylists weren't paid, and people started asking questions. Mr. Hummer hired Nathan two years ago to determine where the money was going. He followed Mrs. Implant for two days before he spotted her entering a casino. Nathan watched her lose over a quarter of a million dollars. That explained why she needed the money so badly; she had a massive gambling problem. On top of that, she was also a raging alcoholic.

Mr. Hummer kicked her out right away. Luckily for her, her daddy is a wealthy CEO who gave her a modest five-bedroom, three-hundred-square-foot house for free as a consolation prize since he never approved of Mr. Hummer anyway.

While they were separated, Nathan did a dumpster dive three nights in a row before the divorce was finalized. In the world of private investigation, a dumpster dive is when the investigator waits until it's garbage night on the block. Once the garbage can is on the curb, it's public domain, and anyone can rummage through it. Nathan would swing by around two in the morning, pull up next to the garbage can, and dump the bags into the bed of his truck. He would then go to the loading area outside a steel warehouse that was closed for the night. It was isolated and well-lit so he could videotape what he found inside for the courts.

Nathan found dozens of cans of white claw inside the garbage bag each day—this woman literally drank a dozen white claws a day. He also found tin foil with hair dye, proving she ran an illegal, unlicensed salon out of her home. Unsurprisingly, Nathan also found stubs for a riverboat casino in Portland as well.

Mr. Hummer won the divorce proceedings, and the court awarded him temporary custody of their daughter until Mrs. Implants went through treatment for her gambling and alcohol addictions. She completed a short stint in rehab, attended a few meetings, and now they split custody. The client still feels that she is still gambling and still drinking. So here is Nathan, back on the job, staked out in front of that consolation prize of a house and watching Mr. Hummer strap his daughter into a car seat in the back of that gaudy SUV.

As Mr. Hummer drives off with his daughter, Mrs. Implants runs to her garage and disappears inside. Nathan can't see what she's doing but knows what's coming next. He hears a massive engine roar to life which he recognizes from the last time he had to follow the woman. Mrs. Implant's rich daddy also bought her a blacked-out Ferrari 812 GTS which suddenly screeches out of the garage, tears down the driveway, and onto the street, leaving black rubber streaks on the asphalt.

Nathan is ready for her this time and has already started driving down the road before she even pulls out of the driveway. He's gotten up to 45 mph in the small residential neighborhood when she flies by him to pass in a no-passing 25mph zone. He keeps a safe distance behind her as she weaves in and out of traffic. Nathan only has to get up to speeds in the 70s to stay roughly 200 yards behind her. Three blown red lights and many angry horns later, he stops at a truck stop. Of all the places he expected to find her, a truck stop was one of the last.

After watching her park, gets out of her car with a flip of her hair and saunters inside. He parks where he can watch her vehicle, the entrance and exit, and a clear path if he has to fly out of the parking lot quickly. Figuring it may be awhile, he leans back and gets comfy. A bag of wasabi cashews from his last stakeout calls his name so he tosses a couple into his mouth; his eyes casually sweeping back and forth, looking for any sign of her.

Two hours later, his bladder has finally reached max capacity. He hasn't seen her since she sauntered inside, so he figures this might be a good time to go in and see what the holdup is. He slides out of his truck and stretches. His faded and well-worn brown boots casually click on the pavement as he walks inside, trying to be casual.

Nathan casually strolls down the aisle, pretending to be looking for snacks, as he looks for Mrs. Implant on his way to the restroom room. But so far, he hasn't seen her. After he relieves himself, he casually checks the aisles again. Still, he hasn't seen her, so he goes to the chip aisle near the women's bathroom. He reads the ingredients on the back of a bag of sour cream and salsa pork rinds until a woman exits the restroom. He turns to her.

"Excuse me, Miss. Did you see my wife in there? Young, pretty blonde girl? Big boobs?"

The woman gives him a somewhat disgusted look and shakes her head.

"No one was in there besides me."

She doesn't give him a second look as she walks to the candy aisle and grabs a peanut butter Snickers. After adjusting his pants and ensuring his black T-shirt is tucked into his jeans, he grabs a bottle of water and goes to the checkout counter. Nathan places the water bottle down and smiles at the cashier as she scans the bottle.

"Anything else?" She doesn't even look at him as she asks.

"Yeah, my wife will get some snacks, too, but I will pay for them. Did she bring anything up? She's young, blonde, and has a big rack." He holds his hands up to his chest in an exaggerated manner.

"Nope. Will that be all?" She still doesn't look up to acknowledge him. He can usually charm his way into getting answers from people, but they need to at least look at him. This woman refuses to.

"No? Haven't seen her, huh? Hmm. Well then, nope that's it." He tosses a few crinkled dollar bills on the counter, grabs his water bottle, and walks out of the truck stop. He stops mid-stride and grits his teeth as that blacked-out Ferrari flies past him; tires screeching as she pulls out of the parking lot and onto the highway. Any chance of catching up to her floats away with the trail of her exhaust. He unscrews the cap from the water bottle, takes a sip, and then tosses the bottle in the direction that Mrs. Implant just drove off to. He heads back inside and back up to the counter.

"Where are your gambling machines?" He asks with a demanding tone.

She's playing on her cell phone and doesn't bother to look up at him.

"We don't have gambling machines. They're illegal in this county."

Nathan smiles and places his hands on the counter.

"Last chance; Where are the gambling machines?"

The cashier twirls her hair around a finger as she swipes on her phone, completely ignoring him now. Nathan drums his fingers calmly on the counter before turning on his heels and heading back to the manager's office. He kicks the handle, splintering the frame and sending it flying open. A shocked manager behind the door almost falls off his chair as Nathan enters.

"What are you doing here? I'm calling the police!" The manager cries out as he stands up. Nathan shoves him back down into his chair.

"Go ahead; I'm sure they'll want to see the same thing I want to see. Security footage. More specifically, the footage in your gambling room."

"No! We don't have a gambling room! That's illegal in this county."

"Yeah, yeah, that's what the bitch behind the register said. I don't believe either of you."

Nathan shoves past him and goes to the computer. He moves the mouse around, makes a few clicks, and smiles as footage of a small smoke-filled back room appears on the screen. Several people can be seen playing a lot of machines. He rewinds until he sees what he is looking for. There was Mrs. Implants, drinking a bottle of beer while pulling the lever repeatedly on a slot machine. Nathan pulls a small thumb drive out of the chest pocket of his shirt and sticks it into the USB port. He turns to the flustered manager and smiles.

"You wanna transfer this footage for me? Or should I wait for the sheriff to show up?

After the manager transfers the footage onto the USB drive, Nathan grabs a bottle of soda on his way out. He contemplates twisting the cap off and taking a sip before tossing a handful of change at the cashier on his way out in a blaze of glory, but he doesn't since he knows he's already pushed the boundaries way too far. Private Investigators have no authority anywhere, especially not kicking down a door, strong arming a manager, and stealing a soda by not paying enough. On top of all that, if one of those coins hit the cashier wrong, he could be charged with assault. Instead, he nods to the cashier and strolls out with a smile. She gives him a fake smile and a middle finger in return. Stay classy, Portland.

Nathan fires up his truck and pulls out onto the highway, finally ready to be done with this job and go home and relax. Halfway home, he pulls up to a red light drumming his fingers on the steering wheel. He glances over at a corner bar and what are the odds? There is a black Ferrari in the parking lot. He pulls in and snaps a few photos of the car with the license plate visible outside the bar. Now, he could go inside and get video footage of her drinking, which is against her court order, but figures he has enough evidence to help Mr. Hummer finally get full custody. That means a pretty payday for Nathan. He doesn't need the money since he doesn't do anything that requires money. He doesn't have any hobbies like golf or flying model planes, and has no desire to collect anything or watch sports. Instead he goes home, trains his dogs, tends to his crops, and hunts his food. What else is there in life? A man really couldn't get much simpler than that. Granted, once upon a time, that was the last type of man anyone would have expected from Nathan.

Within 45 minutes, Nathan is home and turns into a heavily wooded gravel driveway. Forty feet up the driveway is a locked gate that he hops out to open, sticking a key into the lock and moving aside the heavy-duty chain. He gets back into his truck and pulls inside only to hop back out to relock it. Whether it be a salesman or an angry cheating spouse that he investigated, the last thing he wants is them intruding on his property, Inevitably because of his line of work, Inevitably because of his line of work, he's had his run-ins with both.

Once, Nathan was hired to determine whether a man's girlfriend was unfaithful. He let the potential client know from the start that he thought the woman was unfaithful and that hiring him would be a waste of time and money. The client hired him on the spot.

All it took was a casual bump at the fair. The woman was a middle-aged woman who would still be beautiful if she spent more time in the gym and less time at the tanning salon. She stood in line at the county fair on a warm August day when Nathan bumped into her. He acted bashful, rubbing his buzzed-down dishwater blonde hair as he gazed at the ground. He brought out the dimples and steel blue eyes as he smiled and looked up at her. That was all it took. She bought him a corn dog and almost dragged him back to her minivan for extramarital activities. Nathan managed to stop things before it got too far by explaining to the cheating woman that he had his wife at home (a lie) and he needed to get home before she got too suspicious. But, he had her text him a saucy message so he could save it and call her later.

Nathan relayed all this to the client in a very professional report the next day, but the client read it as a work of smut. He came roaring up Nathan's driveway a few hours after sending the report almost running over his dogs. The dogs would have torn him to shreds, but Nathan did not give them the command. As the client ran to Nathan calling him a homewrecker, Nathan stepped off his porch onto the grass and steadied himself. The client was a large male in his late forties, who maybe once upon a time, was something special until he got his trophy wife and let himself go. The man raced forward and tried to bulldoze Nathan; Nathan sidestepped him and let the man face plant onto the soft ground. He then quickly but smoothly mounted the man from behind, twisting and locking one of the man's wrists up beside Nathan's torso and kneeling on top of the man's other arm. It took ten minutes of curses and screams before the man calmed down enough to listen to Nathan. Since then, Nathan has locked his property tightly, and his dogs can roam free.

As he drives up his long, windy driveway, dust swallows the road behind his truck in a large gray cloud. He parks on the grass in front of his single-room cabin. He gets out and stretches as two huge Rottweilers run up to him. Nathan crouches down and prepares for impact as they barrel into him. He laughs and wrestles them off of him; they run in circles around him as he goes into his cabin. The door swings back open as the large Rottweiler heads crash against it, sending it swinging back open as the two tanks charge inside.

He dumps dry dog food into two huge bowls and then grabs a Tupperware dish from the fridge. After popping it open and dropping two huge spoonfuls of a venison gravy mix into the bowls, he mixes it up.

"Tango! Cash! Who's hungry?" He calls to the dogs as he holds up the dishes. Both dogs slam their butts to the cabin floor and sit at full attention; their ears perked and heads cocked to the side. Their giant mouths pant as drool runs down their broad chests. Nathan twists his head slightly, and both dogs drop onto their stomachs. He twists his head in another direction, and they flop around onto their backs.

"Good boys! Here you go."

He places the dishes on the floor and clicks his tongue. The dogs jump up and begin inhaling their food. Nathan untucks his shirt and peels it off his back, tossing it into the laundry hamper. His lean and toned torso is littered with scars. There is a large burn scar along his right shoulder blade which goes down to his waist. He pulls a hoodie on before grabbing his baseball cap and beer and heads back outside.

The Oregon days have been warm, but the nights have grown cooler. He takes a sip of beer and looks up to the sky which is beginning to grow dark. The sun starts descending into the dense forest that covers his 20 acres of land. He walks to a field in a clearing where he has rows of corn, zucchini, bell peppers, onions, tomatoes, and lettuce there. He grabs an onion, a green pepper, and heads back to his cabin. He fries the vegetables and a thick chunk of venison over an open fire in a cast iron pan. He cracks open another beer and sits on a rocking chair on his porch with his plate of food. Tango and Cash lay down on each side of his chair, trying not to be too obvious as they watched him eat. Their attempt to beg inconspicuously fails miserably based on the puddle of drool under their faces, but Nathan ignores it. They're good boys.

Nathan tosses a chunk of steak to each of them and finishes his beer. He props his feet up on the tail of the porch as he looks out into the now-dark sky. An ocean of stars lay above him, and a large white moon started peering above the pine trees as he drifted off to sleep outside in the cool Oregon night air.

CHAPTER 3

"The Uninvited"

Nathan slowly starts to stir as he hears the low and steady growl of Tango and Cash. He's still asleep on the rocker on his porch—baseball hat tucked down over his eyes with his boots propped up on the porch rail. The sun has already risen above Mount Hood, which means it has to be at least eight O'clock. He needs to start sleeping in his bed; he's getting too old to be able to tolerate the hardwood rocker all night after sitting stationary in his pickup truck on assignment all day. His ankles will pop as soon as he stands up, and he'll have to shuffle like a zombie for the first few steps until his body loosens up. The rough life he lived back in his twenties put a toll on his body. He has to split wood today in preparation for the upcoming winter, so that'll be a good little exercise for the day. Maybe, he'll walk around his property to inspect the fence line and ensure there are no holes. A nice twenty acre walk would do his knees some good.

He pushes back his baseball cap from his forehead and rubs his eyes before opening them. It takes his eyes a few moments to adjust to the sunlight as Tango and Cash stand at the edge of the porch. Their growls are a low, consistent rumble from deep inside their thick necks. Their short, black, shiny fur stands like mohawks down their muscular backs. Nathan stands to see what they are growling at. He'll have to quickly get his rifle if it's a bear, but if it's just a deer or a rabbit, he'll command them to be silent and go get breakfast. Or maybe he'll get his rifle regardless of whether it's a deer or bunny, and he'll have some extra meat.

The uninvited intruder is neither a bear, deer, or bunny rabbit.

A woman who appeared to be in her late 20s or early 30s was jogging up his gravel driveway. Her thick, curly brown hair bounces on her shoulders as she runs. It appears she isn't even winded as she completes the long jog up his winding gravel driveway. Her blue tank top doesn't seem to be drenched in sweat, and her freckled face barely shows any glimmer of perspiration. Her lips curve into a large, warm smile as she approaches. She raises a hand in a greeting.

"Good morning!" She calls out in a pleasant tone. She's not out of breath at all. "I'm looking for a Private Investigator."

Nathan stretches, removes his baseball cap, and runs his fingers over his short, dirty blonde hair. He really didn't want to have to talk to anyone today.

"I'm closed for the day. Come back on Monday? You could call too, yanno. My number is listed on my website. Or better yet, send an email."

Her smile continues as she reaches the porch steps, not phased at all by the two 150-lb monster dogs standing feet away from her.

"I did call. A couple times, actually. It always goes straight to voicemail. If you're going to have a phone, keep it turned on. Otherwise, there's no point. Can't get any work if you don't accept any calls."

She reaches the porch and holds her hands out to the dogs. Nathan is surprised that the dogs don't growl, snarl, or even attack. Instead, they start licking her hands.

"Aww, such good boys! What are their names?" She moves her hands from their lapping tongues to scratch along their collars and up to their ears. The dog's tiny cropped tails try to wag, making their stout little butts shake side to side.

"Tango has the blue collar, and Cash has the gold collar," Nathan responds.

"Nice. I loved Kurt Russell back in the day. Snake Plissken, oh my God, what a fuckin babe." She's still smiling. Nathan wonders how someone can be so happy for so long. He doesn't respond. Instead, he just watches her pet his dogs. It's been a few years since anyone besides him has given them attention, and they're good boys. So, he lets them soak up the affection. Cash turns around so she can scratch his butt; his favorite. He moves his hindquarters up and down as Sadie scratches good and hard as he lets out what can only be described as a dog grunt. A half growl, half bark. Tango rolls onto his back to get his belly rubbed. Nathan almost smiles at this but catches himself.

"I'm Sadie, and like I was saying, I'm looking to hire you. Assuming that you are Nathan Taylor, right? The Private Investigator?" She wipes slobber and black dog hair off her hands on the back of her jeans as she stands up, then holds her hand out to him.

Nathan reluctantly gives her hand a short, soft shake. He notices how soft her skin feels compared to his rough, calloused hands. He's caught off guard as his eyes lock on her almond-shaped hazel eyes. Even her eyes seem to smile. Her happiness annoys him.

"Yeah, that's me. But like I said before, I'm closed. And I'm booked for the next few weeks, so I'm not looking to take on any new clients.

"Really? Because it looks like you're just sleeping on your porch with your phone off and not really doing any investigating." She waves her arms at the surrounding porch area, and Nathan finally realizes that her left arm is a complete sleeve of tattoos. Her hair, eyes, lips, and face caught him off guard. Honestly, he feels like he has vertigo in her presence, and he doesn't like it.

Nathan shrugs, not having a witty retort this early in the morning. Then something clicks in his head. He's heard that voice before and that name.

"Wait a minute, you said your name was Sadie? Sadie Koop?

"Ooooh," she smirks and folds her arms against her chest, cocking a hip to the side." You're a fan of the podcast, aren't you? Then you'll work with me, right?

Nathan ignores her and looks down at his dogs, trying to push their noses against Sadie. He snaps his fingers, and Tango and Cash return to his side.

"I may have listened to an episode. I'm not really into podcasts. I find it rather pretentious that anyone thinks their voice is so great that anyone would want to sit for an hour and listen to them talk without any kind of visual stimulation."

"Would you listen to me talk for an hour if you could also stare at me?"

She moved closer. Nathan couldn't tell if she was flirting with him or trying to intimidate him. Either way, he did not feel comfortable but stood his ground and didn't move.

"I think I'll pass on that. Same way, I'll have to pass on your case."

"You don't even know what my case entails." She moves past him and sits on his rocking chair. She pats her lap, and Tango and Cash run over to her to get more pets.

"Let me guess, you want me to dig up information on an unsolved murder. Do you think I have some insider information? Maybe I'm buds with the sheriff. Maybe people are more willing to talk to a Private Investigator than some journalist. Wait, scratch that; you aren't even a journalist. You Google stuff and then talk into a microphone. You're just a podcaster. You need someone who can actually find real information, so you can take what I find and look better to your audience of 20 people. Is that pretty accurate?"

"You're kind of a dick. You know that?" She says it so nonchalantly as if his words had no effect on her. She doesn't look at him; she just scruffs the dog's necks. She playfully pushes their faces away, which gets a significant response. They lean back before launching onto her lap with both giant chests across one of her legs. She laughs, wraps her arms around their necks, and hugs them.

"Yeah, I've been called worse." He turns and walks inside his cabin, leaving her to play with his so-called guard dogs.

"Rude!" she calls out as she shoves the dogs off her lap and stands, pulling her slightly loose jeans back up her hips. Her hand catches the screen door behind him before it closes. Her Converse All-Stars are almost silent on his cabin floors. He's still wearing his boots from yesterday, which almost echo as he stomps towards the fridge. He pulls open the door to grab a beer, just enough for her to peek inside.

He turns to look at her as he pops the top of the bottle and takes a sip.

"What?"

"Man, your fridge is sure stocked there. I saw half a dozen beers, some packages of meat, and a jug of milk. I'm impressed. You're taking this loner bachelor schtick as far as possible, eh? Mr. Lone wolf. He doesn't want friends. Blah Blah Blah. Who are you trying to be? Bronson? Eastwood? Van Damme? What cliche are you leaning on, Nate?"

The name Nate catches him off guard. He hasn't been called that in years. He takes another drink and takes a step towards her.

"It's Nathan! And for your information, I don't need a lot in my fridge because I grow all my vegetables and kill all my meat. My vegetables are still out in the field, and I have enough meat in the fridge until next week when I'll go out and shoot another deer. And yeah, I don't want friends. I don't need friends. I don't need your shit. I don't need your case. I don't need you fucking with my dogs, and I don't need you trespassing up my goddamn driveway!"

"Clint Eastwood! I fuckin knew it, dude!" She laughs at him before lowering her voice to a low, gruff tone. "Get off my lawn!"

She bumps past him and opens his fridge, grabbing her own bottle of beer. She pops the top, takes a drink, and sits at his small kitchen table. The cabin is basically an open concept. It's a large room with a sink, fridge, and wood-burning stove on one wall and a table in the middle of the room with two chairs. Across from that, a small bed and dresser adore the opposite wall. Along the wall opposite the front door, is a small bathroom area with a toilet and a shower over a drain. No walls in his cabin separating any of the spaces; not that he needs any privacy. It's just him and his dogs, after all. Nathan watches her as she sets the beer on his table.

"Comfy?"

"I guess. You wanna hear about what I need you for yet?"

Exasperated, Nathan finally relents. He pulls out the other table chair and has a seat. He folds his hands on the table before him and looks at her.

"Fine. Let's hear it. Then I'll drive you back to the gate and see you on your way."

"So, which episode did you listen to?"

Nathan didn't want to admit that he's listened to quite a few episodes. In fact, her podcast is one of the few podcasts he actually listens to.

"The one based here in Cedar Point. It was the latest one. I assume that's the one you want to hire me for?"

"You got it, Sherlock! Wow, you are a great investigator!" There's that smirk again; plump lips pursed together devilishly.

"Great. Now that we've got that out, I'll give you a ride back to the gate." Nathan begins to stand up, but she doesn't budge.

"So you know it's been almost 50 years, and no major suspects have existed. No new leads. No news coverage. Nothing." She leans back and crosses her legs.

"Yup, damn shame. Happens all the time. That's not the only cold case in America. Please go chase down another one that doesn't involve me. Portland probably has thousands of unsolved cases you can investigate."

"Yeah, I've already investigated most of those. Get this, after I released that first episode, one of her friends reached out to me. Here, I'll let you read the email, and you can tell me what you get from it. "

She slides her phone out of her pocket, taps it a few times, puts it on the table facing him, and slides it forward. Nathan lifts up the phone and looks at the cracked screen. There is an email from Cindy Summers.

Subject: Friend of Lisa Fields

Body: Hey Sadie, I want to start by saying what a great job you do with your podcast. I've been listening since you first started. You are doing a fantastic job spreading the word about Lisa's murder. I was Lisa's best friend when we were growing up. It was my house she was supposed to spend the night at the night she was murdered. She never showed up, and I still blame myself for not looking for her. If you'd like to interview me for the podcast, I'd happily share my story. Keep up the excellent work!

A loyal Listener

Cindy Summers.

Nathan turns the phone to face Sadie and slides it back to her, standing as he does.

"Well, that's awesome for you. You got someone to interview for your podcast. You don't need me at all. You got everything wrapped in a nice and neat bow. So, let's drive you back to the gate."

"I need you because that cunt from New York is here, and she's trying to steal this fucking story from me!" Sadie slams her palms down on the table and sits up straight. Nathan blinks at her outburst but doesn't react. He stays standing there, watching her, letting the smoke settle. She hooks her thick, wavy brown hair behind her ears and exhales.

"Jillian Playmore. She's this bitch podcaster from New York. I've never known anyone so obsessed with where they were born. If I have to hear her say, "I'm from New York, so please excuse my attitude," one more time, I'm going to reach through my phone and fuckin slap her. She uses it as an excuse for fucking everything. "Sorry I'm late; I'm from New York. Sorry, I'm a bitch. I'm from New York. Oh, that racist slur I just said? Yeah, I'm from New York". It's so fuckin annoying."

Nathan can't help but smile. He has to admit that she's pretty damn cute when she's all flustered and worked up with quite the mouth. He doesn't mind a woman who can curse like a sailor but looks like, well, looks like how she does. Sadie continues.

"So Jillian hosts "The Playmore Pod. "I know, really clever. She just used her last name cuz it has "Play" in it. I doubt that's even her name. It's probably Smith or something lame. Anyway, every time I start a story, she swoops in and releases almost the same episodes as mine, except that she doesn't investigate anything. She makes shit up. I was investigating this one case where a girl was found in a suitcase on the side of the road, and she started saying that it was a green suitcase and that there was a name tag on it and all these little details. And yanno what? None of that was true! She made it all up. And she'll call people I interview and try to get them to talk to her. She's a fuckin bitch, and I hate her. I am willing to pay you! Three thousand dollars to help me out here. I just got a new sponsorship deal from Spotify, and I have to get the scoop on this murder. I can't do that with her trying to steal everything from me. So if I get you investigating too, she won't be able to steal from both of us, right?"

Nathan shrugs, scoops his keys up from the table, and swings them around his index finger.

"Sorry to hear all that. That's some unfortunate childish bullshit. I suggest you block her on Facebook or whatever social media you use and forget about her. Come on, let's go."

"God, you are SUCH a dick!" She shoves her chair out from the table, moving the table a foot forward into Nathan's thighs. She's out the door before he knows it, the handle slamming against the outside of the cabin as she kicks it open and then slams shut, the old springs squeaking before the thud. He follows her outside and sees her repeatedly yanking on the handle on the passenger side of his truck.

"Unlock the fucking door! Why do you need to lock your door out here anyway?"

He goes to the driver's side and opens his unlocked door. He leans over and smiles as he pulls up on the lock.

"I don't lock my door. The passenger door has not been opened since I purchased it, so I guess I never unlocked it."

She gets in and slams the door, turning her head away from him and staring out the side window. He puts the truck in reverse, performs a three-point turn, and heads off down his gravel driveway. He hits bumps and potholes, jostling her some. As he hits one more giant rut in the road, something hanging from the rearview mirror slaps the glass, and she turns to inspect it. It's a Green Jade Buddha statue, about an inch tall, hanging from a black cord. She moves it in between her fingers.

"Didn't take you as a Buddhist. Or are you just a fan of Rambo?"

He chuckles, "Good Eye. Yeah, it's the same kind as in First Blood part 2. But I do try to practice a bit of Buddhism."

"Yeah, you're cosplaying as Rambo from part 3. Where he's living in the monastery trying to be all zen and shit but still punishing himself by stick fighting."

She turns and looks out the window, her thick hair bouncing about her cheeks. He doesn't respond to that. She already had him all figured out. She was a pretty good investigator, wasn't she? He has second doubts about not working with her for a moment. Or maybe, it was just the fact that he felt a rock in his gut at the thought of never being able to see her again. He quickly pushes that feeling deep into his being as he stops at the gate.

"Let me unlock the gate and open it for you."

"Fuck you," She states as she gets out, leaving his door open. She easily hurdles the gate and begins walking away. He climbs out and goes over to shut the passenger door.

"Where's your car?"

"I took an Uber here. I'll walk back, fuck you very much, asshole!" She holds up her middle finger as she walks away, hips swaying.

CHAPTER 4

"Cab's Here!"

Sadie pulls her cell phone from her pocket, swipes it open, closes the email, and reopens her Uber app. She places an order to be picked up and slides her phone back into her pocket. She had never worked with a Private Investigator, but she had never expected such a big dickhead. She had seen all the movies where they are gruff and alcoholics and all that Hollywood bullshit, but that's all she thought it was. Hollywood Bullshit. She never expected anyone to actually portray that character in real life. He was the only investigator in the area, and she had struck out. So, while she was waiting for Uber, she pulled up her web browser and searched for Private Investigators nearby.

The only other Private Investigator in a 40-mile radius was still in western Portland. It was Black Tie Investigations. She clicked the link and immediately shook her head. It was evident from the start that this webpage was made with some cookie-cutter template, and the font and colors were changed by someone who wanted to portray a specific image. Unlike Nathan, who wanted to play the lone gunslinger type, whoever owned Black Tie Investigations wanted to play the role of John Wick. The background was black, and all the fonts were white. Below the typewriter-style bold font of the company's logo was a picture of the only investigator. He had long, slicked-back, black hair, black stubble and wore a black suit, a black dress shirt, and a black tie.

"No thanks, Mr. Wick." She closed her phone as the white Rav4 with the Uber sign in the front window pulled up. She hopped into the back seat and smiled at the driver as she reopened her phone.

"Where ya headed?" The driver asked.

"Sunrise Motel, please," Sadie responded, already continuing her search for Private Investigators within a 60-mile radius who might be willing to assist her.

"Where ya from?" The driver continues with the small talk.

"Portland," She answers, not looking up.

"What brings you to Cedar Point? You have family here?"

"Nope. I'm trying to solve a murder."

"That wouldn't be the murder of Lisa Fields, would it?"

That made Sadie perk up and pay attention. She looked up at his face in the rearview mirror. He was an older gentleman, probably between the late 50s and mid-60s. He had shaggy white hair and a short white beard. His eyelids dropped over brown eyes, which looked back at her through the mirror. The man chuckled back at her reflection.

"You wondering how I knew that?"

"Yeah, you a fan of the podcast?" She tilts her head in wonder.

"Podcast? Nah, never listened to one before. I'm not a fan of technology, really. I only got a basic cell phone so I could download the Uber app so I could keep working.

"Keep working? What did you do before Uber?"

"Oh, I was a taxi driver in Portland for several years. Eventually, the company said I was too old and let me go. That was bullshit though. My boss was just a jerk, and we got into it one too many times. My age was just an excuse. So I moved back home, and Dee over at the diner talked me into downloading this Uber app, so I kept working around here."

"So you are from Cedar Point, then? That's how you know about the murder?"

"I am from Cedar Point. Born and raised. I moved out to Portland after high school. Ended up driving a taxi for most of my life. Drove limo for a bit but didn't like how long the damn things were."

Sadie swipes open the recorder app on her phone and hits the record button.

"What did you say your name was Mr...?"

"Bates. Craig Bates."

"Did you know Lisa, Mr. Bates?"

"Just call me Craig. No, she was a couple years younger than me. It was my last year of high school when she got murdered. I remember seeing her in the hallway and whatnot, but I never spoke with her."

"So, how did you know that was the murder I was working on?"

"Well," He chuckled and stroked his beard as he drove. "It's the only unsolved murder in Cedar Point. This ain't Detroit. We do have a missing person wall in the sheriff's Station but that's about it. Mostly runaways. We don't have a bunch of unsolved murders. We have Lisa's death, and that's it."

"That makes sense. Who do you think killed her?"

"Well, I have no idea. I didn't know her or any of her friends. I heard some rumors about some Satanists or Cult kids or whatever. I remember seeing those kids in school too. They just seemed like dorks or whatever you call them."

"So you never heard any rumors afterward or anything?"

"Nope. I kept to myself, I didn't talk to many people, and I didn't gossip or partake in gossip.

"I see." Sadie looks out the window as they pull up to the motel, a small 8-room strip motel with a broken neon sign in front. She pulls a business card and a 10-dollar bill from her pocket and reaches it over to him. "If you think of anything else, will you call me?"

"Sure thing." He takes the card and the bill and slides it into the breast pocket of his flannel shirt.

"Thanks for the ride and the info!" She smiles at him as she gets out and closes the door. She makes a note on her phone after she slides her key into the door and enters the dimly lit motel room.

CHAPTER 5

"Playmore"

Over the next three days, Nathan couldn't get his mind off Sadie. So, he was pleasantly surprised when, while sitting in his truck waiting for a middle-aged married man to leave his house, he got a notification on his phone that the Growing Cold Podcast had released a new episode. He clicked on it, fast-forward two minutes past the paid advertisements, and let out a soft sigh as he heard her voice escape his truck's speakers.

"Welcome back to the Growing Cold Podcast. I am your host, investigative journalist Sadie Koop. Once again, we are investigating the 1977 Devil's Night murder of 16-year-old Lisa Fields in Cedar Point, Oregon.

Only a few reports were made in the newspapers regarding what happened that night. Police reported that a witness saw a two-tone colored car, with a dark blue top, light blue color on the sides, and dark blue on the bottom, leaving the 17th Street area sometime between 9 pm October 30th and 6 am the next morning. It was believed that two white teenagers were driving the vehicle. I spoke to the local sheriff, Jim Dalton, whose father was the sheriff then, and asked him about this. His response was the same for every single question I asked. 'It's an ongoing investigation, and I can't comment.'

An inside source told me that Lisa had been seen with a man at the local Harvest Market around 530pm the night she was murdered. The man was described as being between 35 and 40 years old. He stood about 5 foot 8 or 5 foot 9 inches tall and weighed between 170 and 180 lbs. He had reddish, stiff, coarse hair and green eyes with crow's feet wrinkles. He had a reddish face with long sideburns or a mustache. The witness who gave the information said that the man was driving an older model, 4-door car that was either bronze or gold. The car was possibly recently painted but had a dull finish. The car was also said to be boxy and square in appearance. It's believed that law enforcement may know who the man was. It's unknown whether this report has anything to do with Lisa.

I've come to learn from one of Lisa's best friends, that she lost her father in a tragic car accident the Christmas prior to her death. Next week, I'll be speaking directly with Lisa's best friend and the one who was supposed to hang out with Lisa the night she was murdered. Her name is Cindy Summers. They were supposed to finish their Halloween costumes for the school's Halloween dance the following night. Until next week, I'm Sadie Koop, and this has been the Growing Cold Podcast. Thank you for listening!"

Nathan lifts his phone and stares at the empty unplayed podcast playlist on his phone. He sighs and hits the magnifying icon to search. He types in Playmore and hits search. There's one result, and of course, it's one of those podcasts where the host uses their own face as a logo. That's fine if you're Joe Rogan, but it's tacky if you're a small-time podcaster. Even if you are from New York. Nathan clicks on the newest episode entitled "Warlocks and Private Dicks" and clicks play.

He hears a faint voice in the distance so softly he can barely hear it. Something about sexual performance. He turns the volume almost all the way before he can make out what she's saying. It's Jillian reading off a paid advertisement for a sexual enhancement pill. How classy. He instantly has to reach for the volume and turn it down as dubstep roars through his truck speakers, almost blowing them out. Apparently, they don't know how to even out the audio in New York. After the screeching robot techno music ends, he hears Jillian begin, obviously reading from a script.

"What's up, Playmorons! It's your host, Jillian Playmore, and this is the Playmore podcast! But you already know that cuz you just keep playing these episodes, and when one episode ends, what do you do? you Playmore!" She laughs at her pun, and Nathan is entirely convinced that her name is not, in fact, Playmore and that she chose that just for the puns. She then spends the next 20 minutes, almost word for word, repeating what Sadie said in her first two episodes. Eventually, she gets to something new, and Nathan's attention is perked slightly.

"I have been told by an inside source that there have only been, in fact, two suspects in this murder. It wasn't the kids spotted in the blue car or the mysterious man with the red hair that Sadie Poop reported. Oops, I meant Sadie Scoop. Sorry, that's so New York of me!

Anyway, as I was saying, there have only been two suspects. Two real-life Warlocks! What the fuck is a Warlock, you ask? Well, don't feel dumb; I had to Google it myself. Apparently, they're like witches, except they're guys. They're the male version of witches without the broomsticks. Unless those broomsticks are shoved up their own asses. Pretty gay if you ask me, I'm just kidding! Sorry, I'm from New York, and we say what we say in New York.

Anyways, these two Warlocks apparently were heard talking about sacrificing Lisa because she was a virgin, and on Devil's night, that's like the perfect time, right? So check this out; they go by Oshun Rivers and Willow Bloodmoon. How retarded are those names? Whatever I know retarded is offensive. Well, not in New York!

Anyway, Oshun wrote an entire blog about Lisa's death. It's so bizarre. I'm going to read it for you in the next episode. We're almost out of time right now. But first, I gotta tell you guys something. I got the scoop on Sadie Koop. Apparently, she can't do any investigating on her own. She's so lazy that she actually hired a Private Investigator!

I know, right? How lame is that? It gets better. This PI, named Nathan Taylor, lives in some Unabomber cabin out in the woods off Timberline Trail. He's got a bunch of disorderly arrests in Arizona, Texas, and Michigan. For a Private Investigator, he sure doesn't act like one. Before he moved out to Cedar Point all he did was get drunk and into fights. Now, when he's not spying on people and catching cheaters. He's just a fricken recluse out there in the woods. I bet he's banging Sadie; she seems pretty easy.

Oops, was that slut shaming? I'm from New York. deal with it! That's all for this episode. make sure you click Playmore to hear the next one!"

Nathan's hands grip the steering wheel so tightly that his knuckles are white. His jaw is clenched, and he's staring down at his dashboard as if it was actually the radio that just spoke the words he heard and not that bitch from New York. How did she even know about him? And how did she dig up his arrest record? Those records were supposed to be expunged. While lost in the podcast, the middle-aged man he was waiting for got into a blue El Camino and pulled out of the driveway and into traffic before Nathan could even recognize what was happening.

"Fuck!" he smacked the steering wheel as his target just disappeared into the distance. There was no use trying to catch up to him. Nathan was sure his client wouldn't be paying him anyway. He starts his truck, makes a U-turn without even checking for traffic, and screeches down the road, weaving in and out of traffic until he stops at the Sunrise Motel. The only motel in town. He hops out and walks into the office, rapidly ringing the bell until an elderly woman hobbles out.

"Yes? Would you like a room?"

"No, I'm looking for my wife. She's a pretty thing, about 5'7, with thick, curly, brown hair, and freckles. She looks like she works out and has tattoos."

"Oh yes, such a nice girl. Pretty too! She's in room 16."

"Thanks." He gives her a smile and walks out and down the length of the motel until he reaches door 16. He places a hand over the peephole and knocks on the door, calling out in a falsetto voice, "Management. There's a problem with your room."

Inside, he hears water running in the distance. It turns off as he hears her voice call that she'll be right there. A moment later, Sadie opens the door, wearing a towel. Her wet hair hangs beside her freckles and makeup-free cheeks. Nathan is surprised that she looks even better without makeup. Her eyebrows lift in shock as she sees him, and she clutches the towel tight.

"Dude, what the fuck? What are you doing here?"

Nathan tries to regain his composure, remembering he was angry at her.

"What the fuck did you tell that Playmore broad?"

"Broad? First off, that's super sexist. You can't call women broads. Second of all, she's a bitch, not a broad. And I didn't tell her shit about you or anything else. The only time I ever spoke to her was the first time I found out she was stealing my shit. I told her to stop, she told me to go fuck herself, and that she would do whatever she wanted to cuz she's so fuckin New York. So don't come breaking down my door accusing me of shit."

She smacks his arm and then readjusts her towel, almost losing it in the process.

"I take it you listened to her newest episode? I didn't tell her anything. She also said we were sleeping together. So now you see what a piece of shit she is."

Nathan relaxes a little, letting the anger slowly run down and out of his fingers. He takes a slow breath and then exhales.

"Look, I'm sorry. You're right. I overreacted. Would you mind if I came in?

"Yeah, I guess. Just don't be a dick any more than usual". She turns and walks away from him back into the bathroom. Nathan closes the door after he enters and sits on one of the imitation recliners every budget motel has. A moment later, Sadie reenters the room wearing a tank top, no bra, and gym shorts. She sits on the bed with her back against the headboard and crosses her legs at the ankles.

"Well?" she looks at him, still obviously annoyed with him.

"Well, what?"

"Well, what the fuck do you want? You told me you won't work with me, then accused me of telling Playmore a bunch of shit, then you apologized. So now what do you want?"

"Well, I guess I'll work with you." Nathan shrugs and folds his arms against his chest.

"What makes you think I still wanna work with you?"

"Because you do. I can tell. You know I'm a good investigator. Because you know I can help you; otherwise, you wouldn't have come to me in the first place. Plus, you'll do anything to see Playmore brought down."

She looks at him for a moment before chewing on her bottom lip.

"Fuck, you're right. I really need your help. This is one of the hardest cases I've ever worked on. No one knows shit, no one's talking, it's all so frustrating. So you'll help? $3000?"

Nathan shakes his head.

"Nah, I can't take your money. I'll help you for free. Solving a murder and getting back at that bitch from New York will be payment enough. But there are two conditions you have to agree to:"

"Oh God," she says, rolling her eyes. "This isn't where you try to Weinstein me, is it?"

"What?" He asks, slightly confused. "No. The first condition is that I don't have to talk. Meaning, I don't want to be on the podcast. You can use whatever I find, but I'm not doing sound bites."

She lets out an overly dramatic fake sigh. "Fiiiine. What's the second?"

"You gotta come over and play with Tango and Cash sometimes. They don't get as much attention as they deserve, so I'd like them to get some extra love and affection."

"Everyone needs a little love and affection. So yeah, sure thing, it's a deal." She smiles and gives him a wink.

CHAPTER 6

"First Date"

Nathan stands in front of his grill and watches the meat slowly sweat drops of blood on top of the browned surface. He flips the patties and turns and looks out into the clearing that he calls a yard. Sadie is currently trying to pull a knotted industrial rope from Cash's mouth as Tango runs around them in circles, barking. He has to smile. This is exactly what he envisioned when he was growing up. Woods to wander in, dogs running and playing, a beautiful woman who could wrestle in the mud with the dogs and then clean up, throw on a dress, and go to dinner. Someone who could joke about the couple next to them, making up elaborate fake stories about who they were and what they were doing at the restaurant. Granted, he didn't know Sadie would do that, but he figured she would based on what he'd seen of her. On the other hand though, they were strictly business partners at the moment, and he had to remind himself of that constantly. Restricting the strong attraction he had for her.

When the burgers had finished, he flipped them onto a plate and placed them on the old wooden picnic table he had near the fire pit. He also threw a burger into each dog dish and tossed both onto the ground nearby. He whistled, and both dogs and Sadie stopped to look at him. All three had the same expression on their face, as if asking why he interrupted their play time.

"Dinners done. Come eat!" he gave a snapping sound with his fingers. The dogs came sprinting over and began wolfing down their food. Sadie casually strolled over to him.

"So, was that snapping of the fingers meant for me as well?"

"No, me yelling that dinner is done, come eat, was meant for you. The snap is a command for the dogs." His gruff demeanor wrapped back around him like a safety net as he sat down and prepared his burger.

"You are such a shit house!" She exclaimed as she plopped down across from him, pouring ketchup on her burger and piling on a bunch of onions before taking a big bite. He gave her a half-hearted smile and took a bite of his own burger before swallowing and asking.

"So what's the plan?"

She takes another bite, closing her eyes as she chews, enjoying the perfectly cooked venison, before washing it down with a swig of beer.

"Well, I have to meet Cindy tomorrow at her house to do our interview. I thought maybe you could talk to the sheriff and see what he knows. Figured you'd have the best of luck with him. Maybe we could meet up at Shamrocks Tavern afterward and go over what we've learned? I heard they have karaoke."

"That sounds good except for the karaoke part. If I'm not talking on a podcast, I'm not singing at a bar. I'm also not a fan of Shamrocks. There's a diner down the street from the sheriff's office. We can meet there. Why do you think I'd have better luck with the sheriff?"

"Because you're a private eye, and he's a cop. I figured you two would have a long-standing working relationship, right? Like you scratch his back, and he scratches yours?"

"Yeah, being a Private Investigator doesn't work like that. Cops don't really respect us. It's pretty easy to just get a license; it's not so easy to go through the police academy, graduate, get hired, and work 12 hours a day for shit pay. I can charge what I want and pretty much do what I want. Meanwhile, cops have to follow so many guidelines and laws that it's almost impossible for them to do a good job. So yeah, cops hate us. They would never give us any info, even if it leads to us helping to get a lead in their case. Especially if it helps get a lead. They would flip their shit if I got a lead that they couldn't. It would mean all those tax dollars are getting wasted on public servants when a private detective gets the job done in half the time, with no overtime."

She nods in thought as she chews her burger with a small glob of ketchup stuck on her chin.

"Makes sense. So yeah, the Warlocks. I'm pretty sure that Jillian got that info from Cindy. So, I'm gonna talk to her and tell her not to give that bitch any more information. And while I'm at it, I'm going to get as much information as I can on Lisa, the Warlocks, and every other player in this Shakespearean tragedy."

Nathan takes his napkin and leans forward, wipes the ketchup from her chin, and tosses it down on his plate without as much as a smile. Sadie, on the other hand, stops for a moment then breaks out in a wide smile. Nathan ignores it and takes a sip of beer before talking.

"Good thinking. Alright, first thing in the morning, I'll head to the sheriff's office and introduce myself."

"Wait, you've never even talked to the sheriff?"

"Nope. I never had a reason to. I mostly just catch cheaters and shit. No reason to talk to law enforcement. I don't call them, and I don't break the law, so they don't need to speak to me. I know his name and where his office is. I did my research before moving into town."

"So, you aren't from here?"

"Nope." He states, not giving up anymore information. She takes the hint and changes the subject.

"Thanks for dinner; it was amazing."

"Yeah, sure. You're welcome. Thanks for playing with the boys; I know they enjoyed it."

"Anytime." She smiles and holds up her beer in a toast.

He raises his own salute back and takes a drink. She lowers her beer and stares off into the fire burning in the distance for a while. Eventually, he breaks the silence.

"What's on your mind?"

She rubs her arms with her hands, maybe cold from only a t-shirt, as the night turns black in the crisp northwestern autumn night. Or maybe from the thoughts bouncing in her head.

"How can a happy and healthy girl go from heading to her friend's house to make Halloween decorations to being beaten, stripped naked, stabbed to death, and put on display on a slide at a playground."

Nathan ponders that for a while.

"I think the first person to look at is her boyfriend, assuming she had one. According to your buddy Jillian, she doesn't think the teens in the blue car or the man with the red hair are of any concern."

"Yeah, the guy with the red hair was her history teacher. He's been cleared already. I was going to follow that up in a few episodes. The teens could have been anyone. Kids drive all over, especially on Devil's Night. They literally drive around, causing nothing but problems. It's hard to believe the sheriff still lets it happen nowadays."

Nathan unbuttons his flannel shirt and peels it off, handing it across the table to her.

"You look cold."

"Thank you." She smiles and pulls it around her shoulders, hugging herself in the process. Nathan leans back and continues.

"So what about those so-called "Warlocks?""

"Oshun and Willow? I'm going to assume they are two local nerds who saw the Exorcist one too many times and got all goth before goth was a thing. I'm pretty sure they're just harmless dorks; Oshun does podcasts and stuff. He's still a practicing Wiccan, or Warlock, or whatever the fuck he is. He's written books, I think. I remember seeing him at a booth at a podcast convention. Really out there kind of guy. He's like a Halloween costume of a witch wearing a Halloween costume of a witch, if that makes any sense. "

Nathan nods.

"So, you want me to talk to them too?"

"Sure, if you can find them." The green specks in her hazel eyes dance in the reflection of the fire as she stares ahead.

Nathan nods and finishes his beer. Tango and Cash have finished their dinner and are now lying at Sadies feet. "Traitors," he thinks to himself.

"It's getting kind of late. Do you want me to drive you back to your hotel room?"

"Nah, I'll just crash here if it's ok with you."

"Sure thing. I've grown accustomed to sleeping on the porch. Keeps the nightmares away" He chuckles and cracks open another beer.

"Oh? Due tell! And you are such a gentleman by offering me your bed and not trying to take me to bed." she says in a fake Southern drawl, trying her best to be a Southern belle as she folds her fingers under her chin and bats her lashes at him.

"Nothing to tell." He drains his full beer down his throat and sets the bottle down on the table, keeping his inner demons to himself.

CHAPTER 7

"Serve and Protect"

Nathan's old pickup hums to a stop in front of the sheriff's station. He pulls the keys out of the ignition, slides out, and closes the door behind him. He takes a look down the sidewalk of the almost-dead downtown area. There are hardly any Halloween decorations out in front of the storefronts on the main street beside a stray pumpkin or two. Leaves have begun to fall from the trees planted every twenty feet on the grass between the road and the sidewalk. In no time, Halloween will be upon us once again.

Nathan pulls open the glass door to the sheriff's office and hears the ding of a fishing bell hanging on top of the door jam. His boots click on the wooden floor as he approaches the desk of Mable, the secretary who also serves as the 911 operator and the police dispatcher. She's a middle-aged woman with a tight perm, a floral blouse, and too much makeup. She's filing her nails as Nathan approaches. Just like the clerk at the truck stop, she doesn't acknowledge him as he approaches. He waits a moment, then casually leans over and taps the attendant bell on top of her desk. She sighed and put her nail file down on the desk, none too pleased to have to deal with another person in need of the police. Her attitude changes however, when she looks up at Nathan before her. Her eyes stare at his belt buckle, following the buttons of his denim shirt up his chest to his chin, which is littered with a week's growth of dark blonde stubble. That's not what stops her attention, though; neither is it his dimples when he smiles. Instead, she is stopped by his large grayish-blue eyes.

"Can I... Can I help you?" She manages to mutter.

He smiles and nods, sliding his hands into his front pockets.

"Yes, Ma'am. I'm looking for the sheriff. Is he in?"

"Yeah, but Jim.. err.. sheriff Dalton is on the phone right now. Can I ask who you are?"

"Sure thing. I'm Private Investigator Nathan Taylor. I'd like to talk to him about the Lisa Fields case."

"Who is Lisa?"

"Lisa Fields. Just let him know. I'm sure he'll talk to me." Nathan gives her a wink and turns to have a seat at the hard plastic waiting chairs beside the entrance. Mable, without taking her eyes off Nathan, picks up her phone and dials the sheriff's extension. He can see her put her hand over the receiver out of the corner of his eye. She's relaying precisely what he told her to say; then she hangs up the phone and waves to get his attention.

"sheriff will see you now, hunny," She says with a smile, emphasizing the hunny.

He stands with a smile and a nod.

"Thank you very much, sweetie."

He saunters past her, knowing exactly what he's doing. The sheriff's door is opened, and he is sitting behind a large mahogany desk; a large elk mount with antlers and a bighorn sheep skull with horns are mounted on the wall behind him. A stuffed black bear cub climbs half of a tree in the corner. Beside his desk stands a cougar, and on the desk, curled in a sleeping position, is a stuffed Gray Fox. The sheriff is obviously a hunter. He's on the phone as Nathan enters, so Nathan just stops and waits behind the chair opposite the sheriff at the desk, looking around at all the game animals. The sheriff ends his call and hangs up the phone. He doesn't bother to stand; instead, he just turns in his swivel chair to face Nathan.

"Good afternoon, I'm Sheriff Dalton. And who are you again?"

"Nathan Taylor. Private Investigator. License number..." He's cut off before he can give the sheriff his license number.

"Yeah, yeah, I believe you. What can I do for you, Mr Taylor?"

"I've been hired to investigate the murder of Lisa Fields. I'm hoping you'll let me look over all the police files and autopsy report."

The sheriff chuckles and rubs the thick, saggy, leathery skin hanging from below his chin.

"And why would I do that, Mr. Taylor?"

"Because I'm asking nicely? So can I save the $20 and not have to file a freedom of information act request?" Nathan sits at the swivel chair across the desk from the Sheriff without being invited to.

"It's an ongoing investigation, Mr. Taylor, you should know that. Therefore you should also know I can't give you any information. Whom may I ask who hired you?"

"A journalist from Portland. I guess she's working with Lisa's friends. Maybe her mother, too, I'm not sure. I'm still getting caught up."

"Oh, you mean that podcaster lady, don't you? That Sadie, whatever her name is. The big hot shot coming in from the city, going to swoop down on this small town and do something I couldn't do. Something my daddy couldn't do. Solve an almost 50-year-old murder case. That about right?"

"Your father was the sheriff when Lisa was murdered?" Nathan leans back in the chair.

"Yes, sir. George Dalton was the sheriff of this town for many years. He was a fine man and helped get this town back under control. They got a plaque dedicated to him down on the square. He sent me to a military academy back when I was young and helped get my life under control just like he did in this town. The town happily elected me after he passed away some years back. He did everything in his power to try to find that killer, and so have I. What makes you think you'll do any better, Mr. Taylor?"

"Please, call me Nathan, sheriff.'

"Mister Taylor. What makes you think you'll do any better? You and your city girl podcaster?"

Nathan feels the sheriff's eyes digging into him. He knew he wasn't going to get much help from law enforcement, but he never expected this type of hostility from the sheriff. He almost feels like Rambo in First Blood. This cop keeps pushing. How far is he willing to push? Nathan takes a slow breath and smiles.

"Well, sheriff, I don't expect to solve anything you and your father couldn't solve. I'm only here to provide any assistance that I can. You see, in today's day and age, some people are more likely to talk to a Private Investigator than cops. Cops kind of have a bad image right now, you know. What, with all the shootings and false imprisonments and choking and what not? But even so, I'm not working this solo. Some people would be much more inclined to talk to a journalist or even a podcaster. Most importantly, more people would be willing to talk to a pretty, young woman like Sadie instead of some asshole like me, or a seasoned wardog such as yourself. So we're not here to try and steal anyone's thunder; we're only trying to assist in any way we can."

The sheriff picks up a pen and jots something down. He could be scribbling circles and trying to get Nathan to flinch for all he knew, but Nathan's eyes stayed fixed on the sheriff. He's seen older guys peacock like this before. Give them some authority, and suddenly, they think they are king and are untouchable. But like any bully or wild animal, you can't give in, and you can't show fear. The sheriff stares at him for a moment, then smiles and stands, adjusting his holster and belt as he does so.

"Well, I do appreciate the help, Mr. Taylor. I'll give you a call if I need any more assistance. Until then, I invite you to go back to your cabin and your girlfriend to go back to Portfuckinland." He sneers as he leans over his desk down at Nathan, who is still seated. Nathan looks over at the cougar, staring at him with its shiny marble eyes, and then back at the sheriff. He stands and smiles, reaching out his hand to shake.

"Thank you for your time, Sheriff."

His hand stays out there for at least a minute as the sheriff stares him down before he withdraws his hand and exits his office. He gives Mable a smile and a wink as he walks out, shoving open the doors and exiting into the fresh autumn air.

When he gets to his truck, he stops and pulls out his phone, brings up Sadies number and hits the call icon.

"Hey Nathan, what's up?"

Nathan glances out his window at the sheriff, who is leaving his office and getting into his state-issued sheriff's SUV.

"Not much. I got the standard open investigation bullshit. But besides that, he was pretty hostile. Does not think too much of PI's, which is standard, but he really doesn't like you, or journalists, or podcasters, or women in general, I think. He's probably the oddest sheriff I've ever encountered. What did you learn from Cindy?"

"I'm just wrapping up the interview now. I got the names of Lisa's other friends: Johnny, Deena, and Kenny. Apparently, Deena and Kenny are married now. You still want to get together and come up with a game plan?"

"Sure, remember the diner in town I mentioned? I'll be there in two minutes."

"Are you paying?" He can almost hear her smirking through the phone.

"Yeah, whatever. Just get here when you can get here. I don't feel like waiting all day."

He ends the call and slides the phone into his pocket. The sheriff finally backs out of his parking spot and stops beside Nathan's truck.

"Anything else I can help you with Mr. Taylor" He lets his arm hang out the open window, his arm hair long and white.

"No, Sir. I am just heading up to the diner to get a bite to eat."

"Alright then, well after your meal, I suggest you get back to your cabin. Don't be bothering folks around here. People wanna forget that tragic event ever happened. Cedar Point is a happy town now, and locals don't need you or that girl from Portland to dig up the past. As you know, this is a quiet town, and we'd like to keep it that way. Catch what I'm saying, son?"

Nathan nods slowly, his face emotionless.

"I catch you loud and clear, Sheriff." He gives the roof of the SUV a pat.

"Well, alright then. Try the key lime pie at the diner; it's to die for." He smiles behind his thick white mustache and drives off. Nathan has to take a step back to keep from having his feet crushed underneath the off-road tires.

Nathan turns his head slightly and cracks his neck before beginning the walk down the sidewalk of Main Street towards the diner. Most of the shops are currently closed. He always thought they kept such weird hours. As he passes a bookstore, he notices the neon open sign is still lit, so he steps inside. The doorbell rings as he enters. There is a skinny, young man sitting behind a counter who gives Nathan the standard customer greeting without lifting his head from the novel he is reading.

"Excuse me, where is your occult section?"

The clerk looks up and gives him directions to the proper aisle. As Nathan walks down the aisle, he checks down the alphabetical order until he gets to the R section. He scans the names until he comes to the last name Rivers and the first name Oshun. He pulls the book off the shelf and looks at the cover. "Sacramental Theurgy for Warlocks: Advanced Liturgy Revealed." The cover features a large symbol that Nathan had never seen before, with smoke swirling around it. On the back was the face of the author. A young man in his 20s with short, curly, black hair, a thick, black mustache, tan skin, and brown eyes. He was wearing a black turtleneck with a silver chain around his neck. At the end of the chain was the same symbol that was on the front. He brought the book to the counter and paid for it. $9.99 for the 300-page book seemed a little high to him, but what did he know? He wasn't an author.

The cashier seemed to recognize the author as he was ringing up the purchase.

"You don't look like a Warlock fan to me."

"Probably because I'm not."

"Oh, then what are you doing buying a Warlock book, man? The clerk might be a little stoned right now. Nathan doesn't blame him; he'd have to be high to work in a bookstore, too.

"Thinking about converting, right now I'm just a Private Investigator. Figure being a Warlock might be more lucrative."

The stoned clerk doesnt respond. Instead he hands Nathan the book with the receipt stuck in the middle like a book mark.

"Have a good day, kid." Nathan nods as he turns around to leave.

"That author dude has a blog you might wanna check out. One of his stories is based in town."

"Oh yeah? What's the blog called?"

"How I saved Her Soul: A Dark Murder in my Hometown."

CHAPTER 8

"She Was My Rock."

Sadie gives Tango and Cash a kiss on their heads before she heads down the long gravel driveway. Nathan had already left for his meeting with the sheriff. He was starting to grow on her a little bit. Those dogs definitely helped, being they were the cutest things she had ever wrestled with. Once Nathan let down that false facade, he was actually somewhat enjoyable. As she got into the Uber she gave a big smile.

"Hey Craig! How are ya today?"

"I'm good, Sadie. Where are you headed today?" He gave the rearview mirror a smile.

"Trailer park on the south end of town."

"What's your business down there? Some shady people live down there. Not the safest place."

Sadie chuckles. "I can defend myself, thanks though. I have to interview Cindy Summers. Do you remember her from school?"

"Vaguely." He strokes his beard in thought. "I remember her being a bit of a tattletail."

"I see." Sadie looks out the window, watching the scenery as they drive. She was lost in thought as they entered the trailer park. Most of the trailers looked like they hadn't been washed or even repaired in at least 40 years.

"Remember what I told you. This isn't the safest area. I'll stay nearby if you need a ride back."

"Thanks, Craig. You're the best Uber driver in town!" She smiled as she got up and walked up to Cindy's trailer. It was a green and white single wide. Or at least Sadie thought it was green and white. It might have been gray and white at one point, maybe back in the 70s, but now it was encrusted with muck and growth. The grass was uncut, and the front step was held up by cinder blocks. Sadie gave the door a knock. After a few moments, a plump older woman answered. Her short hair had so much hairspray in it, that it was shaped almost like a beehive. It was obvious she dyed it brown, as she had an inch of gray roots sticking up underneath it. She wore too much blush and had lipstick stuck on her teeth. Her green eyes darted side to side from behind bright, green eyeshadow. She smiled as she saw Sadie.

"Sadie! Darling! Come on in!" She stepped aside and let Sadie in. She gave her a big smile as she entered and looked around. The walls were wrapped in wood paneling, which blended into the dark brown shag carpet that looked like it hadn't been vacuumed since it was installed in the 80s. She had glass curio cabinets with little glass figures and ceramic eggs inside.

"Thanks for taking the time to meet with me, Cindy."

"Oh, of course. I'd do anything to help catch Lisa's killer. Please have a seat, can I get you anything to drink?" She motioned to the small wooden table in the middle of the tiny kitchen area. Sadie takes a seat and places her phone in the middle of the table.

"No, thanks. Do you mind if we get started right away?"

"Oh, not at all!" She sits down, still smiling. Sadie pushes the record button, and the seconds roll.
"So, how did you meet Lisa?"

"I remember the first day of kindergarten. We were all new, and no one knew each other. I was sitting over on the circle rug playing with some Lincoln Logs when I noticed Lisa. She stood out because she was half Hawaiian. Lisa was the prettiest girl ever. She was sitting alone, and I asked her if she wanted to play with the Lincoln Logs with me. The rest is history. We've been best friends ever since."

"What kind of girl was Lisa?"

"Oh, Lisa was just the sweetest girl you'd ever met. She was such a sweetheart. I remember one time, this boy broke up with me, right? Well, Lisa got so mad at him that she went up to him at lunchtime and dumped his food tray on his lap. She was such a tough little one, I tell you! And funny, too. We would just lay outside in the grass, looking up at the clouds and trying to find silly shapes. We would just lay shoulder to shoulder for hours, laughing and laughing until our stomachs hurt, and we had tears running down our eyes."

Sadie smiles. Cindy was getting pretty animated with her tales, and she could see the amount of emotion that she had inside of her at the loss of her friend.

"So, Lisa was supposed to be sleeping over here the night she was murdered?" She looks around at the small two-bedroom trailer.

"Yeah, my parents were never home, so we could stay up later than if we slept over at her house. Obviously, her house was nicer than this dump, but her mom was a stickler for the rules. Especially after her Daddy died in that car accident."

"In your email, you said she never showed up that night. Did you talk to her that day?"

"Yeah, sure. We spoke after school. She said she would have dinner at home, grab the stuff for her costume, and she'd be over before the curfew started so she wouldn't get in trouble. I think she was gonna meet up with her boyfriend beforehand, too."

"And that's the last you heard of her?"

Cindy nods, tears starting to form in her eyes.

"Yup. Never saw her again. If only I went out looking for her. Maybe I would have found her before she got murdered. Maybe we'd be neighbors right now. Or maybe I wouldn't still be living in this shit hole, and I wouldn't have had all the problems I had in my life after her death."

"What kind of problems did you have, Cindy?"

"Well, after Lisa died, I blamed myself a lot. I turned to drugs. I ended up moving up to Seattle in the 80s. I took part in some wild times. I tried to party myself to death. I just couldn't stop blaming myself for her death. I felt like I was the one who killed her."

"Why, because you didn't go looking for her?"

"Yes! As her best friend, that was my responsibility!" She slaps the table, tears running down her cheeks.

"Cindy, you were nothing but a child too. You could have been killed as well."

"Well, that's fine. I didn't want to live anyway. I'm better now, been clean for over a decade now. Now, I want closure and justice for Lisa. She deserves to finally have peace in her life."

"Do you remember any of her other friends? You said she had a boyfriend?"

"Yeah, she was dating Johnny. He was a jerk but kind of a pushover. She didn't really have many friends besides me. I remember a girl named Deena who kept trying to hang out with her, but Lisa didn't really like her that much. Deena was a stuck-up bitch. She was a narc. If the kids were having a party or causing problems, she was the first one to call the sheriff and report him. There was this jock named Kenny that was friends with Johnny. Kenny was a dick. Lisa mostly just hung out with me. That's why she and Johnny were always fighting. He felt jealous that we were such good friends. I think Kenny and Deena are married now. Johnny is just some useless drunk that lives in a trailer down at the end of the lot. They can all burn in hell for all I care. They didn't know Lisa, not how I knew her."

"Did you know the two boys who hung out at the cemetery? They were like witches or dressed in black."

"I've heard of them. Oshun and Willow or something like that. I never knew them. The entire town thinks it's them, but I don't think so. I think it was one of her friends."

"Really? Why do you think that?"

"Because Lisa wouldn't be alone in a park with a stranger. She was too safe for that. She didn't go anywhere or do anything with someone she didn't know and trust. In fact, besides me, the only people she would have gone anywhere with were the people I just named. Maybe it was Johnny? I don't know. He seemed to try to pressure her a lot, but he also seemed pretty in love with her. I doubt he could have hurt her. Kenny was a big bully. He might have done something. Deena is a bitch; she might have been hurt that Lisa did not want another best friend. Maybe Deena was gay about Lisa or something, and Lisa turned her down, and she snapped. I'm not sure, but I really think it was someone she knew very well."

"I see." Sadie nods, taking in all the information, when suddenly her phone rings. She see's Nathans number and hits the answer icon.

"Hey Nathan, what's up?" She speaks into the phone. She gives Cindy a polite smile as she listens.

"I'm just wrapping up the interview now. I got the names of Lisa's other friends. Johnny, Deena, and Kenny. Apparently,

Deena and Kenny are married now. You still want to get together and come up with a gameplan?" She responds. Cindy plays with the hem of her shirt as Sadie talks on the phone.

"Are you paying?" Sadie smirks and then hangs up the phone and places it back on the table.

"Sorry about that, Cindy. I have to get going. Is there anything else you wanna add?"

"No. Just solve this murder and bring me some closure about my friend's death. Please." She gives a sad smile. Sadie grabs her hands and gives them a squeeze.

"I'll do everything in my power, Cindy. I promise."

Cindy gives Sadie a big hug at the door and holds her arms, tears welling up in her eyes once again.

"You are such a good person, Sadie. I know Lisa would have just loved you!"

"Thank you." Sadie chuckles a bit before waving goodbye and heading back to Craig's waiting Uber ride.

"Well, you didn't get shanked or robbed. That's a good sign." Craig said with a smile into the rearview mirror. "Where to?"

"Dee's Diner."

CHAPTER 9

"Dinner and Dancing at Dee's diner"

Nathan walks into the small diner towards the end of Main St. A woman, probably in her early 60s, is serving two plates to a couple off to the side of the diner. She looks tired and overworked, probably underpaid.

"Have a seat anywhere, hon; I'll be with you in a minute or two."

Nathan nods and goes over to take a seat at a small booth along the windows that overlooks the sidewalk on Main street. He pulls out his phone and Google's, "Oshun Rivers blog" and a hit comes up. Before he can start reading, the waitress comes over. He turns off his screen and lays his phone down on the table. She places a glass of water and a menu in front of him, holding a pot of coffee in her other hand.

"Sorry about that. I'm Deena, and I'll be your waitress today. Any Coffee hon?"

"Sure, thank you." He turns the coffee cup over so she can pour him a cup of coffee that has probably been burning since 6 am this morning.

"You know what you want?"

"I actually have someone else coming, so I'll wait for her. Thank you."

"Ok, just holler if you need anything." She gives him a weak smile as she walks away. Her white sneakers squeaking on the floor and graying, reddish ponytail swishing behind her.

Nathan unlocks his phone. He clicks on the first Google result and is greeted by a man who looks a lot different than he did on the back of his book. Oshun still had the same hairstyle, but now his hair was completely gray, and his receding hairline had moved his forehead six inches up his head. He also no longer had a mustache. He sported a full white beard, which was probably grown purely to hide the fact that he's put on probably 40 lbs since his book photo was taken. Before he can start reading, he notices Sadie walking up the sidewalk towards the diner. He puts his phone away and takes a drink of the thick, black, sour mug of coffee.

Sadie comes in and smiles as she plops down across the table.

"This place is so cute! Have you eaten here before? What's good?"

"I have never eaten here before, but the sheriff told me to try the Key Lime Pie. I don't recommend coffee."

"If he's giving you pie recommendations, it doesn't sound like it went all that bad with him."

Before Nathan could respond, the waitress came back over with a pot of coffee in one hand, a water glass, and a menu in the other. She places a glass of water and a menu in front of Sadie with a tired smile.

"Hello, I'm Deena, and I'll be your waitress today. Any coffee hon?"

"No thanks," She responds with a sideways smile to Nathan as if they're the only two in on the joke. Then something clicks, and she looks back at the waitress. "Wait, you're not Deena from Dee's Diner, are you?

"In the flesh." She does a half curtsy and smiles.

"You don't happen to be Deena Fox?"

The waitress chuckles and sets the pot of coffee on the table.

"A long time ago, I was Deena Fox; now I'm Deena Neil."

"You're married to Kenny Neil?" Sadie looks from the waitress to Nathan as if he's supposed to understand what's going on, then back to the waitress.

"Yes, why? Do you know Ken? Am I supposed to know who you are?" She begins to look slightly concerned.

"I'm Sadie Koop, host of a podcast called Growing Cold. Have you heard of it?"

"Oh heavens no. I don't have any time to listen to the radio, let alone a podcast. I'm here from 5am until 10pm. Hour before we open until an hour after we close. Can't find any other waitresses. I'm just glad we still got Lee the cook back there."

"I got you and your husband's names from Cindy Summers. Do you remember her?"

"No, did she work here?"

"No," Sadie shakes her head, thick brown tussles moving against her cheeks. "You went to high school together. She was also friends with Lisa Fields."

The waitress grows a little pale as she hears that name. She wipes a few strands of loose hair from her face, then wipes her hand on her apron.

"Oh my. I haven't heard that name in years."

"So you remember Lisa?"

"Oh, of course. We were best friends. Got into all sorts of trouble together. She was supposed to be sleeping over at my house the night she was..."

She stops mid sentence, as the memories come flooding back to her. Her green eyes begin to well up with tears and she takes a long slow breath. Sadie moves towards the window and motions for Deena to sit.

"I know this can be hard to bring back up. Please have a seat. My partner here is a Private Investigator, and we are working together to try to solve Lisa's murder."

Nathan gives her a soft smile.

"Names Nathan Taylor, ma'am."

"Why do you two wanna solve this? What was Lisa to either of you?" Deena sits beside Sadie and takes a drink from the glass of water that she brought for Sadie.

Nathan shrugs.

"Up until a few days ago, I had never even heard of her. But Sadie seems pretty determined to help crack this case, and well, when I was young, I had a sister who was murdered. They never caught her killer either, so I know how it feels not to have closure. I wish someone took an interest in her case the way Sadie is in your friend's case."

Sadie smiles at him and then places a hand on Deena's forearm.

"I've helped solve cold cases before. The family and friends always ask me the same question you just asked. I always give them the same answer because it's the right thing to do. Because one day, I can tell my children mommy did something good one time. Mommy helped people, and I can go to sleep knowing I have made a positive difference in the world. Not many people can say that."

Deena stares down at the table for a few minutes, pondering what Sadie just said. Letting the memories trickle back into her. Reliving the tragic experience from almost 50 years ago. Finally, she lifts her head and gives Sadie a smile and pats her hand.

"Ok, what can I do to help? What do you want to know?"

"Awesome! Thank you so much. So you said Lisa was supposed to come to your house that night?"

"Yeah, we were gonna work on our costumes for the Halloween dance. I don't even remember what they were gonna be, but I had a sewing machine, and she didn't. So we were gonna make our costumes and talk about boys and yanno, do what teenage girls did back then."

"Do you know who Lisa was dating around that time?" Nathan asks, pulling out a small notebook and pen to take notes.

"Of course, Johnny Olsen. They'd been dating for about a year. Well, almost a year exactly. Their official anniversary was going to be on Halloween if I remember correctly. Yeah, that's right, cuz they were supposed to wear a couple's costume like Raggedy Ann and Andy or something silly like that. But, she said they were having trouble or something. That's why she was coming over, so we could make her own costume. Now I remember. Sorry, it's been so long; it's hard to keep things straight."

"Do you know what type of problems they were having?" Nathan scribbles in his notebook.

"I guess Johnny was getting really impatient with her not wanting to go all the way. She wanted her first time to be something extraordinary, and she didn't want to rush. He was constantly trying to pressure her into doing it and then getting really mad if she didn't."

Sadie brushes her hair behind one ear.

"You said she was supposed to come to your house. I take it she never showed up. Or[1], did she show up and leave?"

"She never showed up. She said Johnny wanted to talk to her first. I don't know, maybe try to reconcile or something? They had broken up and gotten together a bunch of times before this."

"Do you know if they met up at all?

"I asked Johnny at the funeral, and he said he never saw her that night. Rumors went around that she turned him down one too many times, and he snapped and killed her. But I don't believe that. I always thought it was those devil boys that used to hang out over at Gold Lawn doing all their voodoo and nonsense." She waves her hands dismissively at the thought

"Gold Lawn?" Sadie asks, not being familiar with the town.

"Yeah, Gold Lawn Cemetery. It's over off Spring street. Now it's pretty big; it's been added onto so many times. Lisa's buried there along with her daddy. But back then, in 77, it was tiny and had a bunch of woods behind it. There's actually a trail that used to go across a river and end up over at the Davidson Memorial Park."

"Do you think your husband would talk to us? He knew Lisa as well, didn't he?"

"Yeah, he and Johnny were friends. They played on the baseball team together."

Sadie pulls a business card from the pocket of her jeans and slides it to her. This was the first time Nathan noticed that she didn't carry a purse with her.

"Have him call or email; both are on the card."

"I should get back to work." Deena turns her attention towards the couple sitting at the countertop section.

"Of course, thank you so much for your time. Call me if you remember anything else." Sadie gives her a warm smile. After Deena grabs her coffee pot from the table and heads to the counter, she turns to Nathan.

"So what do you think?"

It's interesting that Lisa said she was supposed to see Johnny that night, but he claimed otherwise. Also, didn't you say Cindy claimed that Lisa was supposed to be staying at her house making costumes?"

Sadie smiles wide, snaps her fingers, and points at him.

"Bingo! That's what immediately came to mind. They both tell the same story. So, which one of the two is lying to us about Lisa staying over? And did Johnny actually see her that night?"

"How was Cindy when you talked to her?"

Sadie seems to chuckle as she recalls the meeting.

"It was sad. She's dead set that she was best friends with Lisa. Unlike Deena, she didn't have any trouble remembering any details. She told me about playdates and birthday parties they had back when they were eight. Stuff so far back that I couldn't remember those times in my life if I thought back on them. After Lisa's death, she moved to Seattle and hit the party scene. She said she got clean a decade or so ago. She really, really seems to want to get this solved."

"Who does she think the killer is?"

"She thinks it's someone who knew Lisa. Someone in their little group of friends. She said Kenny was a dick, Johnny was a pushover, and Deena was a stuck-up bitch. She said that Deena was always calling the sheriff on other kids. For example, if she saw them planning a party or something, she would call good old George Dalton to come and put a stop to it. Judging by the Deena I just met, that doesn't really sound like her. But who knows? I mean, people change a lot in almost 50 years, eh?"

"That's true. What about Johnny? Do you have his number or anything on him yet?"

"Nope, just his name. It shouldn't be too hard to find him. I mean, we just happened to have Deena wait on us, and Kenny is her husband. The odds of that happening are astronomical! That just leaves Johnny."

"And this guy and his buddy." He slides the book across the table to her.

"Holy 30 year old virgin, Batman! He looked way different at the podcast convention, still nerdy though." she explains as she looks at the photo of the author on the back of the book, smiling as she reads the synopsis below the photo out loud.

"In the Sacramental Theurgy for Warlocks: Advanced Liturgy Revealed, Oshun Rivers improves upon Warlock symbology of the past sixty-nine centuries. This book can take a disciple far beyond the rudimentary magickal practices of the dilettante and help them to develop a spiritual and magickal discipline that furthers spiritual transformation and conscious evolution. It contains the knowledge necessary for acquiring a competent background in the art of 'complete bullshit,' she laughs, not able to contain herself.

"How fuckin long is this anyways? This description is an entire chapter. Let's see. Blah, blah, blah. 'Oshun Rivers has been working and teaching new forms of magick since he was 15, and assisted in starting a magickal lodge where this discipline was taught and practiced' and probably never got laid in that magickal lodge. Jesus, I can't handle this!" She lays the book down and laughs as she rubs her face.

"Yeah, he seems pretty out there. He has a blog too. I guess about Lisa and her murder. I have yet to read it."

"Do you have it on your phone? Fuckin read it to me! Storytime!!" She accidentally slaps her hands on the table a little too excitedly, then casually glances around to see if anyone is staring at her. No one even pays her any mind. Deena must be back in the kitchen or an office, and the couple at the countertop have paid their bill and left. She looks back to Nathan with a mischievous grin, leaning over the table towards him and speaking in a low, sensual tone.

"Read it to me in a sexy voice, like Keith Morrison."

"Who?" Nathan arches an eyebrow. Sadie rolls her eyes.

"From Dateline. Jesus, you are lame!"

"I don't even own a TV; you saw that for yourself. Why are you so shocked? Whatever." Nathan pulls out his phone and pulls up the blog. "Are you sure you wanna hear this?"

"Heck yes, storytime, baby!"

CHAPTER 10

"How I Saved her Soul"

Nathan takes a drink of his water then looks at Sadie before looking down at his phone. He clears his throat and then begins storytime in his most professional-sounding voice.

"This is a biographical glimpse into the life of a magickal master. An event that powerfully impacted and shaped me along with the entire community I grew up in. This is a tale from when I was a youth many decades ago.

It was just before All Hallows Eve that our tale really began.

One late fall afternoon, when the fog was rolling into town off the white tipped waves of the Ocean, I was practicing the dark arts near the headstones of my ancestors down in the Gold Lawn Cemetery when I was approached by someone whom I would never forget.

The most beautiful and attractive young woman that I have ever laid eyes on came up to me with a couple of her friends. I had never seen this woman before, but her friends were students with whom I had a slight acquaintance.

"This is him! That guy I was tellin' you about! The one who can save us all," one of her friends called out.

She then looked me in the eye and smiled a shy smile, and said rather directly, "I wanna talk to you but not now! I gotta split, man!"

Before I could reply, she and her friends were gone. I thought to myself, "Well, I'll be a goat's head on the sabbath. A nice-looking, petite young female wants to talk to me, the High Priest Warlock of the Dark Arts. This is going to be the happiest of days."

Normally, the jocks and nerds at my local high school didn't want to talk to me since I was becoming a master Warlock, so this was a rare event and one that I remembered quite well, even years later. This is because the woman who spoke to me and told me that we needed to talk was named Lisa Fields.

She may have told me her name just before she ran off into the cool Autumn Eve, or maybe I learned it later, but I didn't remember it, I just knew it somehow. It was a name I somehow had always known. It was imprinted on my soul from birth. Most importantly, I remembered how lovely she looked and how bold and self assured she seemed.

A force to be reckoned with wrapped up in a tight little package, I had pondered.

This happened at the end of September back in 1977. I had all but forgotten that some cute young woman had talked briefly to me and promised to talk more later. I was absorbed in the difficulties and troubles of my own life and had little time or interest to be concerned with anyone else's troubles.

Yet, for some reason, I began to feel a kind of dread. I felt this darkness approaching me and everyone else in town. I told my associate, Willow, that he needed to develop more in order to understand. He was almost a year younger than me and was nowhere near as practiced as I was, nor would he ever be.

Then, on Halloween, October 31st, 1977, our entire high school was thrust into a state of shock, panic, awe, and grief.

It was subtle. Some of the girls were weeping against their lockers while some were standing in bewilderment and talking about some horrible incident. Then there was a hush throughout the hallways of the old school as I entered, the soles of my sneakers seemed to echo on the titles.

I went around to pique my curiosity and discovered that some girl named Lisa had been horribly murdered. Lisa, that tiny little bombshell of sexual arousal, was murdered. I was shocked by the news. The beautiful bullet in a tiny full metal jacket that wanted, no.. needed my help had been brutally butchered and left as a fleshlight on the bottom of a child's play slide. I felt that I had let her down.

A day or so later, Lisa's friends caught me practicing outside in Gold Lawn again. They demanded I help them. I was tall, strong, and imposing, but they literally threw me down and accosted me. They said high-level Black Warlocks were after them. I am a level 99 White Warlock now; back then, I was only level 27. Black Warlocks are the opposite of White Warlocks. We Whites practice everything good. We work hard. We do what is right. Black's only want to riot and cause destruction. They don't want to work for anything; they just want to take it. Black Warlocks are a step above Red Warlocks, which are also evil. Red Warlocks are just more shifty. These girls insisted these Blacks had killed Lisa.

I was shocked and dismayed to hear that this lovely, shy, petite but tough young woman, who had been trying to see me and who had briefly talked to me, had met such a terrible end by dirty blacks. If only I, the White Warlock master, had listened to her back when she beckoned.

Her two friends, one was named Diana and the other was called "Ribbit", because she had a short torso and arms with really long legs, invited me over to their house to discuss how I could protect them.

I ended up in the bedroom alone with these two terrified but beautiful young and vulnerable girls. They wanted me to protect them, to kill the Black Warlocks. But I, being a White Warlock, could not do that. Whites don't kill; only Blacks do."

"Shut the front door. Does he really keep calling the bad Warlocks blacks? Like they're black people or something? Cuz that's racist as fuck!" Sadie interjects, interrupting the story, before taking a sip from Nathan's glass of water.

"I guess so? Not a lot of this makes sense. Who is Diana and Ribbit?"

"No clue! And why does he keep writing like he's the world's sexiest man and everyone wants him?"

Nathan chuckles and shrugs before Sadie starts rapidly twisting her hand around in circles, trying to get him to continue.

"Keep going!"

Nathan takes a sip of his glass, the one that Sadie apparently claimed as her own, and continues.

"I consoled them the only way I knew how. I cleaned their body holes and wiped their meta fillings. It wasn't until after I got home that night, I showered the filth off of me and went to bed, that I was filled with the most intense visions. I witnessed every aspect of Lisa's murder. The assault, the stripping naked, the rape, the stabbing, the posing of the body."

This time, it's Nathan who stops reading. He gazes down at the words on his phone for a moment then up at Sadie.

"Was Lisa sexually assaulted or raped before she was murdered?

Sadie shakes her head slowly.

"No. Everything I read was that she was a virgin and that she died a virgin. In fact, the rumors about Oshun and Willow committing the murder was because Lisa was a virgin, and they needed one for some ritual. And you heard Deena. She said Lisa was a virgin and that Johnny kept pressuring her.

Nathan nods and continues.

"When I woke up, I felt the oddest sensation. I was no longer my tall, muscular, intimidating, magickal self. Instead, I felt like the

beautiful, intelligent, and quirky tiny spitfire who was murdered.

I realized that Lisa was living inside of me. She penetrated my being from behind and wrapped herself around my extraterrestrial existence. She raped my core level and took a shit in my charka. It was no longer just me; I was two.

I began to talk to her. We had the longest deepest conversations that I've ever had in my life. Some turned dirty but most were intellectual. Our souls entwined in the purest form.

Lisa told me that she was afraid and confused. She knew that she was dead, but she didn't know what to do next. I knew what to do, but I did not want to. I was content with this hurricane living inside of my bowels for the rest of my days. The next day, I consulted with Willow to get his uneducated opinion. He surprised me when he suggested I help guide her to the other side. Reluctantly, I agreed and began to prepare for the ritual.

By this time, it was Thanksgiving. I had spent weeks with Lisa, who was living inside me. She was sitting with me in class and washing my nether regions when I showered—helping me learn the art of the Warlock. But alas, I had finally prepared to help her transcend this earth and move on to what else awaits. That night, as the snow fell, I went to her murder site and stripped myself naked. As I stood with my bare feet in the frozen sand, my nipples were as hard as my erect penis. I covered my body in pig's blood that I had purchased from a farmer outside of town. After covering my nude form, I climbed the ladder, the metal rungs freezing my feet. I placed my goose-pimpled buttcheeks on the metal slide, and I slid down until I rested at the bottom where she was found. Positioning myself on my back, with my feet stuck straight in the air. My scrotum resting on the metal slide and my erection peering up to the heavens, I felt myself cross into another realm.

There in the nether realm, we walked together towards a large ball of white shimmering light. Around us was pitch blackness, yet we could see the existence of everything. Our town of Cedar Point was *devastated and lay in ruins around us. The river ran red with blood into the ocean, before it had dried out and been depleted. The Black Warlocks ran the streets. We walked together hand and hand, nude, except for the crowns upon our heads. When we reached the center of the light, she turned and gripped my hand the way a bride holds her groom's hands. She kissed me and smiled as she spoke to me. She said,*

"Don't seek to avenge my death. I was killed by no one I knew. It was a stranger, and I wish him no ill will. I only wish for peace, love, and happiness for everyone. Please, Oshun, forget this terrible event and live your greatest life. I praise the cosmos that I finally found you at last, and now I am going to my final resting place. We have met and intertwined as snakes do during mating, so maybe that's what might have been had I lived, or perhaps more. I have lived inside you, and I wish I had you inside me when I lived. What's done is done, and nothing can change it. I leave you now with a smile and a single tear, my dear."'

Once again, Sadie interrupts Nathan's reading of the blog.

"Get the fuck out of here! He did not write that. This was a 16-year-old girl that was murdered, and he's saying her ghost wanted him to fuck her? What the fuck? For real, what the fuck?"

Nathan chuckles and shrugs, then continues.

"Having said that and stroking my cheek, she turned and walked into the light. It was at that moment I felt her existence leave me, and all my strength and masculinity returned tenfold.

She was gone, forever. But I couldn't help but dissect her words the same way the killer tried dissecting her on the slide.

I believed that if Lisa had not been murdered, something extraordinary and romantic might have happened between us. Who knows, maybe she might have been the mother of the children that I never had. I was not a virgin at the time, but I felt like I was the one meant to take her virginity. I believe that she was, in fact, my soul mate. Never being able to connect with her is the reason I never had a committed relationship afterward, why I turned to drugs and found comfort in thousands of sexual partners over the course of my life.

Lisa was very likely the victim of a serial killer since her spirit was not vengeful, nor did she ever seek any retribution against the man who had killed her. She said that she didn't know who her killer was, but released from the cares and worries of life, she did not want to dwell on it. So obviously, the killer was not from town and was not me, nor was it my protege Willow. I think the rest of the people in town should take a lesson from Lisa and not dwell on her murder. Move on.

She had implored me not to perform any magic against her killer and had implied that the group of Black Warlocks she had known had not been responsible for her death. I promised not to perform any magic against her killer. I easily could have smitten the killer down with a snap of my fingers, but I let my love for her control my hand for the rest of my life.

Her friends had been absolutely terrified, thinking that this group of Black Warlock thugs had been the perpetrators of the murder, and would thus seek to strike again. They sought me out to aid and comfort them, and I did so in the same way I would have comforted Lisa the first time she came to me in the cemetery. Comfort is the only way I know how. "

"Who talks like this? I mean, Jesus..." Sadie lays her forehead down on the table with her hands on the back of her head.

"Apparently a Warlock who has published what.. 14 books? Jesus. Is it that easy to get published? Everyone should write a book then."

Sadie laughs and sits back up.

"Keep going. This shit is killing me!"

Nathan continues.

"I held on to my belief that the Evil Warlock gang had done the deed,

as did Lisa's friends.

During this brief intermission of my life, I befriended some of Lisa's closest friends, including the beautiful purple haired and yellow eyed woman who was slightly older than me named Ribbit. She accompanied Lisa to the cemetery to talk to me.

She was originally from Salem, Oregon, but might as well have been from the original Salem; Ribbit was kind of the leader, and Diana was more of the submissive of the two girls.

A dim recollection of mine is going into a bar with Ribbit and a friend of hers to see where the Black punks gathered. I recall Ribbit pointing them out to me with a certain amount of personal venom spilling out of her tiny but tight little mouth. She even got out of the booth that we were sitting in and went over to where several Black Warlocks sat. Dressed in black shirts and black pants, they were sitting on stools before the bar. Ribbit said something to them that I don't have the heart to share or repeat.

The supposed leader of this gang got off of his stool and stood before Ribbit, saying something to the effect, "We ain't got nuthin' to do with that, Jack!"

I also vaguely remember him looking quite distressed and shouting at Ribbit, "Stop telling folks we did that! We didn't do that!"

I also thought Ribbit may have said something like, 'What are you gonna do about it if I don't? Huh? Stab me too? You wanna rape me also, Blackie??"

At that point the leader backed down, and just said, "Just cool it girl! We don't want any trouble and we didn't do it!"

Sadie, once again unable to contain herself, interjects.

"Ok, this dude is A.) full of shit and B.) totally fuckin racist. Did people talk like that in the late 70s? That sounds like fan fiction Grease meets fan fiction Dolomite. I need a drink after this bullshit. How much is left?"

Nathan skims through the blog a little bit, then continues.

"He's almost done. Let's see. He goes on to say he doesn't believe the Black Warlocks committed the murder. He talks about doing lots of LSD with Willow. Um. Oh, he says later in life, he did a psychic scan of the universe and saw that the killer was no longer alive. So I guess this clears up a bunch."

"For sure! We can cross him and his buddy Willow off the suspect list. Along with anyone else who is alive. So that leaves us with no one." She leans back and laughs letting her head fall backwards.

"So what now, Nathan?"

Nathan strokes the week's worth of dark blonde facial hair growing on his jawline as he ponders this question.

"How about I find out who our two Warlocks are? What are their names? Oshun Rivers and Willow, something or another? I'll find them and get some information. You set up a meeting with Kenny. Maybe try to find Johnny and see if he'll talk too. Hey, is Lisa's mother still alive?

Sadie pulls her phone out and scrolls through before looking up at Nathan.

"Sounds good, and yes. She's still alive. She's in an assisted living facility out in Portland. Should I try and see if we can get in and talk to her?

Nathan nods, locks his phone, and slides it back into his pocket. He grabs his book and stands.

"You got the bill, right?"

Sadie leans back with her hands behind her head and laughs.

"You are such a dick."

CHAPTER 11

"Where the Oshun Rivers Flow"

Nathan opens his phone after he gets into his truck and pulls up the search results for Oshun Rivers. He scrolls through until he finds the contact information for his agent. He clicks on "Call Now" and holds the phone up to his ear. Four rings later, a woman answers.

"Hello, Stacking Stones Management Agency; this is Rita; how may I help you?"

"Hey Rita, my name is Brandon Jones. I'm an executive with Apex Publishing House, and I'm interested in contracting one of your writers. I believe his name was Oshun Rivers?"

"Oh yes, Oshun is a fine author. We'd love to discuss the opportunity."

"Well, here's the thing: we have a very large check with a lot of zeros, but you see, I'm kind of a big fan myself. So I'd like to meet with him first to discuss business in person. Then you guys and our lawyers can hammer everything else out. I know it'll go smoothly; it always has in the past for us."

"Oh, I see; I'm not sure if I'm allowed to make that call or not."

"Well, I guess I'll just have to call another author then to write my book for me. Thanks for your time, Rita."

Before Nathan can even pretend to hang out, she quickly blurts out.

"No, wait, I'm sure Oshun would love to set up a meeting with you. Can I have him call you?"

"No, Rita, I'd like to surprise him. What's his address?"

"Oh, I definitely can't give out his.." Nathan cuts her off.

"Thanks for your time, Rita. Have a good.." She cuts him off this time.

"Ok, wait. Let me look it up. He lives in Portland, on the high rise on the corner of SW 5th Ave and SW Oak St., Suite 80D."

"Thanks, Rita. It's much appreciated."

Nathan hangs up before she can say anymore. He punches the address into Google Maps. Not a bad building. Looks like Mr Rivers has done pretty well for himself. He clicks on the directions icon, 45 minutes without any traffic. He clicks "Go," starts his truck, and heads off towards the highway. On the way, he doesn't listen to the Growing Cold podcast or the Playmore podcast. He just drives in silence since this is what he's grown accustomed to over the past few years. He just prays that the sounds of the engine and the tires on the blacktop can drown out the thoughts in his head.

Fifty-five minutes later, Nathan is at the high rise in Portland. It took him another ten minutes to find a parking spot a few blocks away. It's dinner time, and the rush is on. The sidewalks are packed, and Nathan can already feel his anxiety level rising. This is why he moved to the middle of nowhere. Soon enough, he's at the large glass doors of the high rise, which has a buzzer intercom system. He slides his finger down the names listed beside the suite numbers until he reaches number 80D. At first, he wonders if Rita lied to him because the name beside the number doesn't say Oshun Rivers; it says Oliver Garlicky. Then, it dawns on him that Oshun is obviously a pen name. He shakes his head at his own stupidity and rings the buzzer. A few minutes later, an elegant-sounding man responded.

"Yes? To whom am I speaking?"

"FedEx, Sir," Nathan lies, checking around to make sure they don't have any cameras with the intercom. Luckily, they don't. The man rings back.

"Oh heavens, just leave it in the mailbox. I shan't be bothered now, I'm writing!"

"I have a same-day envelope from Stacking Stones, something or another? I need a signature. I think it's a check or something cuz that's the only time I need to have a signature."

"Oh, fine. Come on up."

The buzzer beeps and the lock clicks open. Nathan enters and heads to the elevator and rides up to the 80th floor. He walks down the hall until he reaches suite D and lightly knocks like a Fedex driver would. The look on Oshuns' face is one of utter confusion and slight annoyance.

"What? Who are you? You don't look like a FedEx employee. Where is your uniform, and where is my check?"

"My name is Nathan Taylor. I'm a Private Investigator, and I need to have a few words with you."

Oshun goes to slam the door in his face, but Nathan's been in this position more times than not. His boot is already between the door and the jam, and he shoves it open, moving Oshun back in the process.

"Mind if I have a seat, Oliver?" Nathan scans the suite as he walks in and takes a seat on the oversized, plush white couch. For a Warlock, this place doesn't have the normal dark magic feel. There are no occult symbols or blood goblets or anything of the sort. There are a few tacky pieces of art hung on the walls and a few pictures of cats scattered around. Oshun is dressed in a long flowing yellow silk kimono robe, which is open, revealing blue sweatpants and a hairy beer belly.

"Get out of my condo! I'm going to call security!" He walks over to an old-fashioned rotary phone on the desk beside the balcony and lifts the receiver.

"Come on, Ollie, we both know that this place doesn't have security. If it did, you wouldn't have buzzed me up. Now put the phone down, have a seat, and let's talk."

"Stop calling me that; my name is Oshun!" He hangs up the phone and folds his robe closed dramatically before tying the belt and sitting on a plush chair across a giant white coffee table. "What does this pertain to?"

"The murder of Lisa Fields."

Oshun rolls his eyes and leans his head back with a loud sigh. "For the love of all that is good and holy, why in the heck are you speaking to me? I had nothing to do with that awful event."

"That's not what the people in town think. Seems like you are suspect number one, and your little buddy Willow is suspect number two. Don't suppose he lives here too?"

"No. I have not spoken to Willow in eons. We went separate paths after high school. I became a Grand Warlock, and he went on to become a Catholic Priest."

"Wow, he gave up one cult for another one, eh?" Nathan pulls out his notebook and starts scratching down information. "What's Willow's real name?"

"William Buchanan. The last I heard was he moved away when he joined the church right after we graduated. Like I said, neither he nor I had anything to do with that event."

"What about your blog post? Sounds like you actually had a lot to do with it. You saved Lisa's soul after all, didn't you? After she penetrated your own soul?" Nathan pushes just a little bit.

"My role was not at all central, and I am suspicious of your intentions, Sir."

"My intentions are to solve this murder. That's what I've been hired to do."

"Who hired you? The sheriff? Doubtful!" He bawks at the idea.

"No, a woman by the name of Sadie Koop. She hosts a podcast called Growing Cold, which helps solve cold-case homicides."

"That sounds rather exploitative to me! And this entire subject seems melodramatic and nonsensical. Like I said, I played no part in the matter."

"In your blog, you wrote that you knew who the killer was, but Lisa made sure you did not retaliate. You also said you used your psychic powers later in life to see that the killer was dead. Don't suppose you'd be willing to tell me the killer's name?"

Oshun crosses one leg over another and leans back in the plush chair.

"I cannot. I was sworn to silence by Lisa before she crossed over. If I told you, I would violate our sacred bond. "

"If he's dead, it wouldn't be retaliating against him. So why not just tell me and close the book on this horrible chapter."

"I shall do nothing of the sort, Sir. Now, I invite you to leave!" Oshun stands abruptly and points towards the door. Nathan stands and moves quickly to him, grabbing his shoulder and placing a boot behind his heel; he spins his face first onto the coffee table with Oshuns arm bent behind his back.

"How about you fucking tell me what I need to know before I dislocate your shoulder."

Oshun lets out a scream of surprise followed by pain.

"I'll have you arrested! Then I'll sue you! You'll be hearing from my.." His words are cut short by Nathan wrenching up on his arm, almost dislocating his shoulder. "Ok, ok, ok. Stop before you break it!"

"Who killed her?" Nathan lets up slightly on the pressure but keeps a firm grip on his arm.

"I have no clue. I never met any of those people. I made them all up. I had never met Lisa, but I saw her in class. I had a crush on her, but I had never even talked to her. "

"So the entire thing was bullshit then?" Nathan lifts up on his arm again, applying pressure.

"Yes! Yes! It's purely a work of fiction! Please stop!"

Nathan lets go and moves back. He picks up his notebook and shoves it into his back pocket.

"So, where were you the night she was murdered?"

"I was with Willow. We were adding symbols to our robes at his mom's house."

"Will he verify that?"

"I don't know. If he's honest, he will."

"I can't believe you wrote that piece of shit blog. You started this entire elaborate career based on a blog that is nothing but lies. You should be ashamed of yourself."

"You're not going to tell anyone, are you? Please, you'll ruin me!"

Nathan just shakes his head as he walks out the door. He can still hear Oshun threatening to sue if he reveals anything as he enters the elevator. On the ride down he Googles Father William Buchanan. He gets a result for a Zion Catholic Church in western Portland.

On his ride to the church, he calls Sadie. She answers on the second ring.

"Whatcha find out with the White Power Warlock?"

"He made the entire thing up."

"Wait, what?"

"Everything in the blog was bullshit. He never knew Lisa. He knew of her but never talked to her. He had a crush on her, and that was it. He used her death as a way to get his shit published. I guess Ribbit and Diana were made up. He might have based them on Deena and Cindy. No idea. His little helper is now a minister with the Catholic Church. I'm heading there now to talk to him. Oliver claims they were working on their robes at Willow's house the night Lisa was killed.'

"Wait, who's Oliver?"

"Oh yeah, Oshuns real name is Oliver Garlicky. Willow's real name is now Father William Buchanan. You found Johnny?"

"Yeah, he works down at the lumber mill. I'm going to have lunch with him tomorrow if you want to join us."

"Where at?"

"I'll give you one guess!"

"I'll see you at Dee's diner tomorrow then. What time?"

"11:30. See you then. It's a date!" She hangs up before he can protest the fact that it's not a date. But still, the word makes him smile as he repeats the words to himself.

"It's a date."

CHAPTER 12

"Forgive Me, Father"

Nathan pulls up to the church and parks outside the front doors. It's an old red brick building, probably from the 1930s, sandwiched between a few early-century two-story homes. He walks up cement steps to the giant double wood doors that adorn the front of the building and pulls one open. Inside is a small entryway that goes directly into the main church area. The carpet is dark red and worn down, the old pews are blonde, and the shine has long been rubbed off of them from decades of people sitting on them. The altar is a large wooden structure with a life-size statue of Jesus dying on the cross. His large brown eyes stare down pitifully at the empty church, begging for the nonexistent audience to help him. Up by the podium, Nathan notices an older man in a black suit with a white collar. He has a ring of gray hair on an otherwise bald head and wire-rim glasses. Nathan crosses himself, shoulder, shoulder, and belly button before he enters the church. He's not religious anymore, but old habits die hard apparently. He approaches the Minister and clears his throat.

"Excuse me, Father, I'm looking for William Buchanan."

The Minister turns to Nathan with a warm smile and a nod of his head.

"Yes, my child, I am Father Bill. What can I do for you today?"

"I'm a Private Investigator out of Cedar Point, and I'd like to ask you a few questions."

The color in the Minister's already pale face seems to drain out, and he turns his attention back to lighting the candles near the altar.

"What kind of questions?"

"Do you know Oliver Garlicky?"

"Many moons ago, I did. Back when I was a completely different person, back when we were completely different people.' He doesn't turn back to Nathan. He keeps his attention on lighting the candles.

"What does that mean, father?"

"Well, I'm not sure if Oliver has changed at all. From what I hear, he hasn't. It means that back when I was a youth, I was easily manipulated. Before I found God, I partook in many evil deeds with Oliver. Oshun, he called himself back then. But after high school, I realized I was meant for a greater purpose. I received a call from a higher power. I closed myself to evil and opened myself to the Lord. I joined the church when I was 18 and I've kept my vows to the Lord ever since."

"What kind of evil deeds did you two commit?"

"Blasphemy. Heresy. Things of that nature."

"Murder?"

The Minister recoils and turns to face him as if Nathan had just thrown a beer bottle past his head. "Oh, my Goodness, no! Never! We never even hurt an animal. We didn't make sacrifices or anything like that. We were young and dumb. We pretended to be Warlocks and foolish things like that. We didn't know what we were doing. We were basically witches without the brooms and hats. Looking back, it was extremely childish. We were simply two loner kids with no friends who found friendship in fantasy. Oliver just read some books and made stuff up on his own. He was very creative but also very foolish."

"I see. Do you remember Lisa Fields"

Father Buchanan nods his head solemnly. "I knew of her, but alas, I never actually spoke with her. Oliver had a crush on her, but he had a crush on most girls. He was an extremely sexually repressed young man. He was more determined to lose his virginity than anyone I've ever met. Even now, with the Catholic Church, I meet some very sexually obsessive young men, but none of them can hold a candle to Oliver. "

"Where were you on October 30th, 1977"

"The night she was murdered? Well, Oliver came over to my house, and we worked on our robes. He made some new symbols that needed to be sewn onto our robes. He didn't know how to sew, and my mother had a sewing machine. The symbols were supposed to make us stronger and more attractive to the girls at our school. Obviously, they didn't work; none of his magic nonsense worked."

Nathan pulls out his notepad and jots down some notes.

"Did you know Cindy, Deena, Johnny, or Kenny?"

One of the names made Father Buchanan cringe, but Nathan couldn't tell which name it was that had that effect on him. He narrowed his eyes a bit as he waited for the Minister to answer. Based on how long it took, he could tell he wasn't being completely honest.

"Again, I knew of them but did not know any of them personally. They were part of their own little group. Too cool for kids like me or Oliver. "

Nathan jots down some notes before stuffing his notepad back into his pocket. He retrieves a business card from his wallet and hands it to the Minister. "Thank you for your time Father, sorry to bother you. If you can think of anything else please give me a call."

"Of course, my child. May God bless you and keep you." He begins to anoint Nathan, crossing his hand on his shoulders and forehead as he speaks. "May his Face shine down upon you for all the days of your life."

Nathan nods.

"Amen"

CHAPTER 13

"Campfire Light In The Autumn Time"

The last leg of a trip is always the worst. Nathan yawns and rubs his face. He pulls his phone out to check the time when he sees an alert that notifies him that the Playmore Podcast has just released a new episode. Reluctantly, he clicks download, and in a few moments, when it's finished downloading, it begins to play. He instinctively skips five minutes ahead, not willing to subject his ears to the super loud dubstep intro again.

"What's up Playmorons! It's your host Jillian Playmore and this is her Playmore podcast! But you already know that cuz you just keep playing these episodes and when one episode ends what do you do? You Playmore!

Boy, do I have a scoop for you today? I spoke with that private dick that Sadie Pooper Scooper hired, and he's actually pretty nice. He informed me that he found Oshun Rivers and Willow Bloodmoon, the two prime suspects in the murder of Lisa Fields. Well, actually, the only suspects in her murder, but whatever! So get this: Oshun is a best-selling occult author. I know, right? Who even knew that people read that nonsense? I guess Twilight ruined everything for everyone! Also, peep this, Playmorons! Willow is now a frickin Minister with the Catholic church! How amazing is that? Both men deny having any involvement in the murder of Lisa Fields. Which, of course, they would be right? They're not gonna get away with it for this long and then suddenly be like, oh shit, you got us! They claim they were together that night designing robes or something gay like that. Whoops, was that not Politically Correct of me? Sorry, you know I'm from New York, right!?!"

Nathan's grip on the steering wheel tightens, and he feels rage shoot down his spine. He's never even spoken to this bitch, and here she is, acting like their best friend. How did she get this information? Definitely not from him! His first instinct is to pull over and check his truck for a tracking device. But first, he had better call Sadie before she had a chance to listen. He clicks stop and dials Sadie. She answers on the first ring.

"You fuckin dick!" She screams into the phone.

"Sadie, listen. I have never spoken to.." he's cut off before he has a chance to explain.

"I should have known better than to trust you. You know, I was actually starting to respect you, and then you pulled this shit. You're a fuckin scumbag, and I hope you rot in hell. Go fuck yourself, you shithead cocknose dick face!"

Click. The phone goes silent as she hangs up on him. Her language would have made him chuckle if he wasn't so angry.

"Shit!" He curses and throws his phone down on the floor of his truck. He curses again and hits his steering wheel with an open palm. He reaches over, picks up the phone from the floor, and hits play on the podcast app.

"I don't expect to be working with Private Dick anymore after this, however, as he made several advances on me. He decided not to keep his dick so private. He told me Sadie was a lame duck, and he wanted to see how a lady from New York was in bed. I had to straight-knee him in his lil balls and tell him to fuck off. You don't treat someone from New York like that! We don't play like that in New York! Stay tuned next week when I bring you more..."

Nathan clicks stop, tosses his phone onto the bench seat beside him, and pulls over. He calms his breathing and gets his heart rate back down. He grabs a flashlight from the glove box and hops out of his truck. He gets down on the asphalt and looks underneath his truck. He checks the wheel wheels and then under the bumpers. Nothing in the bed of his truck or under the hood. He opens his doors and searches under the seats, then under the dash. He feels along the back of the seats and headrests. nothing. After a half hour of searching, he felt safe, saying there was no tracking device or recording device in his truck. He slams the door and heads back towards his cabin.

Nathan slows as he approaches the turn towards his driveway. Surprisingly, his woods seem fairly well-lit despite the fact that they are dusk and should be darker than they are. He notices smoke rising off in the distance, and that's when it all clicks together.

He doesn't bother stopping at the gate. Instead, he floors it and crashes right through the chain. The metal bars flip up over his hood and smash his windshield, spider-webbing the glass. He pins the accelerator to the floor as he gets thrown about inside his truck, it roars over potholes in the gravel and skids around the tight curves. Tree branches snap off on the sides of his truck as he sideswipes a tree. His passenger mirror gets snapped off as a branch from a tree flies through the open window. He moves his foot to the left and slams his boot down onto the brake as he comes to a halt in front of his cabin. Or what's left of it?

The frame of his cabin is in a complete uproar. Ten-foot flames dwarf the structure, reflecting off his eyes. Suddenly, a loud explosion pierces the night sky. Flaming scraps of lumber fly outwards as Nathan turns his face away from the growing inferno. As he feels the air fly past him, he turns back to his cabin with a face of shock, fear, and dread.

Where his cabin once sat was now just a smoldering pile of

ashes. It was burnt entirely down except for the porch railing and steps in front. His rocking chair was smoldering twenty feet in front of the porch or what was left. He falls to the ground and crawls forward, coming to a rest on his knees. His hands run over his head as tears begin to form in his eyes. He could care less about anything in that cabin; in fact, the cabin could easily be rebuilt in a week. He has nothing of value inside. He didn't have any photo albums or souvenirs from family vacations. He didn't have any trophies or awards. Nothing in that cabin matters except for two furry little bastards that he didn't see. The two things in his life that he couldn't replace were his only two friends.

Tango and Cash.

His face fell into his hands as he openly started to weep. The only two constants in his life over the past few years were gone. The two friends were always happy to see him. The two that never let him down. For a couple of years, they were the only two that he talked to and confided in. They were all he had, and now they were gone in the fire.

He let out a scream of anguish and let his elbows and face rest down in the dirt; tears flowed onto the ground below him. It was between choked sobs that he felt something wet run up the side of his ear, leaving a streak of wet goo behind it. He tilted his head towards the source of the liquid and saw a huge black face with tan eyebrows raised and a giant tongue hanging from a monstrous mouth. It was Cash. He gripped the dog around his neck and squeezed him in a way he'd never hugged anyone or anything before. Behind him, he heard a familiar sound, a jealous bark from Tango. He turned with a smile and saw Tango prance playfully on his front paws. He reached over and grabbed the dog, and pulled him in for a colossal double hug.

Somehow, the dogs had escaped the fire.

CHAPTER 14

"Like A Phoenix"

Nathan's hand, black with dirt and soot, curled into a fist, and he rapped his knuckles on the door. Sadie opens her motel door wearing a Detroit Red Wings jersey and seemingly nothing underneath. Her face started with a look of anger but quickly changed to shock as she saw Nathan. His face was caked with dirt and ash except for the trails down his cheeks that the tears cleaned on their way down and his right ear, which had been licked clean by Cash. He reeked of smoke, but before she could even ask, Tango and Cash pushed their way past him and ran up to Sadie, nosing her and rubbing their sides along her hips to try to get all the pets. She struggled to keep her balance as she looked Nathan up and down.

"What the fuck happened to you?"

"Someone burned down my cabin. I'm not sure how, but the dogs managed to get out in time, thank God." Maybe that Blessing Father Buchanan put on him saved his boys. God works in mysterious ways.

"Jesus, are they ok? Are you ok?"

"Yeah, can I come in? I kind of don't have anywhere else to go."

"Yeah, of course!" She steps aside and lets him walk past. She closes the door, locks the deadbolt and chain, and turns to lean her back against it as Tango and Cash demand attention. She leans down and scratches their necks. They both also reek of smoke. "Ooof, you two need baths!"

"I'll take them in the shower with me if you don't mind.."

"You're gonna shower with your dogs?" She gives him a strange look.

"Well, I'll wash them first, then I'll shower. "

"Duh, of course." She laughs at her own stupidity. "Help yourself. The towels are in the bathroom. "

Nathan snaps his fingers and points to the bathroom, and the dogs head inside. He follows them and closes the door. As he showers, Sadie pulls out her phone and searches the fire and police reports for any reports of the fire. Nothing. Which made sense because Nathan wouldn't report it. He didn't have any valuables to report for insurance. He seemed like the type who would just build a new one right next to the old one and turn the ashpit into some kind of garden. She had heard somewhere some time ago that ashes made good fertilizer. Gardening is weird.

After a half hour, the bathroom door opens. Tango and Cash run out looking like huge balls of fur from Nathan trying to blow dry them. He closes the door and hops in himself, trying to utilize the little bit of hot water that is left. The dogs hop onto the bed with Sadie, and she lays between them, stroking their backs as they lay their giant heads on her torso. A few minutes later, Nathan emerges with just a towel around his waist, holding his dirty clothes in his hand.

"Does this room have a washer and dryer?"

"Nope, you'll have to hit the laundry mat tomorrow. I got a pair of mens shorts in the top drawer that you can borrow. Actually, they're too big on me anyways; you can keep them."

He opens the drawer and looks inside. Beside some thongs, lace panties, and booty shorts, there is a pair of black men's basketball shorts. He grabs them, heads into the bathroom to change, then returns and sits down at the fake recliner beside the bed.

"You got anything to drink here?"

"Yeah, I got a 12-pack in the minifridge under the table. Grab one for me, too."

He reaches under and pulls out two cans of Lucky Stripe Lager. He cracks one open and hands it to her.

"Look, Sadie. About what that bitch said in her podcast.."

She interrupts him before he can go on.

"Yeah, I know. I should have known. She's done that before. She was probably following you and just put two and two together. I don't think you're a scumbag, and I don't think you would try to put the moves on her. You might be a bit of a prick sometimes, but I don't think you're that type of person. You seem kind of like an old-fashioned gentleman when you're not putting on the asshole persona." She holds up her beer in a toast and then chugs half of it down before letting out an enormous burp.

"Thanks." Nathan drains his entire beer down his throat and then cracks open another.

"So, who do you think burnt down your cabin?

"I don't know. Obviously, someone connected to this case. Maybe one of the Warlocks? Maybe someone else? I have no clue. Could have been that Jillian bitch for all I know."

"Nah." She shakes her head and takes another drink. "Jillian is pretty fuckin shady, but arson isn't really her thing. She'll burn down your career but not your house."

They both sit silently for a while, drinking their beers. Sadie casually stroked Tango's fur since Cash had already fallen asleep at the foot of the bed.

"Do you mind if I crash here tonight?"

"Yeah, yeah, of course. In the morning I'll go to Gus's store and get you some new clothes. I wouldn't bother trying to clean your clothes. You'll never get that smoke smell out. Then, once we get you looking respectable, we can go meet up with Johnny at the diner together."

"That works. What's his story? Have you learned anything about him?"

"Yeah, let's see" She leans over and grabs her phone from the night stand. She unlocks it, clicks a few things and scrolls down.

"Ok, so John Olsen, aka Johnny. He was dating Lisa, as we know, and was supposed to be the last person to see her that night. The next year, when he turned 18, he dropped out of high school and joined the Navy. He was kicked out a year later. Apparently, he had a severe drinking problem and would get into it with his superiors. One night, he decided to get drunk and tried to take a helicopter for a joy ride. That obviously got him kicked out of the Navy, and he spent five years in a naval prison. After he was released, he returned to Cedar Point and got a job at the lumber mill. Besides several DUIs, he's stayed out of trouble. He's a barfly when he's not working. Never married. So yeah, we'll see if he's sober tomorrow for our luncheon. Speaking of, toss me another beer."

Nathan kills his second beer and grabs a third. He tosses Sadie her second beer. She taps the top before opening it and taking a few big swallows.

"You think me contacting Johnny had anything to do with your cabin?"

Nathan takes a drink from his beer. "I'm not sure. It seems like odd timing that the Playmore podcast was released the very same night my place gets scorched. It's just too much of a coincidence."

Tango hears a car door outside the motel room and sits up sharply but silently on full alert. Cash flips from his back to his stomach and is at attention. Tango's giant head sends Sadies beer flying, spilling half of it on her oversized shirt.

"Shit fuck!" she exclaims as she tries to upright the beer before it spills anymore.

"Floor! Now!" Nathan stands, snapping his fingers. Both dogs instantly leap to the floor with their chins tucked against the floor between their paws. Nathan rushes and grabs a towel; he goes to the bed and starts to pat the wet beer spot on the front of her shirt.

He started to rub and blot at the beer spill, apologizing for his clumsy dogs, when he realized he could feel her hard nipples and small breasts between the towel and wet shirt. He instantly felt his face grow flush as his eyes slowly moved up to hers. Her eyebrows were arched in a state of surprise and amusement. Her hands held out to the side as if to not only say, "Don't shoot," but also say, "What the fuck?" Nathan dropped the towel on her lap and leaned back, standing straight beside the bed.

"I'm sorry about that. I was just trying to help. The boys, Tango and Cash, are very well-behaved Rottweilers. If you didn't know, they are also clumsy sometimes. They don't realize how big they actually are, yanno?" He grabs his beer and finishes it off. Sadie just smiles and picks up the towel. She holds her shirt away from her torso as she attempts to dry it.

"No biggie. Unlike you, I have extra clothes packed."

She twirls off the bed. She goes to the dresser and pulls out another night shirt. With her back to him she peels off the wet shirt and tosses it aside. Her toned and lean back is bare. Her spine leads down to a perfectly heart shaped muscular backside half clad in a pair of tight black bicycle shorts. He notices a few freckles down her spine before she pulls on an oversized gray shirt and turns back around to face him.

"Much better. We should probably get some sleep. I'll get to the store when it opens to get you some clothes. What size are you?"

"Large shirt. 33x32 jeans. You got any toothpaste I can use?"

"Sure. Next to the sink. Help yourself."

Nathan goes into the bathroom and closes the door. He splashes cold water on his face and then stares into the mirror for a moment, catching his thoughts. He cannot catch feelings now. He cannot feel the way he feels about this girl. He doesn't even know this girl. He needs to keep his mind on the case. He puts some toothpaste on his finger and brushes his teeth. He splashes water on his face again before drying it roughly, and then holds the towel against his face for a minute to compose himself.

When he leaves the bathroom, he finds the lights are already off except for the small lamp next to the bed. Sadie lays on her side, her bare runner's leg off to the side as she snuggles up to Tango. Cash lay at the foot of her bed on his back, already snoring.

"I'll take the recliner," He says as he grabs an extra sheet from the shelf.

"You sure? I bet The boys will miss you if you aren't in bed with them" she smiles and pats Tango on the side. His eyes look at Nathan but he doesn't move. Nathan just smiles.

"I don't know, they look pretty comfy to me. Besides, I'm used to a rocking chair on a porch, remember?"

Her smile almost seems to turn into a pout, as if she's sad he's not joining them in the bed.

"Sure thing, cowboy. You enjoy that chair. Don't forget to set an alarm."

Nathan tries to make himself comfortable on the hard plastic chair, still only wearing gym shorts. He tries to cocoon the blanket around his body.

"Alarm? What for? What time? I thought we weren't meeting Johnny until lunchtime."

Sadie laughs and turns off the light before flaring her hair out and laying back on the pillows, stretching her arms out wide.

"I'm kidding. Get some sleep, ya goof ass"

Sadie falls asleep with a look of contentment on her face; the two smokey Rottweilers snuggle against her.

CHAPTER 15

"Swallowed"

Nathan walks across the dying grass of a small front yard. He moves past a giant oak tree and looks at the cookie-cutter 1960s-style house in front of him. He tries the front door but finds it locked, so he moves along to the driveway and pushes the side door, which is hanging off its hinges. The doorway enters directly downstairs to the basement, which Nathan can see is flooded halfway up the staircase. He can't tell for sure, but it almost sounds like someone or something is in the water. The water is black and murky, an occasional bubble rising to the service. To his left, he can walk into the kitchen area.

The hardware floor is worn with huge grooves dug into it. The kitchen is littered with trash, mounds of white trash bags fill the small space. A dead raccoon lays in the sink with flies buzzing around it. He moves into the front room and looks side to side. There are dog leashes hanging by the front door but otherwise the walls are bare. Empty squares show were photos once hung, outlined by the yellowish tint left by decades of nicotine smoke.

In the middle of the room, there is one lone metal folding chair. Its seat is bent so that it doesn't rest entirely on all four legs. He turns and looks down the hallway, which leads to two bedrooms and a bathroom. He can hear movement in one of the rooms. He carefully proceeds forward.

Stopping just before the bedroom to his left, he leans and peers inside. The floor has caved into the basement, which is just a black void of nothing. He turns around and looks into the bathroom. The sink and toilet are practically black, with dark brown and green scum caked onto the porcelain. He carefully pulls back the shower curtain and recoils back into the vanity. The shower is alive with rats, filled to the brim as they twist and turn around each other. Their tails have all become entangled and stuck. Black beady eyes glare up at him as their long front teeth gnash wildly into the air. Eventually, they will start to kill each other and eat the dead rats in order to survive. That will only last so long, and soon enough, they will all be dead. He shoves the curtain closed and leaves the bathroom, closing the door as well.

He leans his back against the closed door and turns his head to the right, down the hallway towards the master bedroom. The hallway seems longer than it did before with the light dimming until it reaches the closed door. There are scratches halfway up the door. Long slim gouges going up and down about an inch apart. He can hear what sounds like a small child giggling and singing a soft song from the other side of the door.

"I wuv you in the morning and in an addermoo. I wuv you in ceeding and unda unda moo."

Nathan recognizes the song and the voice. It's her, the one he needs to save. He tries the doorknob, but it's glowing red and instantly burns his hand. He wrenches his hand back in pain and screams; he tries slamming his shoulder into the door. The singing gets louder, but he can still hear someone else in the room with her. No, something else.

He kicks his boot near the doorknob, over and over, again and again, until finally, the wood begins to splinter around the door jam. With all his weight, he throws his body into the door, and it swings open. Nathan lands face down on the hardwood floor, which is wet with a slimy grayish substance. He pushes himself up to his knees and sees a young girl, no older than 3, in the middle of the room before her.

Her blonde hair is half brushed into a messy side ponytail; the rest falls onto her shoulder in ringlets. She has big steel blue eyes and is still singing her song.

*I wuv you in the morning and in an addermoo. I wuv you in 'eeding and unda unda moo."

Nathan begins to move towards the girl with a handout. Out of the corner of his eye he notices a brownish green snake begin to slither towards them. Its yellow eyes tucked into the sides of its football sized head. The body seems never ending as it coils from the shadows that hide the corners of the room.

"I'm here to help you, sweetie. Can you come to me?"

The girl ignores him, singing her song as she moves her fingers together in the rhythm of the song. The hideous boa constrictor begins to circle the girl, its tongue darting in and out of its mouth. Nathan could swear he saw it smiling.

"Sweetie, I need you to come to me now!"

Nathan begins to move towards the girl, panic filling inside him. The snake begins to curl around the girl's legs and work its way up her tiny body. Nathan can't even see the snake's tail, it's still off in the darkness of the corners of the room. The girl stops singing and looks at Nathan with a big smile on her face.

"It's Otay; I want to be eaten."

Nathan starts to scream as the snake opens its beartrap-like mouth and begins to swallow the girl's arm. She giggles as the snake begins to suck her in. When he gets to her shoulder, her laughing head stays out, smiling at Nathan as her torso bends in half, sucking her legs down and then her other arm before all that's left protruding from the serpent's jaws is her adorable little face. She sings her sweet song one last time.

"I wuv you in morning and in an addermoo. I wuv you in 'eeding and unda unda moo."

The snake swallows the girl, and Nathan lets out a blood-curdling scream.

"Nooo!! Nellie!!"

Nathan falls to the floor with a thud and rolls to his back, out of breath and covered in sweat. He feels the snake's forked tongue against his face. Turning to face the monster he is instead greeted by another lick from Tango up the front of his face.

He pushes the dog away and sits up. He's back in Sadies motel room. Nathan stands and shakes the cobwebs from his brain as his eyes focus. Cash is still sleeping on the foot of the bed, and Sadie is gone. His phone is on the table and he looks to see a text message.

"Went to get you some clothes, be back soon."

Nathan goes to the bathroom and splashes water on his face; halfway in the dreamworld and still stuck in the nightmare that plagues him. It's never the same dream, but it always has the same ending. Some version of his sister dying a horrible death.

He dries his face and turns to leave the bathroom, only to be stopped by his boys sitting side by side and blocking the bathroom doorway. He smiles.

"I missed breakfast, didn't I?"

He pats their heads as he walks past them and grabs his phone, typing out a text to Sadie.

"Grab some steaks for the boys; they're hungry."

CHAPTER 16

"Here's Johnny!"

Tango and Cash are devouring raw chunks of cubed stew meat fresh from the packaging as Nathan steps out of the bathroom, feeling a bit uncomfortable in the clothes that Sadie picked out for him.

"Why are you doing this to me?" He looks at her with pitiful eyes. She's resting on the imitation recliner with her legs propped up on the table. She seems comfortable in a pair of gray jogging shorts and a light kelly green hoodie. While fall is approaching, the days are still pleasant in Cedar Point.

"What's wrong with what I got you?" Sadie smiles as she looks him over. She got him a pair of slim-cut navy blue jeans and a long-sleeved, light blue dress shirt with small pink flamingos across it. The shirt fits a little snug, and he has to roll the sleeves up mid-forearm to hide the fact that the cuffs don't reach his wrists.

"Look at this shit? Have you ever seen me wear anything like this?" He holds his arms out and turns around slowly, not catching her eyes dropping down to his backside as he spins.

"Well, I've only seen you in like two outfits that were damn near identical, besides when you were wearing my old gym shorts. You look fine! Come on now, we gotta go meet Johnny."

Nathan sighs and tucks his shirt into his jeans then slips on his boots. Then when he stands back up he has to retuck his shirt to keep it from sliding out from his jeans.

"This is stupid. Can't we stop by Gus's and exchange this shit for something else?"

"No! All sales are final. You look cute!" She stands and gives his butt a slap, which catches him completely off guard. "Come on now, we gotta go. You're driving. Tango, Cash, be good! Don't eat my hotel room, cuz I doubt I'll get my 25-dollar deposit back."

Nathan shakes his head as he follows her out of the motel room. Not waiting for her to lock the door, he heads straight to his truck and starts it up. Before she can even close the door, he's off and heading to dinner.

"Jesus, you almost made me lose a shoe." She looks at him as he drives. He says nothing, just focuses on the road. The ride only takes a few minutes as the motel isn't too far from the diner. He parks out front and hops out. She gets out and follows him up to the glass doors. "Now let me do the talking, ok?" She says.

He raises an eyebrow as he opens the door for her, and she smiles as she skips past. Sadie waves to Deena, who is pouring coffee for an elderly couple off to the side.

"Hey, hon! Take a seat anywhere you'd like. I'll get you some coffee as soon as I can!" Deena smiles at Sadie.

"No coffee for us. We'll just take some water." Sadie smiles as she walks to a corner table and sits down but doesn't slide over to the middle. Nathan stands there and looks down at her questioningly. She looks up at him with those large, innocent, hazel eyes. "What? Sit on the other side, and when he gets here, I want you in the middle. I don't wanna be next to a guy who might be a killer."

Nathan lets out a slow breath of annoyance but doesn't say anything. Instead, he walks across to the other side of the table and sits down, sliding over toward the middle of the corner booth.

"So you think Johnny is the killer?" He leans back and drapes an arm across the opposite side of the back of the booth from where she is sitting.

"No, but you never know. He's obviously one of the major suspects, but there's something about him. I'm not sure." She glances at the small white digital watch on her wrist. "He should be here soon. Remember. Let me do the talking."

Before Deena can come and bring them their water, a tall, skinny man enters the diner. His face is weathered and wrinkled and he hasn't shaved in a couple weeks. White whiskers start below his shirt collar and continue up his sagging neck to his face. His eyebrows are wild and long above his sunken brown eyes. He wears a beaten Seattle Mariners baseball cap pulled down low. He looks around, a bit unsure of what he's supposed to be doing.

"Mr Olsen." Sadie lifts a hand and smiles at him, politely waving to him. "Over here. Please, come join us!"

He seems to take his time as he shifts his body to the side as if he has to try hard to know where to put his foot to start walking in the right direction. When he reaches the table, he pulls off his hat, revealing long white greasy hair underneath.

"Mrs Koop?" He sheepishly asks.

"No, Not Mrs. Just Sadie. Nice to meet you." She extends her hand to him with that warm, welcoming smile that sucked Nathan in the first time he met her. John Olsen takes her hand in his. His nails are long with dirt caked underneath. His knuckles are bony, and his veins show through his leathery skin. Sadie motions to Nathan, sitting in the middle beside her. "This is my partner, Private Investigator Nathan Taylor. He's helping me out. Please, have a seat."

Nathan extends a hand to him, which is also shaken in a half-hearted manner. "Nice to meet you, Mr Olsen."

"Call me Johnny." He sits beside Nathan, resting his hat on the table in front of him before folding his hands beside it.

"Ok, Johnny, Thank you for meeting with us. If you're hungry, please feel free to order whatever you want. I'm buying!" Sadie smiles that big smile.

"I'm fine, I just want to get this over with" Johnny mutters, not bothering to look up. Instead, he just stares at his beaten hat on the table.

"You sure? I heard the key lime pie here is amazing." Sadie looks to flag down Deena but she's in the back, out of sight.

"I'm sure, dammit, now let's get this over with," Johnny says more matter-of-factly this time. Nathan can see the old man's fingertips turning white as his hands squeeze together.

"Sure thing, Johnny." Sadie's smile fades from her face. She pulls out her phone, hits a recorder app, and presses the record button. "You don't mind if I record this for the podcast, do you?"

"Do I have a choice?" He replies, his cold brown eyes never leaving his baseball hat.

"Of course. In order to record you, I need your consent. Do I have it?"

"Yes," He says coldly, emotionlessly.

"Great!" Sadie purses her lips for a moment after saying the word, then jumps right into things. "How did you know Lisa Fields?"

"We dated," He responds, barely giving up any more than he has to.

"When?"

"Back when we were kids."

"Were you dating in October of 1977?"

"Part of it..." He unfolds his hands and brings them down to his lap. Nathan spots a tremble in his hands.

"What part of it? The first part or the last part?"

"The first part."

"When did you break up?"

Johnny sits silently, his eyes glued to his baseball hat on the table. Sadie glances at Nathan as she waits for a response. Nathan's eyes are glued to Johnny, waiting for any reaction. Said repeats her question.

"When did you and Lisa break up?"

After another few minutes of silence, he finally breaks.

"I broke up with her the night she was killed." His eyes finally move from the baseball hat. They look down at his lap before closing. They remain close as a few strands of greasy white hair fall across his face.

"October 30th, 1977? You two broke up on Devil's Night?"

He slowly nods his head.

"Who broke up with who? Did she break up with you?"

Johnny doesn't move. Nathan can see his thin body growing rigid. He had a slight tremor running through his body. He can't tell if it's nervousness in the old man or perhaps it's been too long since he's had a drink. Nathan could smell the exorbitant odor of last night's whiskey on him when he sat down. And now, sitting down next to him, he could smell the couple of beers the man probably chugged on the car ride to the diner. Sadie turns on the pressure a little bit by letting that little Miss Sweetie persona slip away as she leans forward and rests her elbows on the table.

"Did she break up with you because you kept trying to force her to have sex? Did she get tired of you pressuring her to do something she wasn't ready to do?" Nathan lets his eyes drift over to Sadie momentarily as he listens to her questions before looking back at Johnny. His eyes slowly open, and he looks at Sadie with contempt.

"You don't know shit, do you?"

"No, I don't, John. So why don't you tell me? What I do know is you were the last person she was supposed to be with the night she was murdered. No, the night she was butchered. So you tell me, John. Tell me what I don't know." Sadie doubles down, her eyes locked in on Johnny.

Johnny leans back and grips his hat between his hands, kneading it between his bony fingers.

"I might have pressured her a little bit, yeah. I was a 17-year-old boy, horny all the damn time, and she was a pretty girl. She was my girlfriend. I loved her, dammit, and I wanted to make love to her. Sure. But I never tried to force her. And she knew I wouldn't make her do anything she didn't want to do. Like I said, I loved her."

"Then why did she break up with you?"

"She didn't!" He slams his hand down on the table, eyes wide with anger. Sadie jumps slightly but doesn't move her eyes from him. Nathan remains stoic the entire time, his arm still draped along the back of the booth. The elderly couple across the diner look over at them, a bit shocked and angry that they are interrupting their nice quiet brunch. Nathan notices Deena peeking out from the divider then separates the kitchen from the counter.

"Then what happened that night, Johnny? Did you meet her that night? Did you see her? Tell me what happened." Sadie lowers her tone and speaks more gently now, trying to de-escalate the situation a bit. It takes him a bit to engage, but Sadie gives him as much time as he needs. She sits patiently waiting for him to speak.

"I met her that night." He starts off. His brown eyes started to shimmer as tears formed.

"I met up with her at the playground that night. We had been fighting a lot lately—just dumb kid stuff. You know how it goes when you're a teenager. Every little fight is literally the end of the world. I hated fighting, and I still do." He lets the last sentence sit for a moment before continuing.

"We had broken up and gotten back together so many times already. She was a year younger than me, and I knew that the following year, I was going to turn 18. I hated this fucking town and I still do. There was nothing good in this town back then besides her. Now she's gone, and there's not a damn bit of good in this entire fuckin town. It's all cursed. I hated it here, and I knew that when I turned 18, I was getting out of here. I was going to join the Navy and sail the hell out of this shit hole and never look back! And I knew," He stops, the words catching in his throat as his voice cracks. "I knew I couldn't bring her with me."

He lifts his hands and wipes his face slowly but roughly before continuing.

"I invited her there that night to tell her I wouldn't be going to the dance with her. She already kind of knew it, but I wanted to tell her in person. I wanted to tell her there was no point in us going the way we were going. All the stupid bickering. Me trying to get to 3rd base with her. She wanted things to be more special than I could give her. There was no point. The next year, I'd be a sailor and she'd still be in high school. We'd never see each other again. So there on the swing set, just feet from where she.." His voice cracks again; a tear runs down his wrinkled cheek. "From where she was murdered. I broke up with her. She got so mad at me. She got so mad at me that she slapped me."

He stops and chuckles as he wipes the tear off his cheek. Sadie glances at Nathan, who is intently watching Johnny.

"Is that why you killed her? Because she slapped you?" Sadie asks softly, almost in a whisper. Johnny slams his hand down on the table, then points right into Sadie's face, his finger an inch from her nose.

"I didn't kill her!"

"Let's bring it down a notch!" Nathan grabs Johnny's wrist and pulls it away. Sadie never flinches from him, her eyes locked on his. Johnny yanks his hand from Nathan's grip and rubs his wrist.

"I didn't kill her. I left her there. She slapped me. I told her I guess I made the right decision, and then I went home. I left her there in that park, all alone. So I didn't kill her, but it's my damn fault that she's dead." He hangs his head, tears steadily flowing down his face now.

"So that's why you got kicked out of the Navy. That's why you turned to alcohol." Nathan drapes his arm back across the back of the booth. "You blamed yourself and tried to drink away the guilt. When that didn't work, you wanted to sabotage yourself. But all that got you was some time in sailor jail. "

Johnny lets out a deep sigh as if a weight has been lifted off his shoulders.

"I'm still trying to drink it away. I'm trying to drink myself to death. Suppose I hadn't left her there that night. Hell, if I hadn't invited her there, she'd still be alive. Even if I had gone to her house to break up with her, she wouldn't have been alone in the playground with a goddamn monster."

The seconds tick by on the recorder app on Sadie's cell phone. She looks down at it and then back up to Johnny. She runs her hand through her hair, glances at Nathan, then looks back to Johnny.

"What time did you leave her at the park?"

Johnny swats the air as if he's trying to swat away the question.

"Oh hell, I don't know. It must have been before nine cuz the sheriff had a curfew out that night. He was trying to keep kids from vandalizing the town on Devil's Night. Some good that curfew did eh?"

Nathan leans forward and rests his forearms against the edge of the table, his fingers laced together. He looks at Sadie before turning his attention back to Johnny. She told him to let her do the speaking but figured that just meant let her take the lead.

"Did you see anyone else there that night?"

Johnny mulls it over, replaying the events in his head for the millionth time.

"While we were talking I saw a blue car tearing down the road from Gold Lawn. It was a blue car, I think. I think I had some kids inside. Didn't recognize any of them. I just figured it was kids from school TPing the cemetery or something. I told the sheriff about it the next day when he questioned everyone. "

"How close to you leaving did you see that car?"

"I left right after. She had already slapped me, and I used the car as an excuse to have to go. I told her things were gonna get crazy in town, and I didn't want the sheriff to catch me and think I was doing anything bad. She told me.." He stops, tears welling in his eyes again. "She told me there was nothing worse I could have done than break her heart."

Neither Sadie nor Nathan say anything for a while. Deena approaches with some menus, sensing that the silence at the table might mean they are done and ready to order.

"Hey, Johnny. Long time no see. Anyone want a menu?"

Johnny doesnt look up to her, instead he pulls his hat back on and nods solemnly. "Deena, how ya been?"

She shrugs and hugs the menus to herself. "I've been managing."

"And Kenny?"

"He's good. Still teaching PE and coaching baseball at the high school. He loves it. It's like he never had to grow up; he stays at school and keeps playing sports." She chuckles awkwardly. "Gimme a holler if y'all need anything."

She turns and walks off, her graying red ponytail swishing behind her and white shoes still squeaking on the tiles.

"Johnny." Sadie finally breaks the silence. "Are you sure you didn't recognize the two boys in the car? Could they have been Oshun or Willow?"

"Who?" His eyes are now dry and hollow, looking up at her. "You mean those little devil shits? No idea. I don't even know if they drove a car back then. I just assumed they rode around on broomsticks or whatever. "

"I see, well if you can think of anything, will you give me a call?" She finally offers that warm, caring smile again.

"Yeah, sure." He stands, his fingers still trembling. Sadie stands and offers her his hand. He gives it the same quick, weak shake as he did before and turns and walks away, completely ignoring Nathan's outstretched hand. The doorbell dings as he leaves. Nathan and Sadie look at each other. She hits stop on her recorder and turns off her screen.

"What do you think?" She takes a drink of water. "Do you believe him?

Nathan leans back again and stretches his arm along the back of the booth.

"Kind of, yeah. It all kind of lines up."

"We gotta find out who those two kids were in the car."

"Yeah, except the sheriff isn't giving any information to anyone, especially not us."

Sadie winks at him. "One of my listeners works in the office. They said they could get me some of the files. Hoping to hear back tonight. "

"That's good". Nathan turns his head halfway to the side and cracks his neck. "It seems like every time we start investigating a lead, it instantly goes away. "

"Yeah, except every time our lead goes away, we're instantly given a new lead to investigate."

"Yeah, it seems kind of suspicious, don't you think? Every lead turns into a different lead. First, Oshun led us to Willow. Then Deena, who led us to Johnny, who both led us back to Oshun."

"If Oshun or Willow did have a car back then, it could have been them in the blue car. It doesn't mean they are the ones who killed Lisa, but it does destroy their alibi for the night and place them directly at the scene right before the murder. Maybe you should have another word with Oshun?"

Nathan shakes his head. "No, that'll go nowhere. He's as tight-lipped as the sheriff. "He waves to Deena when she glances over, motioning her over. She smiles and holds up a finger before taking two plates to a young couple a few seats away. After she delivers the food, she comes to Nathan and Sadie's table.

"How'd it go with Johnny? He's looking pretty rough."

"It went better than expected," Sadie responds.

"Did you have a chance to talk to your husband? Will he speak with us?" Nathan asks.

"Yeah, he's a little reluctant. Same reasons I was. He thinks you guys are just trying to get rich off a young girl's murder. But I think I can get through to him. He's more apt to talk to just Nathan, though. He doesn't really respect women too much." She looks down at the floor, smoothing down her apron.

"He works at the High school, right?"

"Yes. He's got classes for the next few hours, but afterward, he's free. He's usually tending to the baseball field, the track, the football fields, and stuff like that. Making sure it's all in order before winter comes. You could probably catch him then."

Nathan nods. "Thank you, Deena."

"Are you guys ordering anything today?"

Sadie frowns. "We gotta go, I'm sorry. Here.. "She pulls some cash from her pocket and slides twenty and two tens across the table to her. "We don't want to use your tables for free. We appreciate everything.

Deena picks up the money and stuffs it into her apron pocket. She smiles.

"Thank you, don't be strangers now. Anything else I can do just let me know. " She walks away, checking on the table where she just served the food to see if they needed anything else.

"Ok cool. You go try to meet Kenny after school and I'll talk to my source and see what she can sneak out of the sheriff's office. Meet back together at the motel tonight? Did I give you the spare key?" She begins to pat the pockets of her jogging shorts.

Nathan nods. "Yeah, you did. I gotta stop at the Harvest Market before I get back to grab some more food for the boys. Do you want me to grab anything?"

"Sure. How about some more beer?"

CHAPTER 17

"Put Me In Coach"

Nathan pulls into the school parking lot, which starts to empty out. It's not a very big high school, as there are only two buses that pull out of the half-circle driveway. Some obnoxious teens who just got their license rip out of the parking lot in their mom's minivan. Other kids are left to walk home by themselves. Nathan wonders when it became socially acceptable for kids to wear their comforters from their bedspreads to school in place of a jacket. He shakes the question from his head, not wanting to be that old "Get off my lawn" fart that Sadie referred to him as when they first met back at his cabin.

That brings his thoughts back to the cabin. Who would have had the most to gain from burning down his cabin? True, it could have been a cheating husband who had gotten caught in the past by Nathan whose marriage was ruined because of his own urges and sins. But Nathan's address wasn't technically on file anywhere. His land was owned under an LLC, and the owner of the LLC was unknown. He legally didn't even technically have a house built on it. Well, not anymore since the fire, anyway. But he never registered the house. There was no address to get mail. All his mail went to a PO box in Portland. If you googled him, he was basically a ghost. He spent months wiping his existence off the internet, and at the first of every month, he would search his name again to see if any information had leaked back onto the web. He was literally off the grid, although Sadie had found him. How did she find him anyway? Nathan had not considered this. Did she follow him somehow? Maybe she was a better investigator than he gave her credit for. She did a good job of locating Lisa's friends, which leads Nathan's thoughts back to Jillian.

How did she find him? How did she get his arrest record from back in Arizona? The judge said that if he went two years without so much as a parking ticket, the arrests would have been expunged like it never happened. Yet somehow, she found it all out. Sadie seemed convinced that Jillian wasn't capable of committing arson. Maybe she's right. But maybe, Jillian has an associate who is a firebug. Or maybe, one of the two Warlocks, Oshun or Father Bill, got a little spooked about Nathan showing up and then hearing their names on the podcast. Or maybe, it was none of them and it was the actual killer trying to ensure that Nathan didn't do any more digging. He makes a mental note to do some digging into Jillian.

Nathan climbs out of his truck, not bothering to retuck in his too-small dress shirt. Fed up, he unbuttons it and forces it off his shoulders and tosses it onto the passenger seat in his truck, content to simply wear the white t-shirt he wore underneath. It was getting a bit chilly as the sun was beginning to descend, but Nathan figured the conversation with Kenny wouldn't take too long. He didn't expect to get a ton of information out of the man, not after what Deena had told them. It didn't seem like many people around here had much information to give up. Everyone seemed so closed off from the event.

He followed the sidewalk to the back of the school, which led back to the old baseball diamond. He doesn't see anyone on the field but can faintly hear voices coming from the dugout. He could hear what sounded like a cracky voice that was obviously going through puberty, laughing and saying, "Stop, stop!" Nathan slowly peeked around the side of the dugout and saw a middle-aged man playfully poking a chubby teenage boy with the end of a baseball bat. The man sported a crew cut and a thin mustache that connected to a thin goatee. If Nathan had to guess, the man only grew facial hair to give his face some defining characteristics. Otherwise, his cheeks melted directly down into his fat neck. He could tell the man at one time was athletic; he had broad shoulders, and his legs were still thin but muscular especially his giant calves. But the man's torso had ballooned out over the years, developing those side breasts that some men got when they switched from regular exercise to a desk job and too much beer and chips at night in front of the TV watching the game.

Nathan took a step into view, and the boy and the man who wore a whistle around his neck came to a sudden halt. The man frowned at Nathan and moved the thick end of the bat to his empty hand, almost as if he was trying to intimidate Nathan.

"Can I help you? This is a private field" The man spoke, his dark blue eyes were beady, his nose slim and pointing.

"Kenneth Neil? My name is Nathan Taylor; I'm a Private Investigator. I believe your wife, Deena, has mentioned me."

The man took a deep breath and nodded slowly. He held the bat out to the teenage boy, who did not appear to be any older than maybe a freshman.

"Here, why don't you go check the outfield for any fly balls we missed? If you finish that, go on into the gym and start sweeping the floor." He gave the kid a squeeze on his shoulder as he walked past then turned his full attention to Nathan. He folded his thick arms against his chest, his forearms resting on his stomach. "Yeah, I'm Kenny. And you're the guy who wants to get rich off the death of a poor young girl."

"No Sir, I just want to help solve it. You were friends with Lisa?" Nathan pulls out that little notepad and starts scratching.

"Yeah, kind of. We weren't besties or anything. Never hung out alone. But she dated my bestie for a year or so. So yeah, I saw her a lot. Got to know her well enough to not want her tragedy exploited."

"By bestie, you're referring to John Olsen, correct?"

"Yeah, Johnny. We played baseball together. He was a damn good pitcher. He should have gotten a scholarship and probably could have, too. But he was so hung up on getting out of town right away when he turned 18. Seemed he was running from something before he even knew how to walk."

"How long were you and Johnny friends?"

"Since before we could walk" He spit a big wad of chewing tobacco onto the ground then kicked some sand over the top of it. "We were always friends, up until Lisa's death anyways."

"Did Johnny tell you anything about that night?"

"Just that he didn't see any use in dating her anymore if they weren't going to be able to stay together after he left. So he broke up with her. She said she got all mad, and then he left. He stopped talking to me slowly after that. He just got really distant. The next thing I knew, he had skipped town. He turned 18, and the next day, he was on a fuckin ship in the middle of the ocean trying to be a sailor. Look how well that worked out for him. Got himself court-martialed and ended up here worse than he was if he had stayed."

"Did he mention anything about maybe seeing anyone else that night? Maybe a blue car with a couple of boys in it?"

Kenny narrowed his eyes for a moment. "Nope, he didn't say he saw nothing."

"What about you? Where were you the night of October 30th, 1977?" Nathan scribbles something down on the notepad.

"I was at home, watching the Mariners game."

"All night?" Nathan doesn't look at him as he writes.

"Yeah. All night. Then I went to bed."

"You remember who they were playing that night?" Nathan finally lifts his eyes and looks at Kenny. Kenny stares back into Nathan's eyes before he spits a wad of chewing tobacco again.

"Yeah, The Yankees. The Mariners won, 6-3."

Nathan nods and jots something else down.

"Did you know anyone by the name of Oshun or Willow?"

"You mean those two faggots who used to play grab ass down by the cemetery? Yeah, I knew those two fruitcakes."

"How did you know them?"

"I knew they were some devil worshipers! I used to beat 'em up in the locker room during gym class. Duct tape their ass cheeks together. Shove their heads in the toilet. Shit like that, yanno? Just fun shit that kids do to nerds like that."

Nathan nods slowly. "I see. So they were the gay ones, but you taped their asscheeks together, right? Do you let the kids in your class bully other kids in a similar manner?"

Kenny puffs up defensively.

"If some little weak pieces of shit can't stand up and defend themselves against an alpha dog, then yeah, I let them. This world will chew you up if you aren't an alpha dog. Those two little freaks were not even beta bitches. They were the bottom of the barrel. I'd slap them both right now if I saw them. No, if I saw them, I'd break every bone in their bodies. Cuz I'd bet a million dollars that they were responsible for Lisa's murder. I'd bet more than a million; I'd bet every dollar in my bank." He nods aggressively to drive the point home.

"Gotcha." Nathan writes in his notepad, closes it up, and stuffs it back into his pocket. "So, who was the kid that was over here? A student, I assume?"

Kenny's eyes narrowed again at Nathan.

"Yeah. He's a good kid but not very athletic. He tries hard though. I had never seen anyone try harder to catch a fly ball than that boy. So, instead of failing him, I let him do a little extra credit after school so he could get by with a C. He helps me paint lines on the field, clean the court, pick up the bats and balls, and replace nets. Stuff like that."

"So he's not an Alpha. Is that what you're saying?"

"No, he's definitely a beta. But he tries, God help him, he tries. And I respect that. Plus, he respects me. He calls me sir and coach and not Mr. Neil like the other little jerks do. Plus, I met his dad. His dad is a little sissy, so the boy needs a father figure. That's how he sees me. He sees me as a hero, something his daddy will never be and never could be!"

"Gotcha. Well, thank you for your time". Nathan pulls a business card from his pocket and extends it to Kenny. "If you think of anything else, please don't hesitate to call."

Kenny eyeballs the card for a moment before snatching it from Nathan's fingers.

"Don't think I'll be thinking of anything else; don't be expecting no phone calls from me."

Nathan just smiles, turns, and walks away.

CHAPTER 18

"I Fought The Law"

Nathan pulls out of the school parking lot and unlocks his phone as he drives. The single-family residents in the suburban part of town near the high school start to fade out into fields as he drives. By the time he finds Sadie's contact and hits call, the fields have grown into the thick forest that the Pacific Northwest is known for. It's growing later, and the red glowing sky is starting to descend west over the ocean. After a few rings, Sadie answers in the way that only she can, with a playful insult that makes Nathan smile.

"Hey Mr. GQ. How'd it go with Coach Kenny?"

"Very Funny." Nathan smiles, glancing over at his dress shirt, which is now on the floor on the passenger side of his truck. If he still had his cabin, that shirt would either be kindling for the fire or a rag for the next time he had to change the oil on his truck.

"I know I am. Now, what did you find out?"

"Well," Nathan thinks for a moment, letting everything that just happened at the dugout register a little bit longer. "Something didn't really add up with him."

"What do you mean?"

"First off, he was really homophobic and kind of a bully."

"Well, that doesn't surprise me. He's a former jock turned high school gym coach." Sadie scoffs.

"Yeah, I know. This is beyond that thought. This falls into the extremely uncomfortable zone. But there are a few other things. Stuff that involves Lisa. For starters, he claims he was watching a baseball game at home the night that Lisa was killed."

"So what? It's a hard alibi to prove unless he knew the score and shit. But even then, it's a hard alibi to disprove. After almost 50 years, he could have googled the score and rehearsed his alibi. So basically, what you're saying is that his alibi, or lack thereof, doesn't advance this story at all."

"Hmm. Yeah." He doesn't indulge in that; he just continues. "He claims that he was watching the Seattle Mariners play the New York Yankees. He even knew the score."

"I don't know much about Baseball, but were the Mariners around in 1977? Is that why you think it's bullshit?"

"Yeah, they were around in 77. It was their inaugural year, actually. But there's a huge problem with that."

"Ok, so what's the fucking problem then??"

Nathan can actually picture her, sitting criss crossed on the bed with both his dogs laying beside her and suddenly leaning forward in anticipation of his deductive skills which cracked the coach's alibi. He shakes the image from his mind and focuses on driving.

"Well, in 1977, the baseball season was over by October 18th. The Yankees beat the Dodgers in game 6. Even if he was watching the Mariners' last game that his old man recorded on VHS, which he hadn't seen yet, that game was played on October 1st. So he has no alibi for the night that Lisa was killed."

"How do you know this shit? Are you a baseball nut?"

Nathan closes his eyes, wishing he had a free hand to rub his face.

"No, I just looked up the schedule after I left."

"Oh shit, the plot thickens. Do you think he could have killed Lisa? What would have been his motive? Maybe he had a crush on her too? Maybe he hit on her after Johnny broke up with her, and she slapped him too? Since he was a big dumb jock, maybe he freaked and killed her?"

Nathan thinks about this a moment as he drives with the thick, dense forests rolling past the side windows.

"Maybe? I'm not sure. He's definitely covering up something. It's just hard to..." Nathan stops as he notices cherries and berries light up in his rearview mirror. He looks in the mirror and sees the flash of red and blue lights on top of an SUV. "I gotta call you back; the sheriff is pulling me over."

"No fuckin way!" Sadie tries to get out before Nathan ends the call and tosses his phone on the dashboard of his truck. He glides over onto the gravel shoulder of the road and turns his truck off. He rolls down his window, places one elbow on the door of his car, and rests his other hand on top of the steering wheel as he waits for the sheriff to come up.

He waits, and he waits. He glances at his wristwatch. It's been over 25 minutes since the sheriff pulled him over, and he has yet to come up to his door. He rests his head back against the headrest and closes his eyes. He feels his toes against his boots and lets his thoughts run up his heels and into his calves. The thoughts of his existence run up his stiff knees that are still bent in the seated position, then to his butt, which is starting to grow tired of the truck seat. He takes another slow breath and feels his chest rise and fall, feeling the seatbelt against his sternum. He focuses on his hand gripping the steering wheel with his elbow across the open window of his truck. The air inhaling through his nose lingers in his lungs before he lets it out through his slightly parted lips. Finally, the sheriff is here.

sheriff Jim Dalton gives a good hard rap against the door with his nightstick, causing Nathan to snap his eyes open. He looks out at the man who is now at eye level with him.

"Hey, sheriff. Fancy meeting you here."

"Funny boy, you know why I pulled you over?" He adjusts his belt and holster under his aging stomach.

"I can only assume you read my reviews on Google and realized I'm a pretty good Private Investigator. You thought I'd be an excellent addition to the force and you want to recruit me to be a deputy? Maybe one day, take over and be sheriff when you retire?" Nathan gives a fake cheesy smile. The sheriff does not smile back.

"Your windshield is broken. Now that's gonna be a $120 fine."

"That's all, sheriff? Put it on my tab. I'll drop by on Friday and give Mabel a check."

"That's all fine, boy, but you're also missing a side mirror over there." He points his nightstick through the open window, inches past Nathan's face, towards the passenger window.

"Yeah, I know. Damnedest thing. I was trying to fight a forest fire and clipped a tree. "Nathan tries to lean his face back from the nightstick, letting his smile slowly fade. The sheriff pulls the nightstick back out from the window and slides it into the holster on his belt.

"Funny. Funny. Now, that mirror had better be fixed by tomorrow, or I'm going to have to impound this old truck. "He drapes an arm across the top of Nathan's door and leans in so close that Nathan can tell he had Classic Lay's potato chips with vinegar for lunch.

"Sure thing, sheriff. I'll swing by Autozone as soon as I get back into town and get that fixed. Is there anything else I can do for you?"

"You're a little old to be lurking around the high school. What are you doing up that way?"

"Oh, I was just talking to Coach. I heard they have a pretty good football team this year, and I wanted to get his thoughts before I bought season tickets." Nathan gives the sheriff a big smile, which lingers only a short time after the sheriff pulls out his nightstick and smashes out Nathan's driver-side mirror.

"Well, guess I got two mirrors to fix now. Huh." Nathan nods slowly, looking at the broken mirror.

"You'll have a lot more than that to fix if you don't learn to watch your mouth! As I told you, this is a quiet town now. We don't need you and that city bitch stirring up old memories and causing problems. You start harassing people having lunch in a diner, in a bookstore, and a high school; I hear about all this, you see. And I don't like it. I don't like people causing problems in my town. So consider this your last warning, son." Jim Dalton sucks in his stomach and puffs his chest as he adjusts his utility belt.

"Sure thing sheriff. I hear you, loud and clear." Nathan looks forward calmly. His hands lightly gripped the steering wheel at 10 and 2. The sheriff clicks his nightstick on the top of his truck.

"Good to hear. Now get back to that motel and tell your girlfriend the same thing."

Nathan can't even respond, as the sheriff is already halfway back to his SUV. Nathan grips his wheel in a release of anger, then lets out a deep breath. Next thing he knows, he hears gravel flying from underneath spinning tires as the sheriff's SUV pulls out quickly beside him and tears down the highway. He finally smiles and runs a hand over his head. He realizes he needs a haircut. And maybe a shave. Looking at his phone, he sees he has a text from Sadie. It's actually a picture of her and his two dogs.

The caption below the photo reads. "Don't forget the dog food and the beer."

CHAPTER 19

"An Inside Source"

Nathan is greeted at the entrance of the motel room by two extremely energetic and hungry Rottweilers. He knees past them and drops the 50lb bag of dog food off his shoulder onto the floor. He places a paper bag of groceries and a 12-pack of beer on the table next to Sadie's laptop and scattered papers. He pulls out two extra large metal dog dishes from the bag and plops them on the floor. The dogs instantly sit at attention. Nathan rips open the bag of dry food and pours some in. The dogs patiently wait as he opens the cellophane wrap on the deli meat, which he tosses on top. A click of his tongue and the dogs begin to eat. Removing two beers from the case he puts the rest in the fridge. Nathan cracks the top of a bottle open for Sadie and takes his own over to the fake recline where he plops down and takes a drink.

Sadie takes a swig of her beer and sits at the table in front of her laptop.

"What happened to your dress shirt?"

"Burst at the seams. Had to throw it in a piss hole off the highway."

"Funny Mr. T-Shirt. Are you just going to wear those pants and that shirt for the rest of your days?"

"Nah." Nathan shakes his head and takes another sip from his bottle. "I stopped by Gus and got some clothes for myself."

"Whatever. Damned if I know anything about fashion, right?" Sadie shakes her head playfully.

"Well, right now, you're wearing a black Motorhead t-shirt with the sleeves cut off and red jogging shorts. So no, it doesn't appear you have much of a sense of fashion."

"Whatever dick. So what did the sheriff have to say when he pulled you over?"

"Same shit. Don't ruffle any feathers. Don't bring up the past. What did your inside source have to say?"

Sadie smiles wide and holds up a small stack of papers.

"I got the Autopsy report. It doesn't reveal too much more than what we already know. The papers reported her injuries pretty accurately. It does reveal that she was sexually assaulted, but they did not obtain any DNA. They did not find the murder weapon. In fact, the crime scene itself was pretty damn spotless. They checked for fingerprints and discovered every piece of playground equipment was spotless. Not a single child's fingerprint on any handle or rail or anything. It's like someone spent the entire night wiping every surface down."

"Interesting. Do you think there could have been more than one killer?"

"If there wasn't more than one killer, then the killer at least had a helper."

"Or a protege?"

"You thinking Mr. Rivers and Father Bill?"

"It's looking more likely that they might know more than they were letting on. I do believe that Oliver made up all of his little stories just to sell books, but I think he might know something else."

"Me too, so I did a little more digging. In the original police report, they interviewed Oliver Garlicky and William Buchanan. They both told the same exact story that they had given us. William's mom verified his albi, saying they used her sewing machine. But get this, William's Dad drove a two-tone blue car."

"Same kind of car that Johnny saw leaving the cemetery that night. What were they doing down there? Maybe a ceremony with their new robes? Or a ceremony before they started sewing on their new symbols?" Nathan rubs the back of his neck.

"Maybe. I'm not sure. I just know there are just too many coincidences going on here. People know more than they are letting on about. I don't trust any of them."

"Yeah, me neither. So where do you want to go from here?"

"You want to go out for dinner?" Sadie finishes her beer.

"Not really in the mood to go out and deal with the general population after today. You want to just order something?"

"Sure. Pizza or Chinese?"

"Either is fine with me." Nathan finishes his beer and stands. "I'm going to grab my clothes from the truck then take a shower."

Nathan walks out to his truck, casually surveying the parking lot as he walks. He grabs the two bags of clothes from Gus's and closes his door. He notices a tan 4-door sedan in the back of the lot as the engine starts. It starts to pull away without turning its lights on. Nathan drops his bags and starts to jog after the car. When its lights turn on, it peels out of the lot and down the street. The back license plate had been removed, and Nathan was unable to get a look at the driver. He picks up his clothes from the pavement and goes back to Sadie's motel room. She's scrolling through her phone while chewing on a nail.

"Just noticed a strange car out in the lot. The driver took off when I noticed it." Nathan tosses his bags of clothes on the dresser and pulls out a pair of shorts and a T-shirt. "Keep your eyes out for a tan 4-door sedan while you're going and about. No back plate."

Sadie looks up at him.

"Will do. Jillian posted another episode. I saw it when I was looking at the Main Moon restaurant's menu. I was waiting for you to get back inside to listen to it. You wanna hear it?"

"No, but also yes." He grabs two more beers from the fridge, handing one to her before he takes a seat across from her at the table. "Let's hear this. Make sure you skip ahead 3 minutes or so. I don't want to hear that damn intro music."

Sadie chuckles and skips ahead and presses play, laying her phone down in the middle of the table so they both can hear.

"What's up Playmorons! It's your host Jillian Playmore and this is the Playmore podcast! But you already know that cuz you just keep playing these episodes and when one episode ends what do you do? you Playmore!

So you know that I have all the inside sources in the world, right? I have inside sources inside the inside source, and Cedar Point is no different. I have an inside source inside the sheriff's department, and this source, we'll call her Sable, gave me Lisa's autopsy report and the original police reports from Devils Night back in 77!"

Sadie slaps the table with the palm of her hand.

"Fucking bitch!" Sadie screams.

"Who, Jillian? Or Mable?"

"Both! Although Mable is probably going to get her instant fuckin karma once the sheriff catches wind of this. I can't imagine she's still going to have a job once he learns that she's leaking shit to Jillian. Hopefully, he doesn't realize that she leaked it to me, too."

"The autopsy report confirms all the injuries that I've already reported on, but the key difference is that Lisa was raped! She did not die a virgin. She was fucked before AND after her death! I imagine Oshun Rivers, the main Warlock, probably took her virginity before they murdered her, and then he let his little butt buddy Willow have his sloppy seconds after she was already dead.

I also have the police interviews from back then. Contrary to what I believe happened, Oshun and Willow stick to their claim they were sewing pride symbols onto their gay robes, and their mommy confirms it. Oops, is that homophobic? Well, not in New York! So deal with it!

The police reports also state that Johnny Olsen met with Lisa that night at the playground and broke up with her. Apparently, after she slapped him, he left. You go girl, slap that sorry son of a bitch. Lisa was too good for him anyway. Nowadays he's just a useless alcoholic. So good on you Lisa!

Also, Kenny claims he was at home watching baseball or some shit, but we all know baseball was over by then. So he must have been mistaken. Maybe he was watching hockey or some other lame sport. So everyone has an alibi now except for Cindy Summers and Deena Fox. That's right, Playmorons! The owner and only waitress at Dee's diner on Main Street in Cedar Point! You see, both Cindy and Deena claim they were waiting at home for Lisa to come over and finish her Halloween costume at their house. So who's telling the truth? And who's lying? We got some fishy bitch shit in Cedar Point! Oops, that wasn't very nice. Oh well, I am from New York, Yanno!

I also got a good word that Nathan burned down his own cabin in order to shack up with Fadie Poop; oh, sorry, my New York accent got a little strong there. I meant Sadie Koop. Turns out he had to burn down his cabin in order to get her to forgive him for trying to rape me! That's right, they're probably currently laying in bed snuggling together, listening to the Playmore Podcast!"

Sadie hits stop aggressively with her middle finger, then flips off the phone.

"Fucking bitch!" She chugs down the rest of her beer, then tucks her hair behind her ear and gets up to grab a third beer from the fridge. "How does she get this information? How is she always right on the same goddamn level that we are on?"

"Maybe it's time I have a word with her?" Nathan rubs Tango's furry ear as he rests his head on Nathan's lap. Sadie sits back down in front of her laptop and starts punching something into the keypad. After a few minutes of clicks and swipes, she smiled.

"She's staying at the Hilton on the outskirts of Portland. It's only a half-hour ride from there into town. God forbid she actually stays in a fleabag motel like this."

"You want to go now? Or wait for the morning."

"Wait for the morning. I'm getting drunk tonight!" She chugs down her third beer and lets out a long loud burp followed by a laugh. The beer obviously already started to have an effect on her.

"Grab me another beer cowboy!"

"Sure, then I'm going to take a shower. Don't get too drunk. I don't need you all hungover tomorrow when we confront her." He grabs his clothes and slings them over his shoulder before grabbing a beer from the fridge for Sadie. She takes it and slaps his butt as he turns to walk to the bathroom.

"Thanks for the advice dad! Like I've never had a beer before and you gotta watch out for me." She laughs and takes a drink from the bottle. She tilts back on the chair and smiles innocently.

Nathan just shakes his head with a smile and heads to the bathroom. Twenty minutes later after a shower and a clean shave, he emerges. Sadie is sprawled out on the bed on her back. Her hair is splayed out and Tango and Cash are both lying besides her. She looks at Nathan's clean shaven face.

"Look at your baby face! Wow, you clean up nicely. Wish you still had those clothes I bought you. You'd be a babe."

Nathan chuckles and sits at the table.

"Thanks. So, what are we thinking right now? Who's our main suspect in this entire thing?"

"Well," Sadie sits up slightly, leaning back on his elbows. Her speech was a little slurred. "I think we can rule out Deena and Cindy. Unless they're secretly like the chick from Sleep Away Camp, I don't think they're sexually assaulting anyone. And even if they worked together, they're not killing Lisa in such a violent manner and then cleaning everything up."

"Good point." Nathan agrees. "So what about Kenny and Johnny? They were friends. Maybe Johnny snapped and then got Kenny to help him out?"

"That's a big maybe. However, it does make a lot of sense. What about the Warlocks?"

"That's what I can't figure out. It seems pretty logical that the Warlocks, or at least someone driving Father Bill's car, were there that night. Johnny saw the car but not the driver. He did say there were at least two kids inside. "

"So maybe the Warlocks circled back and got Lisa before she could leave?"

Nathan just nods slowly, deep in thought. He knew there were still huge holes in the story but he just couldn't figure out which of the suspects could fill in those gaps.

"Which person do you trust the most?"

Sadie flops back onto the bed again and lifts her legs up into the air, slowly moving them side to side and occasionally spreading them and moving them in random circles.

"Probably Johnny. He seems pretty genuine and eager to help."

"Who do you trust the least?"

"The fucking bitch Jillian!"

CHAPTER 20

"That's So New York"

Nathan drives down the highway towards Portland. The sun is rising over Mount Hood off in the distance. Sadie is curled in a ball on the bench beside him with her sunglasses covering her eyes and the hood of her gray hoodie pulled tightly over her head. She lets out a soft groan as they hit a bump in the road. Nathan takes a sip of coffee from his tumbler and smiles.

"A little hung over there champ?"

"Do not speak. Please." She croaks out, raising a hand to show him.

"I told you not to get too.." He's cut off as she shakes her hand at him and sits up.

"Wait, stop."

"What?" Nathan raises an eyebrow at her.

"Pull over. Now!" She holds her hand to her mouth. Nathan abruptly pulls off to the side of the highway and puts the car in park. A cloud of dust from the gravel shoulder engulfs the truck as Sadie opens the door and falls out onto the grass. Nathan takes another drink of coffee and listens to her water the grass with the contents of her stomach. Wrenching and straining, she proceeds to vomit up the remainder of the beer and bile. In all the anger and frustration after they listened to the Playmore podcast the night before, they had forgotten to order dinner.

Sadie had consumed over half of the 12-pack of beer and had ended the night trying to teach Tango how to do an actual Tango.

After a few minutes of silence following what sounded like a very painful attempt at hurling, Sadie finally emerged from the grass and climbed back into the truck, still holding a hand over her mouth.

"Got any gum?" She asks.

"Check the glove box. You feel better?"

Sadie finds a pack of gum in the glove box and shoves a few pieces in her mouth nodding as she chews. Nathan continues down the highway toward the hotel where Jillian is staying. As they approach the city of Portland, Nathan finally breaks the silence.

"So, how do you want to approach this?"

"I want to punch her in the nose when she opens the door."

Nathan laughs.

"I don't think that's a good idea. Ever hear the expression 'you catch more flies with honey than you do vinegar'?"

"A pile of shit attracts the most flies," Sadie retorts.

"True. But we can't just bum-rush her if we want to get information. I think the best approach is the Trojan horse method."

"What? Use a condom?"

"No. We go and try to befriend her. Act like we need her help. Play to her ego. Make it seem like she's the only one who can solve the murder. She's smarter than you and I. We lull her into a sense of false confidence and use that to get as much information as we can. Then we steer her in the completely opposite direction."

"Oooh, that's a good idea!" Sadie takes off her sunglasses and tosses them onto the dashboard. She pulls down the visor and looks into the mirror, tossing her messy hair as she speaks. "Jesus, I look like shit. Don't suppose you have any makeup in the glove box?"

"Negative. And you look fine. I mean, besides the smell of vomit, the bags under your eyes, your messy hair, and the clothes you obviously slept in." Before Nathan can continue, she playfully slaps him on the chest.

"Rude!" She laughs trying to fix her hair but eventually just gives up and pulls it back into a ponytail. She takes off her hoodie, revealing a tight black tank top with a white Shamrock on the front.

They come to a stop in the hotel's parking lot. Unlike Sadie's cheap motel, you can't access the rooms from the outside. You have to go through the front doors and past the desk clerk.

"You ready?" Nathan asks as they get out of the truck. He stretches as they walk towards the door.

"Yeah, but how are we getting past the desk clerk?"

"Just act like you belong here." He smiles and wraps an arm around her shoulders drawing her against his side. She instinctively wraps her arm around his waist as they casually walk through the automatic double doors. Nathan smiles and waves to the clerk as they walk straight past the stairs. Once the stairwell door closes, Nathan removes his arm from her shoulders, which brings a slight pout from Sadie. Nathan ignores it.

"What floor is she on?" He asks

"Third floor. Room 302."

They walk up the three flights of stairs and head down the

hallway until they reach room 302. Nathan gives the door a polite knock. Sadie takes a long slow breath. After a few moments the door opens.

Jillian is standing before them, her purple hair cut into a Pixie cut. Her hair is cut into petals that outline her face, which lead up into short bangs with crown layers on top. Her skin is tan and she has a nose ring. Her wardrobe can only be described as a rainbow. The look on her face is a combination of shock and amusement at the same time. She laps her thighs and opens her mouth wide.

"Oh my gawd. If it's not Batman and fuckin Robin. The dynamic duo!"

"Hello, Jillian," Sadie says through gritted teeth.

"Miss Playmore, I'm Nathan Taylor, but I assume you already knew that. Since, according to you, I gave you a bunch of information right before I tried to sexually assault you?"

Jillian laughs and waves her hand dismissively at him.

"Oh, whatever. I gotta add some spice to the podcast. Otherwise, it would be as boring as Growing Cold."

Nathan can sense Sadie's urge to tackle the woman and beat her into a bloody pulp. He places a hand on the small of her back to help calm her. He can feel her warm skin from the small space between her tank top and her shorts.

"So what, you two came here to set the record straight? Maybe you wanna beat me up? You can try to but don't forget that I'm from New York. In New York, if you don't know how to fight by the time you can walk, then your ass is toast!" She takes a step back and holds up her hands in what is supposed to be a fighting stance. Nathan, having been in hundreds of fights in his life, can tell by the stance that Jillian has never been in anything more than maybe a hair-pulling catfight in her life. He gives her a smile.

"We did come to set the record straight, but not with that. I get that you do what you have to do to get ratings. I do the same thing when I'm working as a Private Investigator. You say what you have to do to get the job done. We wanna get the job done and solve this case, but we haven't had much luck. Even when working together, we always feel like we're a step behind."

"Yeah? So? What's that got to do with me?" Jillian brings her hands down to her sides and seems to relax a bit. Nathan gives Sadie a nudge with his hand on her back, causing her to think that it's her turn to talk. Reluctantly, she smiles.

"So, you always seem to know exactly what we know and maybe a little more. It just seems... that.. It seems that you are better than both of us combined."

Jillian holds her stomach and lets her mouth drop open.

"No fucking way did you just admit that. Finally, You finally admit that I'm the better podcaster?"

Nathan can feel Sadie's back tensing up.

"We just feel that three minds are better than one. If we can work together, the three of us can figure this out once and for all. And once we do, you can post it all on your podcast, and we'll go on with our lives."

"Yeah. On your podcast, Jillian." Sadie grudgingly spits out.

Jillian ponders this for a moment placing a finger to her pursed lips as she dramatically pretends to mull this over. Finally, she steps aside and holds her arm out to the inside of the hotel room inviting them in.

"Well, come on then. Take your shoes off. I don't want any filth on the floor. They'll take my security deposit."

Nathan slides off his slip on work boots and Sadie bends down to untie her Converse Allstars. She quickly moves to take a seat at the fake recliner in the corner of the room. Even more luxurious hotels apparently have fake recliners as well. Nathan takes a seat at one side of the small table which has Jillian's laptop and stacks of folders and paperwork.

"So, how did you always manage to stay one step ahead of us, Jillian?" Nathan asks as he glances at the paperwork. On top is the autopsy report that Mable smuggled out.

"I got followers of the podcast. Playmorons, as I like to call them. I just put out on my Facebook group that I wanted people to follow you, too, and report back to me. The next thing I knew, I had dozens of people reporting on your every move. It was great. All I had to do was kick back by the hotel pool and let my listeners do my job for me." She smiles and sits on the other side of the table.

"That's pretty clever." Sadie sarcastically states. "So what do you have that isn't in the podcast?" Do you have a smoking gun yet?"

"No, nothing even close."

"You think Oliver and William are the prime suspects though?" Nathan asks.

"Oh fuck yeah. Those two little queers are definitely the prime suspects." She notices Nathan's eyebrow raise at her slur. She smirks. "Sorry, that's what we call people like that in New York."

Nathan nods. "Of course you do. So, what evidence do you have that those two are the killers? Even the sheriff didn't have anything. No fingerprints, no murder weapon, nothing."

"Nope. They got nothing, and I got nothing. So yanno what I'm going to do?" She smiles and waits for them to answer her question.

"No clue, what are you going to do Jillian." Sadie reluctantly states, not actually asking the question. Just saying what she knew she was supposed to ask.

"I'm gonna frame those little pricks, and I'm going to catch them, and I'm going to get all the glory. I bet there's a reward, not that I need it. I got a good sponsorship deal from Blue Ball Male Enhancement."

"How do you plan on framing them? And isn't that a little unethical? If they aren't the actual killers, then you are putting two innocent men in prison and letting the real killer walk free."

"Unethical my ass. That's how we roll in New York! Those two aren't innocent of anything. Have you read any of that shit that Oshun prick wrote? He's definitely killed other people besides Lisa. And his little butt buddy Willow is a priest now, so he's probably banging altar boys all day long. Both of them deserve the death penalty." Jillian lights up a cigarette in spite of the hotel's no-smoking policy. She was worried about dirty shoes but apparently not the smell of smoke.

"So, how are you going to frame them, Jillian?" Sadie coughs.

Jillian blows a cloud of smoke in Sadie's direction and smiles. "Don't you worry about that? You'll find out when it's plastered across every news channel across America. Brash New York Podcast Host solves the 50-year-old cold case!" She holds up her hands as if it's a marquee.

"What's to say that we won't let law enforcement know that you're framing them?" Sadie folds her arms across her chest.

"You can tell Law Enforcement whatever you want. sheriff Jimmy Pop doesn't like you two anyway, and I doubt he'll believe anything you say. You're just a shitty podcaster and a hermit private dick. No one's gonna believe anything either of you say, and no one's gonna care about you after this is all said and done. I'm the star of this story and I'm the hero. You two are just NPC's."

Nathan looks at Sadie and then back to Jillian. Jillian laughs.

"NPC means Non-Playable Character. You stupid fuck. Haven't you ever played a video game?"

"Not since I was a kid. Thanks for your time Jillian. You've been a lot of help" Nathan stands and grabs his boots, slipping them back on. Sadie gets up and ties her shoes back on. Jillian finishes her cigarette and drops it into a half drinken cup of Starbucks on the table.

"Sure thing. You two are so cute together. Useless people belong together." She starts to give Sadie a mocking smile, but that facial expression quickly changes to shock. Her eyes are wide as blood starts to run down her nose from both nostrils.

"What the fuck? Did you just hit me?" Jillian starts to raise a hand to her face, and Sadie pops her again right in her mouth, splitting her bottom lip. Jillian falls to the ground and holds her arms up defensively. "Owie! Stop! Fuck!"

Sadie doesn't hit her anymore; she just shakes her head and looks down at her. "You're pathetic, Jillian, even for a New Yorker."

Nathan puts his hand on her shoulder and leads her out of the room, closing the door behind them as they hurry down the stairs.

"Think she'll call the cops on you? That was assault." Nathan comments.

"No way. She doesn't want to look weak. I bet you that in her next episode, she'll talk about how we came to her hotel room and begged her for help. She'll say she whooped my ass and threw us both out onto the street."

"How's your hand? You threw a good punch."

"Hurts, but in a good way." She smiles at him and wraps her arm

146

around his torso as they reach the ground floor.

Arms wrapped around each other and laughing, they casually stroll past the front desk like they owned the place.

CHAPTER 21

"Dempe"

Nathan and Sadie drove in pretty much silence the entire ride back. Sadie rode with her window down and the wind blowing her hair back as she watched the beautiful scenery. The leaves were in their full autumn glory. The landscape looked like it was on fire as trees of red, orange, and yellow blankets the rolling hills in the countryside. Nathan glanced over at her and smiled as he drove.

When they got back to the motel Nathan scanned the lot for any suspicious cars and found none. Maybe Jillian called back her hounds after their little meeting. Inside the room they were greeted by two overly hyper Rottweilers who had not had much outside time since the cabin was burnt down.

"You poor boys must be bored out of your doggy minds being cooped up inside the motel room all day and night!

"You want to take them for a walk?" Nathan asks as he scratches Cash's neck.

"Sure! That sounds fun! Where do you want to walk them? Wait, do you have leashes for them?"

"They'll follow your lead and your command. They don't need leashes. You can walk them wherever you want."

"Wait, you're not coming? Where are you going?"

"I'm going to go have another word with Coach Kenny" Nathan

gives Cash a pat on the butt.

Sadie looks a little disappointed.

"Fine, whatever. I'll go walk your dogs and you can just go investigate I guess."

"Thanks, I appreciate it." He gives her a smile as he walks past her into the parking lot. After another scan of the cars in the lot, he still doesn't see anything suspicious. He feels she would be safe with his dogs anyway. He hops in his truck and drives off, not noticing Sadie standing in the doorway of the motel room, looking more than mildly annoyed.

It only takes five minutes for Nathan to reach the school. The lot is empty except for a couple vehicles. It's after school hours, so Nathan didn't expect it to be very busy. He hops out of his truck and heads over to the dugout, looking for the coach. The dugout was empty. Nathan heads across the track field towards the gymnasium. On his way he sees two Rottweilers running across the field towards him.

"Tango? Cash? What the fuck?" He then notices a woman also running towards him. It's Sadie. He calmly shakes his head as she approaches.

"How dare you?" She gives him a shove as she approaches."

"You got a great set of lungs to make it here that fast, shove me, and yell all without even being winded." Nathan chuckles as he stumbles back. She really shoved him hard.

"Yeah, well, I like to keep in shape!" She responds angrily. "We're supposed to be partners. I'm not some fuckin dog walker! If you want to go talk to someone we can do it together, as a team!" She gives him another shove. This time, he grabs her wrists to calm her down.

"You're right! You're right. I'm sorry. I should have brought you. I'm just used to working alone." He can feel her heart beating through her wrists. He guesses her raised pulse isn't from the jog. He lets his hands move down her wrists to grip her hands. "We are a team, and I won't do that again."

Nathan can feel his own heart pulsating almost through his chest. Sadie's hands are sweating as they hold onto his own. Her eyes locked on his own. Nathan snaps himself out of the moment, much to Sadie's dismay.

"Coach isn't outside. Might be in the gym." He turns his head to Tango and Cash. "You two stay outside."

The dogs sit outside the gymnasium doors and Sadie and Nathan enter. Her shoes squeak on the freshly buffed basketball court. Midcourt, Nathan stops and holds a hand out to stop Sadie from walking. She stops and looks at him. She starts to speak, and he holds a finger to his lips to stop her. She listens, not hearing anything. She mouths the word, "What?"

"I hear water running." He speaks quietly and motions his head towards the locker room doors. They walk quietly over and crack the doors open slightly. The smell of dirty gym shorts and body odor whiffed out the doors along with steam from running showers.

"I think I should wait outside. I'm not about to invade the boy's locker room. I don't want to see anything that happens inside there." Sadie whispers to him. He nods and slips inside.

The locker room is small, with a bench in the middle. Around the corner is the bathroom with two stalls, three urinals, and a large circular sink in the middle. Past that is the locker room. He can see the steam lurking along the ceiling as the sound of water fills the enclosure. Nathan quietly begins walking into the bathroom area, careful to not make a sound. He turns the corner into the shower area when suddenly he's face to face with a very naked and very shocked coach Kenny Neil.

Kenny quickly grabs a towel from around his neck and drapes it around his bloated stomach, hiding his nether regions. He's still dripping wet, and his face is red with rage.

"What in the Sam hell are you doing in the locker room??"

"I was just about to ask you the same thing, Coach." Nathan moves his head past the coach to try to look into the shower area.

"What's it look like? I'm taking a goddamn shower. This school has better shower pressure than I do at home, especially when Deena takes her goddamn half-hour-long shower." He adjusts the towel under his stomach to keep it from falling down. As he speaks, the teenage boy from the dugout comes out of the shower. Nathan looks away as the naked boy hurries past, grabbing a towel from the rack as he heads shamefully to the locker area. Nathan looks at Kenny and raises an eyebrow.

"What? You never showered in gym class? Have you ever even played a sport in your life, Mr. PI? Guys shower together all the goddamn time. It's perfectly normal."

"Maybe when everyone is on the same team. Or in the same grade. Or even the same age. But I don't know how appropriate it is for a grown man to be showering with a little boy like that."

"He's not a little boy! He's a teenager."

"How old is he? 13 at the most? You really think that's appropriate, Coach?" Nathan folds his arms across his chest.

"Get the fuck out of my locker room!" Kenny pushes past him and goes to the locker room. He picks up his white briefs and pulls them on. Then, he grabs his golf shorts and pulls them up under his stomach. The boy has already dressed and is heading out the doors into the gym. When he opens the door, he's greeted by a very surprised Sadie.

"What the fuck? Who are you?" She asks the boy. He doesn't respond. Instead, he just takes off through the gymnasium and runs out the door. She steps inside and looks at Nathan and

Kenny in confusion, and then it all starts to click together. "Oh shit. You sick fuck."

"Fuck you bitch, you don't know what the fuck you're talking about. Why don't you go."

He's cut off before he can finish. Nathan throws a straight right hand into the side of the Coach's cheek, spinning his head to the side and dropping him to the tiled floor next to the bench. He sits up groggy and places his hand on his cheek. Nathan stands over him.

"Don't you ever call her a bitch again? In fact, if I ever hear you call any woman a bitch again, I'll break your goddamn jaw. You hear me, you fat piece of shit?"

"Fuck you" He spits at Sadie and stands, moving pretty fast for a big fat guy. He slams Nathan into the lockers, pinning him against it with his broad, beefy chest and shoulders. With Kenny still wet from the shower, Nathan manages to slip an arm out from underneath him and bring an elbow crashing down onto Kenny's collarbone. Kenny yelps out in pain. He rears back and then slams his shoulder into Nathan's midsection, slamming his back against the steel lockers again. Sadie starts raining down hammer fists onto his back, but the big boy is pretty solid. Nathan drops another elbow onto the Coach's collarbone. He yelps in pain again and gives Nathan just enough space and time to call out one word.

"Dempe!"

Within ten seconds the two Rottweilers burst through the door and skidded past on the wet slippery tile floor. They regain their foot and turn back to the ensuing fight. Kenny instantly releases Nathan and jumps back against the lockers, holding his hands and a foot out to try to fend off the two dogs. He yells out in surrender as the dogs snarl at him.

"Call 'em off! Call 'em off!"

Nathan snaps his fingers and the dogs sit in front of the quivery man who appears to have soiled his golf shorts. Sadie blinks wide eyed in surprise.

"Wow, what does Dempe mean?"

"It means 'subdue' in Norwegian. I have them trained in a few different languages." Nathan adjusts his shoulder as he straightens himself. "Now, Kenny, are you going to turn yourself into the sheriff, or should I have my boys here escort you down to the sheriff's office?"

"Fuck you!" He spits at the dogs. Tango barks at him which makes him jump. "Ok, fine. Yeah, I'll call the sheriff tonight. Tell him everything that happened here."

Sadie looks at Nathan in shock. "No way you're going to let him walk out of here and trust he's going to turn himself in?"

Nathan shrugs. "If he doesn't, we'll just go talk to the boy's parents and let them call the sheriff themselves."

Sadie goes to protest, but Nathan puts a hand on her back and leads her out of the gym. He clicks his tongue, and the dogs follow behind him. He can hear the coach start to sob as they exit the gymnasium.

CHAPTER 22

"When Doves Cry"

After they got back to the hotel, Sadie convinced Nathan to take the dogs out for a walk together as a team. So together, side by side with the dogs walking beside them like bookends, they walked down the side roads of town. The conversation was limited. Instead, they opted to just enjoy the companionship. The air was as fresh and brisk as the sunset was gorgeous. The leaves danced across the sidewalk. Orange, red, and yellow figures twirled among the headstones as they made their way into Gold Lawn Cemetery. They headed straight forward, following the road to a slight left until they hit a giant oak tree on the right side of the road. There, beneath it, lay the Headstone of Lisa Fields. The dogs sniffed around the grass as Sadie and Nathan stood before it, taking it all in.

"Do you think we can solve this?" Sadie asks, hugging herself as a chill begins to envelop the evening.

"I think everything can be figured out. How long does that take? I'm not sure." He notices her shivering as she's still only dressed in a tank top and jogging shorts. He puts an arm around her shoulders and pulls her against his torso, rubbing her arm with his other hand. She melts against him. Neither of them says anything as they memorize the letters on the headstone.

A large crack of lightning interrupts the moment. It fills the sky with bright light before returning to the dark. Another large crack followed a few seconds later. Nathan looks off into the distance.

"We should head back. It's gonna get nasty out real soon."

Sure enough, it got nasty really quick. They were both soaking wet as they ran into the motel room. Tango and Cash tried to run in behind them but Nathan gave a command that stopped them just before the door. Underneath the overhang they were safe from the storm but still outside. He went and grabbed a couple towels as they shook themselves off outside. He went and dried them off before letting them inside.

After he followed them in, he peeled his wet shirt off and looked over at Sadie, who was already lying on the bed with her back against the headboard. She has a Pepsi can filled with wine and her hair, still wet from the storm, is hooked behind her ears. She had changed out of her wet clothes and was wearing just a white motel-issue robe. Nathan went to the bathroom, removed the rest of his wet clothes, and changed into a pair of sweatpants. Upon exiting the bathroom, he took a seat at the table and started doing research on Sadie's laptop. His dogs were already fast asleep on the floor, sprawled out and snoring. After a while, Sadie asks,

"Do you really think that Kenny is going to turn himself in?"

"Nah." Nathan shakes his head. "Even if we turned him in, I doubt the sheriff would believe us. This is a good old boys kind of town. Both seem like they're cut from the same shitty cloth. The best we can hope is that we scared him enough to get him to stop. I wonder if Deena knows."

"Doubt it. I'm sure he still makes her put out once a week like a good, obedient wife. He probably just gets his rocks off on grooming young boys. I wonder how long he's been doing it?"

"No way of knowing." Nathan closes the laptop and rubs his eyes.

"Finally ready to call it quits for the night and relax a bit?" Sadie asks.

"Yeah. You got any wine left, or you drink it all?" Nathan cracks his neck.

"You can share the can with me if you want?" She smiles, swirls the wine in the can, and pats the bed next to her. Nathan chuckles. Outside the motel curtains, lightning can be seen lighting up the sky. The sound of pouring rain beats against the glass of the window.

"I think there's a couple beers left in the fridge." He goes to the fridge and finds one bottle left. He pops it open, takes a sip, and sits on the bed against the headboard beside her.

She lets her shoulder rest over against his arm and sips the wine from the can. He takes a long, steady drink from his bottle. Eventually, she breaks the silence.

"Back when we were talking to Deena. She didn't want to trust us and you mentioned something about your sister."

Nathan doesn't say anything, but she feels his muscles tighten. It was obviously a sensitive subject. He takes another drink from his bottle before responding.

"Didn't you look that part of my life up before you hired me?"

"No, I tried looking up where your office was. Quite quickly, I found that you had no office and no address; in fact, you had no presence online at all. You were a ghost. I just happened to be inside a truck stop when I heard some asshole kicking down a manager's door. What were the odds, eh?"

"No Shit," Nathan says matter of factly. Kind of dumbfounded.

"Well, it gets even better. I didn't have a car; I had taken an Uber and then walked to the truck stop in hopes of hitching back to Portland to save money. That sponsorship deal I was telling you about wasn't all it was cracked up to be. In fact, if you had wanted that $3000 I promised you, I probably wouldn't have been able to pay this month's rent or even afford this shitty motel room for another night. So I couldn't follow you. By the time I found someone to give me a ride, you had already left. I went in the direction you left in and to my surprise, I saw you sitting outside a bar on a corner taking pictures. I sweet-talked to the guy giving me a ride to follow you back to your cabin. I gave him a sob story about you being my baby daddy and owing child support money. He honestly wanted to go and beat you up. Obviously, you would have won that fight, but he was a sweetie for the offer. Anyways, The rest is history."

Nathan nods. It all makes sense now. That still didn't explain how Jillian had found out so much information about him though.

"So you said that your sister was murdered... Can I ask what happened?"

Nathan doesn't say anything. His emotions rose, and his memories flooded back in. That snake is slithering out from the corner, and his sister is crying inside his head. Sadie brings a hand to his chest and looks up at him with those large eyes.

"You don't have to tell me if you don't want to."

Nathan takes a long slow breath, inhaling through his nostrils and exhaling through his lips before he responds.

"No, it's fine. I trust you, I think."

"Well, I'd fucking hope so." She nudges her body against his playfully with a smile. Nathan gives a half-hearted smile back before his somber tone returns.

"I was 16, maybe 17 years old. I know I had my driver's license. Nelsa, or Nellie as I called her, was younger; she was 10. I don't remember a lot because I didn't pay attention too much back then. I had already started getting into trouble. Mostly stupid teenager shit, you know? Like shoplifting from the mall, sneaking vodka from my parent's liquor cabinet, and smoking some pot with my friends."

Nathan lets out a breath which catches slightly on the exhale. Sadie notices and reaches down and entwines her fingers with his, resting her head against his shoulder as he continues.

"So one day, she comes up to me and says she wants to go to the edge of town to ride her bike to this abandoned Grocery store. Apparently, there was this ramp out by the loading area she heard the older kids in town talking about. This was around the time the X games were becoming really popular. She thought she was going to be some big BMX star even though she just has this normal little girl Huffy bike with tassels on the handles." He chuckles softly, loft in memory.

"We didn't have any kind of skate park or anything in town. So, mostly I would just build her a little ramp or whatever, with half a sheet of plywood and some 2x4s, or she would try to Pop wheelies around town. Anyways, this old abandoned grocery store had a loading ramp that ran up against part of the parking lot that almost served as a halfpipe, at least in the mind of a 10-year-old. So she tried to convince me to drive her out there. "

Sadie finishes her wine from the can, watching him intently.

"It was a Saturday afternoon. I was supposed to meet this girl at the mall later, but I wanted to take a nap first. She begged and begged me, but I thought she was just being an annoying little sister."

Nathan is silent after that as he stares off into the distance. Replaying the memories in his mind.

"My last memory is of her telling me she hates me as she pedals off on her own to find the store. She was so mad at me, saying I never did anything for her and that I was a jerk. I told her she was a little brat and that I was gonna tell Mom and Dad that she was going off on her own. That night, she never came home."

His eyes start to redden as he looks away. Sadie squeezes his hand and looks up at him.

"The street lights came on and my parents started getting worried. They asked me if I knew where she was." Nathan closes his eyes as he's transported back in time. Back to his teenage years.

"I remember it being dark out and at least 50 of our neighbors walking down the street checking ditches all the way to the edge of town. They thought maybe she fell off her bike or was hit by a car or something. They called the Hospital, but no one fitting her description was there. It was like she had just..... vanished."

"Did they ever find her?"

Nathan nods solemnly.

"Yeah, about four days later. They found her down by the wash. I can't even bring myself to say what happened to her. We had to have a closed casket, so I couldn't even see her one last time to say I'm sorry. I have to live with that last memory of being an asshole who caused the death of my baby sister."

"You can't blame yourself! You were what a teenager! Hell, you were basically still a child yourself! There is no way you couldn't have known what was going to happen. Even if you did know what could you have done? What if you had gone with her? Maybe you would have been killed too, Nate."

"Don't call me Nate! Only Nellie can call me that!" Nathan snaps at her. It makes her jump and sit up, startled. Nathan instantly regrets it, his shoulders slumping. "I'm sorry"

Sadie regains her composure and runs a hand through her now dry but wildly curly hair.

"It's ok. I get it. I won't call you that. It's a special name. Can I call you Magnum Teapot?"

Nathan looks at her with a look of confusion. "What? When the fuck did you ever call me that? What does that even mean?"

She just gives that big warm smile and shrugs her shoulders. "No idea what it means, and I never called you it. But I can if you want me to."

Nathan chuckles and lightens up. "You can call me whatever. I'm sorry, it's just a touchy subject and has engulfed my entire life. It's the reason I became a Private Investigator. To try to get answers. When I couldn't, I just got into fights. I ended up moving here because she said she always wanted to live on the ocean in the Pacific Northwest. She wanted a cabin in the middle of nowhere. So I've been trying to honor her wishes my entire life."

Nathan closes his eyes and tips his head down. He feels Sadie's hand stroke his cheek and grip his chin, lifting his head back up. He opens his eyes and is greeted by her warm hazel eyes. His head tilts slightly, and their lips meet. Warm and dry at first. They press slowly together and close letting the moisture slowly overtake them. Nathan's arm reaches under her and up around her back as her hands slide over his shoulders. She climbs on top of him as their lips part, tongues darting together as their lips glide against one another. His hands run up under her shirt along her back feeling her warm, smooth, silky skin under his hand. Her thighs grip his sides as she leans down tight against him. His hands slide her shirt off over her head and then entwine in her hair pulling her head back, his lips grazing her neck, biting ever so softly. Her fingernails dig into his shoulders as she cranes her head down to mash her lips back against his.

That night, they fell asleep entwined with each other in a sweaty heap. The next morning, they woke up in almost the same position. Tango and Cash are sitting on the floor at the end of the bed, staring at them and wondering where their breakfast is.

Sadie lifts her head, looks at the dogs, and lets out a laugh before burying her face into Nathan's chest. Nathan lifts his head and chuckles before dropping his head back onto the pillow.

"I'll feed them." He slides out of bed, slips his sweatpants over his naked bottom, and grabs the dog's empty metal dishes. Sadie pulls the sheet to her naked torso and reaches over to grab her phone absentmindedly scrolling through her news feed. Suddenly, she stops and lets out a gasp.

"Holy fuck, Nathan."

Nathan sets the food dishes on the floor and signals the dogs to eat before turning to Sadie.

"Huh? What's wrong?"

The look on her face says it all. The color is gone, and her eyes stare blankly at him. She holds out her phone, unable to talk. He goes over to the bed and takes the phone from her hand. Looking at the news article on the screen his eyes skim it briefly, not yet registering what it all says. He scrolls back up to the headline.

"Popular New York Podcast Host, Jillian "Playmore" Jones, Found Murdered In Hotel Room."

CHAPTER 23

"Play No More"

Nathan scrolls through the news report again as Sadie quickly gets dressed and can't believe what he's reading. Below the headline is a bright and smiling picture of Jillian when she was younger, presumably when she first started podcasting. Her hair is a plain mousy brown and her bangs are longer; more sweeping across her face like curtains. She does not have a nose ring and her wardrobe seems a lot more modest and less flashy. She doesn't look so 'New York' here.

"Is there any update or anything new on what happened?" Sadie asks as she sits down beside Nathan at the table.

"Same thing. Someone reported a struggle last night. There was shouting and fighting. The guest next door reported it to the front desk clerk. Management went to check on it and found her lying on the floor in her room. She was bleeding from multiple stab wounds to her chest and throat. Flight for life was called but quickly canceled as she succumbed to her injuries about 3am this morning." Nathan skims through the report giving the cliff notes version.

"Jesus, I still can't believe it." Sadie takes a sip from the mug of instant coffee that Nathan had made for her. She gazes blankly across the room at nothing in particular.

"This has to do with the investigation." Nathan lays his phone down on the table and looks at her.

"Oh, One Hundred Percent!" She nods emphatically.

"What are the chances that if we call Portland PD that they'll give us any information?" Nathan wonders outloud.

"What are the chances that they'll be knocking on our door soon, asking what we were doing in her room yesterday?" Sadie pulls her knees up to her chest and rests her heels on the chair's seat.

"We should probably beat them to it and give them a call." Nathan grabs his phone and googles the number for the Portland PD Non-Emergency number. After a few rings, a female dispatcher answers.

"Hello, my name is Nathan Taylor. I'm a Private Investigator for the state of Oregon. I may have some information regarding the murder of Jillian Jones." It still felt strange using a last name that wasn't Playmore when he spoke of her. "Can you transfer me to the homicide Detective in charge?"

The dispatcher placed him on hold, and after listening to some updates on the Fall Festival the police department was holding the upcoming weekend, a voice answered. He sounded younger, maybe new to the homicide department. Not a seasoned old war dog like the sheriff of Cedar Point.

"Detective Holes, How may I help you?"

"Hello Detective. My name is Nathan Taylor. I'm a Private Detective out of Cedar Point. I'm working on an investigation with another Podcaster named Sadie Koop. She's here with me at the moment. Last night, we went to visit Ms. Playmore. Err." He corrects himself. "Ms. Jones. So you will likely find our prints in the hotel room. We figured we should reach out to you right away."

"I see." The Detective responds and then waits in silence. A typical police tactic. Let the silence linger, which makes the suspect feel uncomfortable. The suspect then starts to try to fill in the silence by talking, most likely talking too much and letting valuable information slip. Nathan doesn't take the bait. He waits for the Detective to resume speaking. He can hear people talking in the background, so it was more than likely that the Detective was still at the crime scene. Eventually, the Detective continues. "Are you able to make a statement?"

"Sure thing. Do you want us to come down to the precinct in Portland?

"No, I'm going to be out for a long time running down leads. Why don't you text me when you get into Portland and I'll tell you where to meet me."

Nathan jots down the Detective's personal cell number on a scrap of paper lying on the table and hangs up. He looks over at Sadie.

"I fuckin knew her name wasn't Playmore" She finally smiles for the first time this morning.

Nathan chuckled and ran his hand through his hair, which was starting to get a little longer than he had buzzed.

"We should head to Portland soon."

"Let me do something first." She slides her laptop over to her side of the table and flips it open. She pulls up Facebook and starts typing.

"What are you doing?"

"I'm putting out a post on her Facebook group. She has tons of minions, but there has to be someone who actually works close to her. Maybe someone who has access to her notes or something. Something that can give us some kind of details into what she was working on before she was murdered. Maybe someone can access her calendar and see if she was supposed to meet anyone when she was murdered."

"Don't you think the police are already doing all that?"

"Yeah, but people don't want to talk to cops. They want to talk to Podcasters. They'd rather get famous for their help than just help a cop catch a bad guy. Plus, they'd rather talk to cute female podcasters. So I think I got a better shot at getting information than Mr. Homicide Detective."

"Good point." Nathan takes a drink from his own mug of coffee. "Wish I had thought of that."

"What does that mean?" She gives him a sharp look. Nathan just smiles and shakes his head.

"I said something similar back when I first spoke to the sheriff."

"Great minds think alike." She smiles at him before resuming her Facebook search. Nathan goes to the curtains and pulls them open. The rain had stopped, but fall was in full swing now. The once bright and fiery trees were now almost completely bare. The sky was gray and overcast with no sun in sight. The sidewalks and roads were covered in wet red and orange leaves: making a soggy but beautiful carpet in whatever direction you were heading.

As Nathan drinks his coffee and gazes out the window, he spots that tan four-door sedan again parked in the back of the lot. Nathan slowly moves off to the side of the window, out of view. He calls to Sadie.

"Don't move, but that car I saw is back."

"The one you think was working for Jillian?"

"Yeah. that tan sedan. I got an idea. I need you to go get some ice from the ice machine down the way."

"Yeah, sure." She stands and pulls a heavy white hoodie over her tank top and pulls black sweatpants over her underwear. She sticks her feet into her Adidas slides, grabs an ice bucket, and opens the door. As she opens it, Nathan crouches down and sneaks out the door before she closes it. As she heads down to the ice machine, he sneaks along the sides of the cars, out of view of anyone sitting in a car. He knows the person is most likely watching Sadie anyway and has no idea he's even out of the motel room. He reaches the sedan and crouches as he sneaks up the side of it. He can see a face in the side mirror, which is in fact watching Sadie, and is oblivious to the fact that Nathan is reaching out to the driver-side door handle.

Nathan rips open the door and instinctively pins the driver back against the seat with a forearm to the chest, while simultaneously reaching through the steering wheel with his left hand ripping the keys from the ignition. The middle-aged woman sitting behind the wheel lets out a blood-curdling scream.

"Help! Help! FIRE!"

Nathan looks at her confused and removes his forearm from her chest. He stands back from the car, still holding her car keys. "Relax, you're not on fire. And I'm not gonna hurt you. Who are you?"

"You're supposed to yell fire instead of rape or help. People are more likely to help with a fire than they are with a violent encounter," The woman says sheepishly.

"I see. That's good to know next time I'm being sexually assaulted. So, who are you? And why are you following us?"

"My name is Liz, and I'm Sadie's number one fan!"

CHAPTER 24

"Make Me A Fan"

The woman sits on the fake recliner inside the motel room. She looks nervous; her knees are together, and she's playing with split ends in her pale blonde hair. She's in her late 40s or early 50s. Wearing faded blue jeans with a Growing Cold Podcast T-shirt, she seems too nervous to even look at Sadie or Nathan who are sitting beside each other at the table, looking at her.

"You said your name is Liz?" Sadie asks.

"Y-yea... Liz Arnold." She quietly responds.

"So you're not following us, you're just following Sadie?" Nathan asks.

"I'm not following her. I just wanted to meet her and maybe help her with the case. I've been listening since she first started. I gave you a five-star review, Sadie!" She finally looks up at Sadie with a nervous smile.

Sadie gives her a compassionate smile. "Thank you for that. Why are you following me, though? You could have just met me at one of the podcast conventions? Or, you could have reached out to me on social media. I talk to fans all the time."

"I did all that." She hangs her head. "I met you last year at the Portland True Crime Convention. And I've sent you messages on Facebook. Sometimes, you respond, but most times, you just give me that big blue thumbs up symbol. Sometimes the thumbs up are really large and sometimes they are a normal size. Honestly, it confuses me. Why do you give me the thumbs up symbol?" She tilts her head and looks up at Sadie inquisitively.

"Well, I'm pretty busy, you know, doing the podcast and investigating the stories I tell on the podcast. So, I don't have a lot of time to make small talk online. I want you to know that I read your message and that I appreciate you sending them, but I just don't have the time to have a full-blown conversation. You understand, right?"

Liz nods slowly, playing with the hem of her shirt.

"Do you want to have lunch with us today, Liz?"

The woman perks up with the excitement of a kid who was just informed that they were not going to the dentist, but rather they were heading to Disney World.

"Oh man, that would be great!"

Nathan looks at his watch and then at Sadie.

"I don't think today would be a good day for lunch, Sadie. We gotta get to Portland, remember?"

"Shit, you're right." Sadie looks at her phone and then at Liz. "Liz, what's your number hun?"

She timidly recites her phone number, and Sadie enters it into her phone. Within a few seconds the woman's phone pings, signally she had received a text message.

"I just sent you a text so you have my number. Save it, hun. I'll text you tomorrow morning, and we can grab breakfast together. That way, we can have real conversations like friends. How does that sound?"

"That sounds amazing." She scrambles to grab her phone and looks at the text, almost in awe.

"Great!" She stands and smiles. Nathan stands as well. "Well, we gotta get going now. You're not going to be following us anymore, right? Since we're going to be having breakfast tomorrow."

"No, I promise. No more following. I'm sorry if I made you feel uncomfortable, Sadie. I didn't mean to do that." She stands as well, getting the hint and meekly heading towards the door.

"It's ok Liz. I'll text you tomorrow morning." Sadie follows her out the door and gives her a hug. Liz seems to melt into a puddle before dripping down the sidewalk to her tan four door sedan. Nathan locks the motel room door behind them.

"You think it's a good idea to give her your number and meet up with her?"

"She's harmless. She's probably just lonely and needs a friend. I became that friend because she listens to me every week and feels like she knows me." She gives him that warm smile as she gets into his truck. "Besides, you'll be there with me in case she decides to get all Single White Female on me."

"Great. Sounds fun." He starts the truck and pulls out onto the road heading towards Portland. When they enter the city limits, he texts the Detective that they are in town while stopped at a red light. He tosses the phone onto the bench between him and Sadie and turns to her.

"So you live in Portland, don't you?"

"I do," she responds while looking out the side window.

"You want to stop and get anything while we are in town?"

She instantly shakes her head. "Nah, that's alright. I got enough stuff for another week."

Nathan makes a mental note but doesn't push the envelope anymore at that time. The light turns green, and he continues towards the hotel where Jillian was staying assuming the Detective will still be working there or nearby. Sadie lifts her phone after it makes a robot zapping sound, signaling a message.

"Holy Shit!" She exclaims.

"What? What's wrong?"

"Nothing wrong. We just hit the jackpot! Jillian's Producer just reached out to me. He's willing to help us. Let's see. He says he always liked my podcast and didn't understand why Jillian had such a hatred for me. He has access to all her notes and calendar." She types something on her phone and then waits for a response. Once she does, she continues. "He says she had no meetings set for that night. Earlier in the day, she tried to meet up with Kenny, but he turned her down. Today, she was going to try to talk to Deena at the diner. The day before, she spoke with Johnny, but he was too drunk to be of any use. This is amazing Nathan!"

Nathan's own phone dings and he looks at it. The Detective texted him the address of a coffee shop on the west side of Portland. Insomnia Coffee Company. He exits on Bethany Blvd and turns into the parking lot. Sadie is still reading the messages she's receiving from Jillian's producer outloud.

"He is sending me a link to access her notes. This is so huge, Nate we might be able to crack this thing!" In her excitement, she doesn't even realize that she called him Nate instead of Nathan. But it doesn't bother him this time. Her happiness brings him his own joy. She brings him a feeling that he hasn't felt in years. He lets it go because he's sure that Nellie would be happy that he has someone who likes him enough to call him Nate.

"That's great. I think I see the Detective inside already."

"How can you tell? You know what he looks like?" Sadie looks up from her phone and goes through the broken windshield into the coffee shop.

"No, but I know how Homicide Detectives dress. I've talked enough in my years. Come on, let's introduce ourselves."

They exit the truck and walk up to the coffee shop. The logo is large and black in the middle of a black awning. In place of the O in Insomnia is a view looking down into a mug of coffee. Inside is dimly lit with strands of white holiday lights strung around the place. Sitting at a small counter-high table is a man who appears to be in his late 50's based on his white hair, but his baby face makes him look more like he's in his early 20's. He's wearing a light gray suit with a light blue dress shirt and a shoulder holster. Nathan walks up to the man and extends a hand.

"Detective, I'm Nathan Taylor. This is my partner, Sadie Koop."

The Detective stands and shakes Nathan's hand firmly and professionally with a tired smile. After he reaches his hand over to Sadie, he shakes her hand, not as firm but still professional.

"Nice to meet both of you. Thanks for meeting me here. I've been up since 5am yesterday and could really use a cup of coffee. Or a glass of whiskey, but it's too early to tell which will be more helpful." He chuckles as he sits back down. "Please, have a seat. Can I get either of you a coffee? It's paid for by the city."

"No, thank you, Detective," Nathan is cut off before he can continue.

"Please, call me Paul. So you two were friends with Ms Jones?"

"Alright, Paul." Nathan continues, not used to law enforcement being this friendly. He hasn't experienced a friendly police officer since he was interviewed after his sister went missing. "No, we weren't friends. I only met her once. Sadie here knew her, but they weren't friends."

"We were both podcasters. I guess you could say it's kind of like rivals. She would steal my work and add a bunch of fake shit into it and try to pass it off as fact."

"So you two were enemies?" The Detective pulls out a notepad and starts scribbling as she talks.

"Kind of? Not really? I mean. I didn't want her dead, that's for sure. I just wanted her to get her own stories and be a little more ethical."

"Mhmm." He nods as he writes. "So why did you go to her hotel last night?"

"We wanted to see what kind of information she had regarding the Lisa Fields Murder. That's what we are currently investigating." Nathan tries to decipher the upside scribbles on the notepad. So this is what the suspects felt like when he was interviewing them.

"What time was this?"

"Um. I don't remember. It was before the storm rolled in cuz we got caught in it back in Cedar Point walking the dogs." Sadie checks her phone, hearing another notification ding.

"And she was alive when you left her?"

Sadie doesn't respond. The Detective stops writing on looks from her to Nathan.

"Sadie may have punched Jillian before she left. But I can assure you that while Jillian's pride was hurt and her nose might have been bleeding, she was alive and well."

The Homicide detective nods and jots down a few more notes before closing his pad and stuffing it back into the inner breast pocket of his suit coat.

"Well, I appreciate you talking to me. Do you have any idea who might have wanted to kill her?"

"So that's it? We aren't suspects?" Sadie asks, surprised.

"You never were. The desk clerk recognized you as you two

tried slipping past the front desk. Apparently, he's a fan of your podcast; he was just too nervous to talk to you because you were with Nathan. He also saw you leaving. We checked Ms. Jones's social media and she was active after you two left, so we know she was still alive. Also, the scuffle didn't happen until much later in the early morning of the next day. I spoke with Jim Dalton, the sheriff in Cedar Point, and he verified that he saw your truck at your motel in the morning. So you couldn't have had enough time to go back, kill her, and get back in time for the sheriff to see your truck parked."

Nathan nods, curious as to why the sheriff was driving past the motel early in the morning. Maybe he was just doing a routine loop through the motel to ensure there weren't any kids partying or drug dealing going on.

"Damn, you're a good detective. How long have you been working Homicide?" Sadie swipes open the recorder app on her phone." Do you mind if I record you?"

"I'd prefer it if you didn't. I dont have anything that I can put on record. This is a very fresh and new investigation. I worked Homicide down in Contra Costa county for about 15 years and just transferred up here to begin my retirement parade. Another 5 years and I'm retired and going to open up my own flower shop."

Sadie's mouth drops open. "Wait, did you say flower shop?"

The Detective chuckles. "Yeah. I like flowers. They smell good, they look good, and people always need to buy them for one reason or another. Gardening is very calming, especially after working with dead bodies and murderers all day long.

"Makes sense," Nathan responds, knowing all too much about trying to find Zen in your life. "So, do you have any suspects yet?"

"Nope. It appears that Ms. Jones might have been expecting her killer. She let them in from a side door and walked with them up to the hotel room. We pulled the CCTV footage and saw her welcome the unsub into the hotel." He stops and looks at Sadie. "Unsub means unknown subject."

"No shit." She laughs. "I do true crime podcasts for a living, remember?"

Paul chuckles before sipping his coffee. "Oh yeah, my mistake. I apologize. Anyways, the unsub was wearing a bulky jacket with a hood pulled over their head. They appeared to be bigger than Ms Jones, but that doesn't mean much, considering she was only 5'3. The unsub was wearing a bulky down north face coat with the hood pulled up, black jeans, and white sneakers. Sound like anyone you know?"

"Sounds like half the people in Portland." Sadie leans back in her chair and folds her hands on her flat stomach.

"Well you got my number now, call me if you learn anything." He finishes off his coffee, stands, and buttons his suit coat. He offers his hand one more time to Nathan and Sadie. "It was a pleasure to meet you both."

Nathan and Sadie both shake his hand and then follow him out and get back into Nathan's truck.

"Well, now what?" Sadie asks after she slams her door closed and settles back in her seat.

"Wanna go to church"? Nathan fastens his seatbelt and glances over at her

"Ugh God no. Why would I wanna do that?"

"You really don't have any sins you want to confess?"

"Well, yeah. I have a lifetime of sins that would probably make the Virgin Mary weep like a baby. What does that have to do with anything?"

"I wanna go talk to Father Bill and see if he has anything else he needs to confess." Nathan starts his truck and pulls off onto the road.

CHAPTER 25

"Amen"

Sadie and Nathan climb the cement steps leading up to Father Bill's church. When they reach the top, Nathan tugs the door but finds it locked. He tries the other door and finds it also locked.

"That's weird. I thought churches were supposed to always be open?" Sadie muses.

"They are. Let's check the side door."

They trot back down the stairs and swing around to the side of the church. Near the back end by an alley there is a wooden back door. Nathan tries the handle but finds it too is locked. He gives it a jiggle and sees that it moves quite a bit in his hand. He grips it firmly and twists it as hard as he can. He jams it downward, then back up, and he hears a small snapping sound. He gives the handle another turn and finds it spins freely in his hand. Giving the door a gentle push, it swings open into a stairwell that descends into the basement.

"Well, look at you MacGuyver. Where'd you learn that trick?" Sadie smirked as they began to walk down the stairs.

"What trick? Breaking and Entering? Growing up an angsty teen, I guess."

The basement of the church is a wide open area with folding tables and chairs set up. It's obviously where the church holds functions such as Spaghetti dinners and fundraisers. Off to one side is a counter, and behind it is an industrial kitchen area. They quietly walk through the area with Sadie's Converse squeaking on the tile floor. As they reach the stairwell and go up to the church, they hear the organ begin to play. They walk up and peer inside the main congregation area. The candles are all lit and the lights are dimmed down, but the pews and podiums are empty. Nathan motions his head towards a smaller circular stairwell that leads up into the balcony area where the choir and the organist sit. Nathan leads the way as they quietly make their way towards the balcony. "Amazing Grace" echoes out through the church. As they reach the balcony, they see Father Bill sitting on the organ, his head resting back and his eyes closed as he plays the hymn.

Sadie walks down along the balcony railing as they approach him on the opposite side of the organ. Nathan walks up and waits for the Minister to open his eyes. When Father Bill does open his eyes they are big as saucers. The look on his face was pure shock and surprise. The music abruptly stops and the church is filled with silence until he speaks.

"What in the heavens? What are you doing up here? The church is closed!"

Nathan raises an eyebrow. "I didn't know churches closed, Father. What happens if one of God's children needs to confess something at two in the morning?"

He takes off his wire-rimmed glasses and wipes sweat from his face before tying the stems back behind his ears.

"What can I do for you? I thought I answered all your questions."

"You did Father, and I think your little blessing helped me. But I have some more questions. You got a few minutes to spare?"

Father Bill shifts uncomfortably on the bench; his body hidden behind the church organ. He doesn't bother to stand or move.

"Yes, of course. I have a few minutes before I need to attend to a few things. What can I do for you?"

"What kind of things do you need to attend to, Father?"

"Oh, you know, just church duties. What can I do for you?" He repeats his question again, obviously eager to get this conversation moving and over as quickly as possible.

"When we spoke, I named off a few names. One of them upset you. I want to know which name and why."

"I don't know what you are."

Nathan cuts him off before he can finish.

"Was it Deena?" Nathan asks, watching the Minister's eyes. He doesn't react except with confusion, so Nathan continues.

"Cindy?" Nathan watches closely. Sadie takes a seat on one of the balcony chairs down by the railing. The Minister shakes his head slowly at each name.

"Johnny?" The Minister shakes his head again.

"Kenny?" Father Bill tenses up at the name, his eyes slowly closing.

"How did you know Kenny?" Nathan rests his elbows on top of the organ and leans towards the Minister. He doesn't respond. Instead, he gets up and starts to walk away.

"I need to go, uh, attend, to uh." He tries to shuffle across the rows towards the stairwell. Nathan cuts him off and stands in front of him.

"Kenny Neil. How did you know his father? It doesn't seem like you two would have been friends. Not now, nor back then in high school. So who is he to you?"

"He's no one to me!" The father snaps at Nathan. The first time, he has been anything but meek and timid.

"Who was he to you!" Nathan snaps back, moving closer to him. He tilts his head as he gets up in the Minister's face. "Kenny. Who was Kenny to you?"

"He was.." The Minister looks down, flustered. His face and balding head grew a deep shade of crimson.

"He was what?" Nathan repeats.

"He was..." The minister stammers.

"He was what!" Nathan shouts, his words echoing through the church.

"He was my first love!" The Reverend shouts back! Spit flies from his mouth as his eyes glare at Nathan.

Sadie's mouth drops open as she watches intently. Slowly, she raises her hand up to her chin and closes her own mouth, covering it with her fingers.

"You two were.." Nathan begins to ask.

"Yes." Father Bill responds.

"Lovers?"

"Yes."

"Who knew that you two were gay back then?"

Father Bill sits on a seat and removes his glasses. He pulls a handkerchief from his pocket and wipes his face before blowing his nose

"Oliver was the only one who knew. At first, he seemed weirded out. But then he got really into it. He used to have me tell him stories about what Kenny and I did together. I'm not sure if he got off on it or if he just enjoyed the... the dirtiness of it all."

Nathan glances over at Sadie. She gives him a big smile as she lifts her phone partially into view from behind the backing of a chair. She has her recorder app open, and the seconds are rolling as she records everything. He looks back at the man of the cloth before him, confessing his own sins.

"How did it start? How did someone like Kenny, the big bad bully, the high school jock, begin a gay romance with a nerdy self-proclaimed Warlock back in 1977?"

Father Bill looks off from the balcony down at the statue of Jesus hanging from the cross. He looks lost in thought as he relives everything.

"Kenny used to bully me really bad. I would always try to run from him or hide, but one time... after school. He saw Oliver and me at Gold Lawn Cemetery. He chased us into the woods. Oliver got away; he was a bit older and faster than me. I tripped, and the next thing I knew, Kenny was on top of me. He hit me in the stomach a few times until I stopped struggling, and I just lay there crying. He laughed at me and called me a little sissy. He said I was basically a girl. And since I was a girl, I should. You know.." His eyes never move from the statue of Jesus. "I should do things that girls do."

Nathan doesn't interrupt or force the questioning. He lets him tell his story at his own pace.

"I was a chubby kid, and he tore my shirt off. He started playing with my chest like they were boobs. I was so humiliated. But at the same time, he started to be nice to me. He started telling me I was so fuckin hot. He was kind of being nice to me, and I started to not be as scared."

"What did he do to you that day?" Nathan asks softly.

"He didn't do anything to me. I did something to him. I saw a video that Oliver had shown me of a girl performing oral sex on another man. Oliver loved watching dirty videos like that. So I, since it was the only thing I thought I could do, since I didn't have girl parts. I ... I did that to Kenny." Tears start to stream down the Minister's cheeks. He wipes them with his handkerchief and continues.

"Kenny was never nice to me in public, but he didn't bully me anymore when we were at school. When I saw him, I didn't have to run and hide anymore. He would just ignore me. But then he would catch me alone and tell me to meet him in the woods between the playground and the cemetery, and we would do stuff. You know, fool around. Eventually, we would talk afterward like we were friends. He could be very soft and tender afterward; it was as if I had a girlfriend, or rather, I was his girlfriend. But it was a feeling that I didn't get when I was hanging out with Oliver. It was a deeper connection."

Eventually, he would start bringing me little gifts when we met up. He gave me a foul ball he caught at the Mariners game. Or some playing cards or something. It was always sports-related. I didn't care about sports at all, but I enjoyed the effort. You know, they say it's the thought that counts. It was so strange to have this boy who tormented me for so long think of me randomly and buy me something. It made me want to do it. Extra... things for him. "

"How long did this go on for?" Nathan asks.

"Oh, maybe about 6 months or so?"

"When did it end?"

The Minister doesn't respond. Instead, he just lets out a sigh and leans back in the seat, crossing his legs at the knees and folding his hands on his lap.

"When did you last spend time with Kenny in the woods, Father?"

"Devil's Night." The Minister finally responds.

"The night Lisa was murdered... It was you in that car.." Sadie quietly says to herself a few rows away at the front of the balcony. Father Bill turns and looks at her.

"Yes, my child. The sheriff had a curfew that night, so we knew we couldn't be walking around the street. We'd definitely get in trouble, and then our little secret would be out. So I told my parents I needed to borrow the car to pick up Oliver and bring him over to work on our robes. I did, eventually, yanno, pick him up and bring him over. That's why my mom said we were there all night working on our robes. She didn't want the sheriff to know that she let me go out when there was a curfew, so she said Oliver and I were there all night. But yes, Kenny and I were down there the night Lisa was killed."

"What did you see that night when you were leaving?" Nathan asks.

"Not much. I saw Johnny sitting on a swing, and Lisa was standing in front of them. She hauled off and slapped him, then turned away from him. Kenny was trying to duck down as we drove past. I saw Johnny rubbing his cheek, and Lisa was crying. That's all I saw."

Nathan looks at Sadie trying to read her expression. She clicks the stop button on her recorder app and slides the phone into her pocket. She stands and walks over and places a hand on his shoulder.

"Thank you for opening up to us Father, it must not have been easy."

"It wasn't, but it was the right thing to do. My relationship with Kenny is what drove me to join the church. I knew it was wrong; it was a sin. I mistook his love for true love, but now I know the only love I truly need is the love of our Lord." He crosses himself and kisses the rosary beads held in his hands.

"If you remember anything, will you give me a call?" Nathan asks.

"Of course." He stands and blesses Sadie in the same way he blessed Nathan last time. "May the Lord bless you and keep me, may his face shine down upon you and protect you all the days."

Sadie smiles, "Thank you Father."

Nathan and Sadie descend the spiral staircase and they hear the church organ begin playing again. As they enter the truck, Sadie looks at Nathan and ponders out loud.

"Seems like Kenny has been grooming kids for a lot longer than we thought."

"Much longer."

"Should we go to the sheriff with this information?"

"Not yet. We need to get more information before we give him anything if we want him to take us seriously."

"So what now?"

"We go back to the Hotel. We got a breakfast date with your biggest fan, remember?"

Sadie laughs. "Oh yeah. Fuck."

CHAPTER 26

"Breakfast of Champions"

The bell above the door at Dee's diner dings as Sadie enters with Nathan holding the door and then following in behind her. They both look tired as if they had not slept at all last night and who could have after what they learned the night before. Nathan is still twisting and churning the information around in the washing machine of his mind, trying to figure out how Willow and Kenny's homosexual teenage relationship plays into the murder of Lisa Fields. Deena smiles at them as they enter.

"Sit where you want, sweeties, I'll be over shortly."

Sadie smiles, "Thanks Deena." Then proceeds to go over to a booth near the windows that look out onto main street. Nathan sits across from her but Sadie quickly gets up and sits on the outside of the bench next to him, blocking him into the booth.

"What are you doing?" Nathan asks with a raised brow. He turns over his coffee cup, signaling he wants a cup. As horrible as the coffee is here, any caffeine is better than no caffeine.

"We are meeting my biggest fan and or a crazy, deranged stalker. She seems nice enough, but I don't want to take chances. I'd rather sit next to you and across from her. Plus, I don't want her to be between me and the exit, yanno, just in case."

"Just in case? In case what?"

"You don't know. She could have a gun, or maybe she's like a 9th-level jiu-jitsu black belt or something and tries to attack me."

Nathan chuckles. "I thought you worked out?"

"I do CrossFit, not mixed martial arts, Dick.." She gives him a playful elbow in the ribs. Deena makes her way over with two glasses of water, two menus, and a mug of coffee. She places the glasses in front of them along with the menus, then pours coffee into Nathan's mug. She looks at Sadie with a smile.

"Well, it looks like you two are getting cozy. Sitting all side by side. Any coffee this morning, hon?"

Sadie blushes slightly, and Nathan smiles as he looks out the windows, watching Main St towards the sheriff's station. Sadie turns her coffee mug over and responds.

"We are meeting a fan of mine. Just setting up the seating arrangement in advance. And sure, I'll take a cup this morning. Thank you!"

Deena pours the thick black coffee into her mug with a smile.

"Ok, well, I'll grab another water and another menu when your guest arrives. Take your time. You know how to get my attention if you need it."

"Just holler?" Sadie asks.

"You betcha!" Deena swishes away from the table towards a young family of four seated over in the corner with her white sneakers squeaking on the tile floor.

"So what are we thinking about the bombshell that Father Billy Boy dropped on us last night?" Sadie takes a sip of the coffee and curls her lips down with a disgusted frown before forcing another sip.

"I mean, besides what we discussed last night? Who knows. Maybe Kenny felt that she saw him and went back and tried to get her to keep her mouth shut. Things went wrong, and he tried

185

making it look like a serial killer. Maybe Father Bill thought the same thing, and then he went back. Maybe neither of them did anything, and it has nothing to do with it." Nathan shrugs and plops a few ice cubes from his water glass into his coffee mug.

"What if Johnny tried to talk Lisa into keeping her mouth shut, and he went too far?"

Nathan sips the coffee, his face staying stoic as usual. "I just don't think Johnny is capable of it. He doesn't seem like the type."

"Maybe his drinking problem isn't from guilt based on breaking up with her, but rather his guilt of killing her."

He nods, mulling that over. As he considers it the bell on the door to the diner dings. He sees Sadie's head shoot to the door with a look of concern only to let out a sigh of relief when it is just the family of four leaving, not the fan entering.

"Why are you so scared? You're the one who invited this woman to breakfast."

"Yeah, I didn't know what else to do. I've had a few scary... Experiences in my time."

"Oh? Spill it. Let's hear." Nathan places his coffee mug on the table and drapes his arm along the back of the booth, turning to face her. She sighs and tucks her hair behind her ears, leaning forward slightly over the table and leaning her head back at the same time.

"So... I was working on this missing persons case. It was a young teenage girl who went missing. Obviously." She seems flustered, trying to get the information out too quickly so she doesn't have to talk about it anymore. "So she was supposed to be dropped off by her boyfriend one night at her house, except it turns out he didn't know she moved. So he claimed he dropped her off at her old house, which was vacant at the time. His phone was off most of the night, and he's got a rap sheet. The only problem is his parents had money and got him a huge lawyer, and he never answered any questions."

"So why does that make you afraid of fans?"

"I'm not afraid of fans; I'm afraid of stalkers. Anyway, there was this guy who was always a big part of the discussion boards and posts. He would go out and look up any information that I asked for. He always talked about how he couldn't wait to meet me. That wasn't really the weird part. So he was middle-aged. Kind of like you but older."

"Hey," Nathan opens his mouth, faking insults.

"I'm kidding. He's in his fifties. So he would send me messages when he was obviously drunk, complaining about his wife and all this stupid shit that I could care less about. That was all just normal everyday shit when you are a semi-popular podcaster, except when I would report that I would have random meetups to put flowers on graves with mourners or do missing-person events to raise awareness. He would get super pissed that I didn't let him know about the events. Like when I am planning on going to a teenage girl's grave to put flowers on with the parents, my first thought is, 'Oh hey, I should let Michael know. He's definitely going to want to attend this.' Especially since I had no fuckin idea who he was!"

She was obviously getting frustrated. Nathan places a hand on her back and lets his nails run slowly up and down her spine. Nathan hasn't learned everything about her since they met, but he did learn that nails up and down her back literally made her melt. He could instantly feel the tension in her muscles relax.

"Oh God, that's heavenly.." She closes her eyes and smiles before continuing. "So where was I. Yeah, I didn't know this dude, and he was acting like a jealous husband. It kept escalating until I put out that I was going to be heading to investigate the vacant house where this girl had reportedly been dropped off. I went there pretty early in the morning since it was August, and it was like 90 degrees out. I had my handheld recorder and was walking around just reporting what I was seeing, making mental notes, recording sound bytes, yanno. The normal podcast shit. I went around to the backyard, and boom!" She slaps her hands together to emphasize the point. "There he is!"

She looks wide-eyed at Nathan. He is still calmly scratching her back, listening intently.

"I tried to talk to him and make nice, but he was really pushy. I kept walking backward, and all that shit I talked about on the podcast went straight out the window. Everyone thinks that they are going to kick Jason Voorhees in the nuts and run away and not get killed until they are scared. Then you are literally liquid fucking jello stuck to the floor without a thought in your head. He tried attacking me, and I screamed. Thank God for the landscapers working a few houses down. They heard me over the sounds of the lawnmowers and came running. He had ripped half my shirt off by the time they tackled him. They beat the ever living shit out of him, and he deserved every goddamn bruise."

Nathan lets her sit for a minute, allowing her to move past that horrible moment in her life and back towards a better place before he asks.

"How much time did he get?"

"Seven months. Which aint shit. Do you know what is really fucked up? The landscapers who saved me, yanno, what did they get? They got fucking deported because they were here illegally. They literally saved my life, and their reward was to go back to the horrid shithole hell that they were working for pennies to try and escape."

She rubs her face. Nathan gives her shoulder a squeeze.

"That's pretty fucked up, to say the least. I can promise you that this fan is not going to..." He goes to say more when the diner door dings. He turns and sees Liz enter the diner with a look of bewilderment on her face. Her wide eyes darted side to side, looking for Sadie. When she spots her and Nathan, she hops slightly into the air, and her hands come up to her chest in excitement. She scurries over to them and slides into the booth across from them.

"Oh, my fuckin God. I'm sitting across from Sadie fuckin Koop. The world's greatest podcaster!"

Sadie fakes a big, warm smile, trying her best to tuck down her worries.

"I don't know about all that." She laughs uncomfortably. "Maybe words most okayish podcaster."

"Oh my God, shut up." She swipes her hand across the air to dismiss her statement. "The amount of details you put into your episodes, how you write and edit everything yourself, you are literally a one-woman show! You are like the best. Other people have teams of editors and producers who are part of a network that advertises for them. Nope, not Sadie Koop!"

Sadie finally smiles for real this time.

"Well, I'll do my best. I appreciate the kind words and I appreciate you listening. How did you stumble upon my podcast?"

"Well, I tried every other true crime podcast I could find. They are all the same. Two people, usually friends, talking. Sometimes, it's girls and wine, or men in garages, or husband and wife. They try to make some sort of pun with their names or make it rhyme with crime. Like True Crime out of Time or Get drunk on wine and true crime. They're laughing during the episodes, and it's like." She tosses her head back in exasperation. "Oh my god, guys, this shit is serious. It's not time to talk about the movie you just watched or some stupid shit your cat just did while you were recording. I don't want jokes during my murder podcast. I want facts. I want to know what I can do to help. I

189

want to feel that the host respects the subject matter!." She slaps her hand down on the table, obviously passionate about what she's saying. Sadie jumps a little. Nathan takes a sip from his coffee before interjecting himself into the conversation.

"So, Liz, are you from around here? Portland, maybe?"

"Oh no. I'm from Kokomo."

"Wait, the fuckin beach boys island?" Sadies mouth drops open. Liz laughs, obviously hearing that before.

"Oh no, it's a shithole in the middle of Indiana, about an hour north of Indianapolis. It's redneck central, more strip clubs than Starbucks, that's for sure."

"So, what brings you out to Cedar Point?"

"Well, I knew Sadie lived in Portland, and from what I read, it seemed like a decent enough town. So I packed up and moved out here and gave it a shot."

"You just randomly packed up and moved halfway across the country?" Nathan laces his fingers together and folds his hand on the table, going into investigator mode.

"Well, I kind of had to move anyway. I could have picked anywhere, really. Portland seemed like the nicest place."

"What seemed nice about it? The constant rain? The coffee?"

Liz laughs uncomfortably, folding a straw wrapper left on the table.

"Well, I read some interviews with Sadie, and she talked about living in Portland. And it seemed really nice."

"What made you move from Kokomo?"

Liz just looks down at the straw wrapper, knotted up in between her fingertips.

"Liz, What made you move from Kokomo?" Nathan repeats the question. She sits there for a few moments, absentmindedly twisting the wrapper and avoiding the question. Finally, Sadie speaks up.

"Hon, you can talk to me. I'm not one to judge. You've heard my podcasts. I'm here for you." She reaches forward and pats the woman's hands. Eventually, Liz looks up with tear-filled eyes.

"Do you remember that episode you did about Dave Hankes?"

Sadie thinks about it for a moment before she snaps her fingers as she remembers.

"Yes! He's that guy who had trapped twelve prostitutes down in his basement. He kept them all chained in a circle. He went years without being outed. Seven of the women died but stayed chained to the other five until they decayed enough that the bones slipped through the neck restraints. The police never released the names of the women. Why do you... Oh.. no.." Sadie's mouth drops open. "No. Don't tell me."

Liz nods slowly.

"Yeah, Hankes lived in Indy. He would sometimes go to Kokomo or Lafayette, or Bloomington to get hookers. I was one of the ones he got."

Nathan and Sadie sat speechless for a while, letting this sink in. Nathan was sure that Sadie no longer feared Liz but rather pitied her and regretted how fearful she was before Liz sat down. Sadie had worked on hundreds of cases during the duration of her podcast, but that episode was so depraved that it left her shaken. David Bryan Hankes was a contractor out of Indianapolis. He lived on a quiet, dead-end street in a nice neighborhood. He was never married and kept odd hours. It was to everyone's surprise when one Sunday morning, while David Hankes was at church, 5 women, chained together by the neck, broke free from the back door and ran for help. A few of the neck restraints still had hair and flesh stuck to them from where the women had decomposed and slithered out. The remaining women were extremely starved and beaten. The heaviest woman, at 48 years old, weighed the same as a healthy seven-year-old girl. They had objective names burned into their bodies. Anything and everything that David could find he inserted into every cavity on the women, and more often than not, made them inflict torture on the woman to their left.

When David Hankes returned home from church he noticed his street was blocked off by a swarm of law enforcement officers, reporters, and onlookers. He didn't try to flee and he didn't try to argue his innocence. He took the coward's way out. He placed a Luger .357 snub nose 5-shot revolver to the roof of his mouth and painted the inside of his 1987 Dodge Daytona red and gray with blood and brains.

Liz opens her blood eyes as tears escape onto her cheeks.

"After that, I decided not to return home to Kokomo. My boyfriend was my pimp who would beat and sell me rather than take me someplace fancy, like Red Lobster. I had no family. No friends. I had just been tortured for almost a year. I had nothing to my name. I ended up getting a laptop at Goodwill and a pair of headphones. I'd go to Starbucks and yanno; they won't kick out homeless people. I'd just look up stuff. One day, I stumbled upon your podcast. It changed my life. I saw that I wasn't the only victim in the world, and I saw there were people like you who cared about people like me. Eventually, the manager at Starbucks took some pity on me and gave me a job. She taught me how to make coffee. I saved up enough and finally transferred out here to Portland."
Sadie takes a long, slow breath, collecting herself. She gives Liz's hand a squeeze.

"There are a lot of people like me who care a lot about people like you. I'm glad you moved here, and I'm glad that you found me. It's probably shitty of me to say anything, but if you ever wanna come on my podcast and talk about what happened to you. Maybe get it off your chest and tell your story. I'd be glad to have you. "

"Oh. My God…" Liz looks at her, jaw practically on the floor. Sadie can't tell if she's happy or mad. Soon enough, the emotion is obvious as Liz starts to bounce up and down her seat, clapping her hands with glee. "I dream almost every night about sitting across a table from you, wearing headphones and talking into those furry microphones. That would be so great Sadie!"

Nathan can't help but smile. His attention shifts as he watches Deena approach with a glass of water and a menu for Liz and that damned pot of coffee.

"Looked like you all were in the middle of something deep, so I figured I'd wait. Judging by the clapping now is as good a time as any. Any coffee, hun?" She holds the mug out to Liz. Liz tilts her head at her.

"I know you."

Deena smiles, a little uneasy. "No, I don't think you do. Unless you've been in here before, and maybe I waited for you? Cuz I don't know you. Now, can I get y'all anything to eat?"

Liz doesn't respond. Sadie just looks at her. Nathan takes the cue and responds to the two of them. "I'll take another cup of coffee and then i think we're good on the bill Deena, Thank you."

"Sure thing. I'll bring it right now. "She pours some coffee into Nathan's mug while side-eyeing Liz. She turns and walks away to ring up the tab. Nathan directs his eyes back to Liz.

"What do you mean you know her?"

"I've seen her. I don't know her by name or anything, but I've seen her before."

"Where? Where did you see her?"

"The other night, when you went to that fancy Hotel in Portland? Well, I was following you two then."

Nathan nods slowly and leans forward slightly, intently listening as Liz continues.

"After you two came out of the Hotel all arm and arm, I figured you two were going straight back to your motel, so I didn't see any use in following you anymore. Especially since you looked kind of sick going in." She sheepishly looks at Sadie, not wanting to insult her. "So I hung out in the hotel room parking lot for a while, just relaxing and people-watching. I ended up falling asleep in my car. I woke up early in the morning when someone next to me slammed their car door. "

"What did you see Liz?"

"I saw that waitress put on a big puffy black North Face coat and meet a bitchy looking woman at the side door of the hotel. By the time I cleared the cobwebs out of my head and thought I was awake enough, I saw her come running out of the hotel. She hopped into her car and drove out of the lot like a bat out of hell."

CHAPTER 27

"A Brick In The Wall."

Neither Nathan nor Sadie says anything else. Within a moment, Deena returns and hands Nathan the check. "Good seeing y'all again. Have you learned anything new about Lisa?"

Sadie stays quiet, and Nathan responds.

"No, we're still investigating. It doesn't seem like much makes sense, and we haven't learned much of anything since we started. It seems like a dead end." He shrugs and puts a twenty-dollar bill on the check. Sadie gets the hint and slides out and Nathan follows suit. "Thanks again for all the help, Deena."

"Sure thing. See ya next time." She smiles and walks out of sight into the back office. Liz looks up at them like a lost and lonely puppy.

"Did I say or do something wrong?"

"Huh?" Sadie asks, confused before it dawns on her. "Oh, no, honey, I'm sorry. We just gotta get back to work. We got a big lead that we gotta chase down. It was so nice to sit down and talk to you. Shoot me a text, and we'll arrange a time to sit down and do your interview. Or we can just have another breakfast date." She gives the poor woman a smile. Liz smiles back as she stands by herself.

"That sounds good. Thank you so much for everything." As she gives Sadie a huge hug, Sadie stiffens at first but quickly lightens up and hugs back. They wave at each other outside the diner as they go their separate ways down Main street. Small snowflakes are now falling onto the sidewalk which is not terribly uncommon in this part of the country in late October. Sadie hooks her arms through Nathan's for warmth more than anything else.

"So Deena was at the hotel the night Jillian was murdered..."

Nathan nods and hooks his arm back against hers.

"If Liz is to be believed, I don't have a big reason to not believe her. Then yes, Deena was the last confirmed person to see Jillian alive."

"What do we do? Go see the sheriff?"

"No," Nathan says quickly. He unlocks the passenger door for Sadie. She climbs inside and rubs her thighs to warm up. Nathan hops behind the steering wheel and starts the engine. "We go see Kenny. School's closed, so I bet we can find him at home, especially since Deena's at work."

"Why the fuck are we gonna go see that pedophile fat fuck?"

"I figured it was a good time to question him about Father Bill and ask him if he knew where his wife was the night Jillian was murdered. He seems to keep a close eye on all his property."

"Hmm Yeah," Sadie says, not paying attention to him anymore. She's engulfed in the contents of her phone. Judging by how much her eyes are darting around, there is much information to take in. Nathan just drives as she reads. As they enter the subdivision where Kenny and Deena live, Sadie finally speaks.

"Pull over here. You gotta hear this shit before we go see Kenny."

"Alright." Nathan pulls off onto the gravel shoulder of the road a few houses from Kenny's and parks the truck.

"So I'm going through Jillian's Producer's notes. Cindy seemed to be feeding her information for much longer than she was talking to us. In one of the emails Cindy sent me, she tried sending me a pic of her and Lisa together when they were 12. No matter how many different ways she sent it to me, I could never open it. Judging by these notes, that photo was fake. A Trojan horse put spyware on my laptop and my phone since I tried opening it on both devices. That fuckin Jillian could read every text, email, every Google search, every damn number I dialed. That's how she was always on the same level as me, if not one step ahead."

"If you weren't before, you should really start doubting Cindy's motivation with all this. Think about how she and Deena both have the same exact story for the night of Lisa's death. The odds of everything we've found are already through the roof. The odds that they were both best friends don't add up." Nathan laments.

"So do you think she has nefarious reasons for helping?" Sadie ponders.

"I think she's a fame junkie now. She wants the notoriety, and she thinks that Jillian can, or could, have helped her. I doubt she even knew Lisa. Same as Oshun. He used her death to write books and develop a career except Cindy isn't talented or smart. She just latches herself on to someone who is." Nathan shrugs.

"Fuckin bitch." Sadie shakes her head. "Whatever, let's talk to Kenny and see if he knows where his wife was." She stops talking as a red hummer roars past them and into Kenny and Deena's driveway. The license plate is a vanity plate that reads 'COACH.'

"Guess Kenny just got home." Nathan watches as the Hummer turns off. He jumps out of the vehicle, opens the trunk, and pulls out a 24-pack of Coors Light. Nathan is surprised to see that young boy from the dugout get out of the passenger side and follow him to the door. Kenny hands the beer case to the boy so he can unlock the door. He holds it open, and the boy enters first with Kenny giving him a slap on his butt as he enters.

"No fuckin way," Sadie says in complete disbelief. "What do we do? Call the sheriff? Or just run in there, guns blazing. Wait, I never even thought to ask. Do you carry a gun??"

Nathan shakes his head slowly, eyes still fixed on the house. He can see the two walk through the front room. Coach Kenny draws the shades to keep out prying eyes. "I have a gun, but I don't carry it like Dirty Harry. I don't think we call the sheriff yet. I say we knock on the door and chat with Mr. Neil."

Nathan gets out and closes his door as quietly as possible. Sadie hops out and slams her door shut. Nathan closes his eyes tightly and lets out a sigh. She raises her hands questionably.

"What?"

"Nothing. No sense in sneaking I guess. It's the middle of the day and he's got the shades drawn anyway." As they approach the house they hear Limp Bizkit blasting from inside. Nathan stands off to the side of the front door and rings the bell. They wait a few minutes before Sadie gives it a ring herself. Nathan opens the screen door and knocks on the security door hard and deliberately.

"What do we do if he doesn't answer?" She asks.

"Let's go around back and see what we can see."

"You can just go into people's yards as a P.I.?"

"No, but if he's diddling a young boy, then I'm going to break a few rules to stop him." Nathan starts around the side of the house. There is a large privacy fence surrounding the yard. The music gets louder the closer they get to the backyard. Nathan crouches down as he approaches the fence so that his head doesn't stick out above it; Sadie doesn't need to. They place their hands against the fence and try to peek between the wood cracks to get a glimpse into the backyard.

There is a large shed in the back of the yard with a large wooden deck that leads out into the backyard, complete with a tiki bar, a huge grill and smoker combo, and an oversized hot tub that takes up a large chunk of the deck. Kenny walks out from the back door onto the porch, clad only in a leopard speedo. His bloated stomach, side boobs, and thighs are almost blinding white in contrast to his tan neck, face, arms, and calves. He's wearing a black cowboy hat and has a beer in his hand, which he begins to chug. The beer flows down his chest as he drinks as fast as possible. He tosses the empty can aside and grabs two from the cooler on the deck. Nathan's eyes follow Kenny's over to the back door.

They can barely believe their eyes as they watch. The young boy emerges from the back door with a towel wrapped around his body. He drops it and is clad in a two-piece pink girl bikini swimsuit. Sadie has to forcibly cover her mouth to keep from making a noise. Kenny grabs the boy and pulls him against him for a rough-looking kiss. The prepubescent teen accepts willingly.

Nathan's hands ball into fists. He stands, grabs the top of the fence, pulls himself onto the top, and then over before Sadie can even register.

"Nathan, wait!" she yells as she runs down the privacy fence, looking for a way in. At the back, she finds a gate but struggles to raise her arm to click the opening mechanism. By the time she gets it and runs into the backyard, she sees the teen boy huddled in a ball on the deck, the towel wrapped around him, and he's crying.

Nathan is trapped underneath Kenny. He had tackled the man, but his size and football experience helped him flip over on top of Nathan. Nathan grabs the coach's left wrist and holds it down on Nathan's right side as he arches his hips up and slips his legs in a triangle shape around the man's thick neck. He pulls down on Kenny's head with all his might and squeezes his legs until the man stops fighting and goes limp. He lets go and shoves the half-naked monster off of him.

Nathan gets to his knees and slaps Kenny until he wakes up.

"What? What happened? What the fuck are you doing here?" He begins to ask as he regains consciousness, only to feel his nose break from a direct punch of Nathan's fist.

Nathan straddles the man with his left hand on the man's throat and his knees pinning down his arms. He rains down punch after punch onto the molester's face. Thick, wet thuds blend into the Nu-Metal blasting from inside the house. Nathan can feel the man's teeth loosen and eventually fall into the blood-soaked hole that is his mouth until finally, he feels Sadie's arms around him. Her words were a distant echo in his ears as the world blurred around him. The only thing in focus is Kenny Neil's broken, battered, and bloody face. His eyes were already growing swollen and half closed. His pointy nose was crooked and smeared across his face. Nathan looks down at his blood hand, pretty sure he might have broken a few of his own bones in the process. He slowly stands and looks at Sadie blankly.

"Nathan, it's okay now. Stop. It's over." She places a hand on his cheek, and his muscles lighten up. He looks down at the pedophile lying motionless on the deck. His gurgles and chokes can be heard over the music. Nathan turns him onto his side so he doesn't choke to death.

"You got your phone on you? Call the sheriff."

"Yeah, okay." She reaches into the back pocket of her jeans and pulls out her phone. He dials the number of the sheriff's office and is greeted by an unfamiliar voice. Apparently, Mable got herself fired after all.

"Cedar Point sheriff's office, how may I help you?" The kid says, probably a recruit from the Police Academy interning until he gets hired.

"Yes, my name is Sadie Koop. I'm at 3237 Sawyer Lane. We witnessed the attempted sexual assault of a minor. There was a struggle, and well, an ass whooping... conveniently for you, we have the sick fucking pig subdued."

"3237 Sawyer Lane? Isn't that Coach Neils' house?" The voice from the dispatch asks.

"Yeah. Kenny Neil. He was trying to molest a student from his school. Private Investigator Nathan Taylor got into a struggle with him and subdued him. You might want to send an ambulance because Kenny's not looking too well. Honesty, he might need a dentist, too."

"I'll let the sheriff know that he may need medical assistance. Anything else I can do for you today."

"Nope, we're all good I guess," Sadie says and hangs up her phone before she can slide it back into her pocket.

A gunshot rains out into the air and Sadie instinctively drops to the ground and covers her head. The music stops, and she doesn't hear anything else. She lifts her head and notices that the boy has already run away. Maybe he went inside to get dressed or grabbed his towel and ran as far away as possible. She looks over, and Kenny is still lying on his side, wheezing with each breath. Sitting up, she can see the Coach's large frame blocking Nathan. He lays face down on the ground, blood slowly leaking from underneath him.

Everything seems to slow to a crawl with time melting like molasses. She gets up and begins to run to him, only to stop when she sees a red and gray ponytail in front of her. The person turns to face her, and Sadie is struck in the face with a pistol. She feels her eyebrow split open, and blood runs down into her eye as she drops to her knees. She looks up at Deena Neil, pointing a gun down at her. Deena slams the heel of those white sneakers down on Sadie's phone, smashing it in the process. She sticks the barrel of the pistol against Sadie's cheek, digging it into her skin.

"Get up, you fuckin bitch. You're coming with me!"

CHAPTER 28

"They See Me Rollin."

Deena shoves Sadie face-first against the hood of the car and pushes the barrel of the pistol into the back of her head. The blood stings Sadie's eyes as her hair sticks to her cheek. She tries to blink it away, but her vision is still blurry. The hood of the car is warm against her face. Deena leans down and screams into her ear.

"Put your hands behind your back."

Sadie complies, and Deena slides her belt off and wraps it around Sadies hands, buckling it as tight as she can. She grimaces as she feels the blood slowly being restricted. Deena grabs a handful of her hair and drags her to the passenger side of the car, and forces her onto the floor with a smack on the head from the butt of the pistol. Sadie curls into a ball on the floor and covers her head with her arms as Deena closes the door and quickly makes her way to the driver's side. As soon as the door closes, Sadie can feel the barrel digging into her head again.

"Don't move. Don't talk. Don't look up. Don't do anything but sit there or so help me God, I'll shoot you in your goddamn face!"

Sadie hears the tires squeal off the driveway as the car races onto the road. She doesn't dare lift her head, but she does speak.

"So you killed Jillian to stop her from discovering what your sick fucking husband was up to, didn't you?"

"I said shut the fuck up!" Deena shoves the barrel of the pistol down into the side of Sadies head, causing the car to swerve slightly as she does so. "You wouldn't understand anyway!"

"Help me understand, Deena! How could you let him do that to those children? I mean, God, they were children."

"Of course, you don't get it with your perfect face and your perfect body and your perfect fucking P.I. boyfriend!"

"He's not my..." Sadie starts, but Deena slaps her with the pistol barrel, and she stops with a grimace. Deena continues.

"Try being a middle-aged nobody with graying red hair and a fat middle-aged body. I didn't have any other choice. Kenny was the best thing that could have ever happened to me. He was smart and funny and super attractive and athletic. I felt like I had won the lottery."

She stops for a second, and Sadie hears her sniffle. "Or like Cinderella with a glass slipper."

"When did you find out?" Sadie hesitantly asks, expecting another smack from the gun, but instead there is a long pause followed by a deep sigh.

"It didn't happen overnight. Kenny started letting himself go. He was drinking pretty heavily every night and started getting a big belly. I didn't care because it's not like I'm a supermodel or anything. The pot can't talk shit to the kettle. You know what I mean? Then he got the job coaching and started giving me less attention. At first, he just had trouble in bed, you know... finishing. Then he had trouble getting it started in the first place."

Sadie takes a chance and looks up at Deena from the passenger seat floor. Her face is matted with blood and hair.

"I can't imagine how hard that must have been for you," Sadie says in a sympathetic voice.

"No, you can't.." Deena's voice cracks as she holds back tears. "I thought it was just me, you know. I'm getting fat too as I get old, so I start eating less. I try to do jazzercise. I dyed my hair, but the roots kept returning and he kept losing interest in me. And then, one day, when I was cleaning up his office, I bumped his mouse, and his computer screen turned on. He was watching..." Deena stops, her words caught in her throat.

"Was it men or children?" Sadie asks.

"It was just gay porn. I didn't know what to do. So I just, you know, offered to try things with him."

"Like what?"

"I didn't know which part of the whole, you know, gay part he wanted to be. If he wanted to be the boy or the girl."

"I'm not sure that's really how gay sex works, Deena." Sadie interrupts, only to have Deena slam the brakes momentarily, which bounces her head off the dashboard.

"Shut up! You know what I mean. So, I would try exploring parts of his body that I never would have dreamed of touching with my finger or tongue. Well, let me tell you. He did not want anything to do with that!" Deena laughs softly.

"I tried to offer myself to him in 'manly' ways. I would put my hair up so it looked like I had short hair or I would come to bed in a flannel and sweatpants. I even offered to let him go in my," she whispered the last word, "butt. Nothing worked. He acted aloof like he didn't know what had gotten into me. So, I finally decided to confront him. Oh, he got so mad. He hurt me so badly. He said he was only married to me because he pitied my fat ass and had a reputation to uphold. He would stay married to me and allow me to live the life I was currently living if I kept my mouth shut. Kenny has a lot of money from his parents. I was basically free to do whatever I wanted as long as we pretended to be a happy, normal husband and wife. So I agreed. I thought he would just meet men in the city on weekends. I never could have guessed it would have gotten to this point."

"Why did you cover up the child abuse?"

"Because I was living the perfect life, you stupid bitch!" Deena lashes out at her. "I told you, in the eyes of everyone in town, I had the high school hunk! I had won in life! Plus, with Kenny's money, I could buy what I wanted or go on vacations! But you and your stupid boyfriend had to stick your pretty little noses where they didn't belong and ruin everything!"

"I told you he's not my boyfriend!" Sadie lurches from the floor of the passenger seat and drives her shoulder into the side of Deena, slamming her head into the window. She presses her feet against the passenger door and pushes with all her might. Deena screams in rage and pain, and the car starts to swerve left and right. Sadie hears a horn honk before the entire world starts to spin creating a carousel of pavement and blue sky carousel around the shattering windows of the car. Sadie and Deena both bounce up and down from the seat to the ceiling in a manic dance as the car cartwheels off the highway and through the farmer's field, eventually coming to a stop on its roof. Smoke starts to seep from various parts of the underbelly as Sadie's eyes close to darkness.

CHAPTER 29

"Baby Ruth"

Sadie blinked slowly, her vision sharpening as she took in the sterile surroundings of the hospital room. She could hear a guy down the hall softly wailing and gnashing his teeth. Memories flooded back—the confrontation with Kenny, Nathan laying face down on the ground after being shot, and the terrifying moments when Deena had forced her into the car at gunpoint.

"Sadie," he said, his tone curt. "How are you feeling?"

"Like a toddlers favorite stuffed animal that got dragged behind a car and thrown through a blender. Is Nathan okay?! What happened after the crash?"

He leaned against the door frame with his arms crossed. "I apprehended Deena on scene. En route from your 911 call, I spotted the car flipped over in old Ted's cornfield. Kenny, well, he's on the 2nd floor here getting treatment for his injuries. After he heals up he'll be placed in custody. Seems there's a lot more to his past than anyone knew."

Sadie's brow furrowed. "No shit sheriff Sherlock. You're welcome by the way."

Dalton doesn't respond, instead he rolls that toothpick from one corner of his lips to the other side.

Sadie's IV drop is the only sound for a few moments until she breaks the awkward silence. "And Nathan?"

"Nathan's being treated for his injuries. He took a bullet to the left shoulder. He's lucky for multiple reasons. For one, the damn gun was an old 22. It could barely kill a squirrel. Also, I read in his medical file that he said the wrong thing to the wrong gang of people and got beat up pretty bad in his past. Broken ribs, collar bone, and skull fracture. They had to mend his collarbone back together with a metal plate along with a plate in his head. That metal plate sent the bullet up through his shoulder instead of down through his lung. He's lucky but goddamn stupid. His aggression might complicate things. We'll have to see how this plays out," sheriff Dalton said, his gaze steely.

Suspicion crept into Sadie's mind. "What do you mean by 'complicate things'? He was just trying to stop Kenny. Granted, he got a little carried away, just still! Dude stopped a pedophile."

Dalton shifted, his jaw tightening. "You two shits aren't above the law! There are procedures that must be followed. People see violence, and they start asking questions. You can't just go around assaulting people. Doesn't paint Nathan in the best light, does it? Especially not with you two running around digging up dirt on that Fields girl."

Sadie couldn't shake the feeling that the sheriff was more interested in maintaining the status quo than seeking justice. "Are you saying Nathan's the problem here?"

"I'm saying he's not a saint, and neither are you," he shot back, his voice sharper now. "You've stirred up quite the hornet's nest."

Her anger flared. "Kenny is a monster, sheriff. We were trying to expose him!"

"It doesn't matter what you were trying to do. You've put yourself in danger which also puts others at risk. This isn't just some podcast project. Why don't you go back to Portland, do your Googling and keep those pretty little lips glued to your microphone instead of stirring shit up in my town!" he snapped.

Sadie clenched her teeth and glared at him. "I'm not just some dumb bitch who mumbles into a microphone."

Dalton rolled his eyes. "What makes you so goddamn special? Do you think you're the first to uncover something like this? You want to go catch old Hank making moonshine down by the creek? Maybe Florence accidentally forgot to pay for the toilet paper at the bottom of her cart at the grocery store. Lock her up right?! Open your damn eyes. There are layers to this town, Sadie. Layers you don't understand."

Sadie's suspicion deepened. "You're saying you knew about Kenny and did nothing?"

"Don't put words in my mouth," he said, his voice lowering. "The truth doesn't always set people free. Sometimes, it locks them away, or worse."

As he turned to leave, Sadie felt her insides wrench as anger filled her. Was the sheriff protecting Kenny, or was he simply trying to maintain his reputation? She needed to know more, but right now she only had doubt and a sense of urgency. Her body ached. She could feel the bruises forming all over her skin and the bandage holding together the stitches on her eyebrow.

Once he was gone, Sadie leaned back against her pillows and started to piece together the information, her mind racing. Deena's car flip had been chaotic, but now it felt like a catalyst. She couldn't shake the feeling that there was more to the sheriff's investigation—or lack thereof. The man supposed to uphold justice seemed more invested in keeping the town's secrets buried.

She spent that night in the hospital with her mind constantly replaying the events. After she was released, she went down to the Police Department. After twenty pages of paperwork and all the money left in her bank account, she bailed Nathan out.

As Nathan stepped out from the Police Station, the warm light of the setting sun softened his rugged features, but the tension in his shoulders spoke volumes. His arm was still in a sling, and his eyes looked over affectionately at Sadie. She stood outside leaning against his truck, arms crossed with a triumphant grin lighting up her face. Her long, wavy hair caught the sun, casting a halo around her head which was a stark contrast to the grim atmosphere of the jail.

"Look who finally decided to join the world," she teased, her voice bright, though a hint of worry lingered.

Nathan's expression was a mix of relief and irritation. "What can I say? It was starting to feel like home in there," he replied, trying to mask his gratitude with bravado.

"Yeah, well, you can always hop back into the cell, and I can take that bail money and go take a trip to Vegas or something," she shot back, her eyes sparkling with mischief.

He chuckled, shaking his head. "Thanks for bailing me out."

"Of course," she replied, Tango and Cash pushed their heads out at the sound of Nathan's voice. They both echoed a series of excited barks, drools launching from their mouths as they bounces with excitement. Nathan smiles and gives them both a large hug.

"Hey boys, I missed you. Sadie has been taking good care of you?" He smiles as he pushes them aside to get into the passenger seat. Sadie follows suit and climbs in behind the steering wheel and starts the engine.

"So now what?" She asks, staring off at the Police Station.

"Let's go see your 'inside source.'" Nathan said, his tone turning serious. "I hope they have something useful."

Sadie nodded. "She will. I trust her completely. She has found things for me that no one else could."

As they drove through the small town, Sadie's eyes flitted from familiar sights to the shadows lurking beneath them. The diner and the park all felt like backdrops to a story far darker than she'd ever imagined. Each corner they turned felt more suffocating than the last with the weight of unresolved mysteries pressing down on her.

They stopped at the hotel to drop off the dogs. While they were there Nathan took the chance to shower off the jailhouse stench and change his clothes.

After a short drive out of town, they arrived at a greenish house. The peeling paint and overgrown lawn gave it an air of neglect, but Sadie felt a flicker of hope. This was where truths often lay hidden.

Sadie parked and turned to Nathan. "You ready"

"Let's do this." he replied, glancing around to ensure they weren't followed.

They approached the door, and Sadie knocked. Moments later, a black woman in her late fifties opened the door, her expression warm and inviting. "Sadie! Come in."

"Hey, Ruth!" Sadie said, stepping inside. Nathan followed, closing the door behind him. The interior was cluttered with books, photographs, and assorted knickknacks. The air was thick with the scent of herbal tea and something sweet baking in the oven.

"Are you okay?" Ruth asked, her gaze flicking between them and their injuries, concern etched on her face.

Sadie took a deep breath and smiled. "Nothing a little bit of R&R can't heal."

Ruth's expression shifted dramatically, her brows knitting

together. "R&R? Girl! When was the last time you took anything close to R&R?"

Sadie chuckles. "Good point. Once we solve this case, I promise I'll go on a long, long vacation. Ruth, this is Nathan, the P.I. I told you about."

Ruth smiles at Nathan. "Oh, honey, you weren't lying when you said he was easy on the eyes. Now, this boy looks like a keeper!"

For the first time since Nathan met Sadie, he saw her blush. He smiled and chuckled sheepishly and nodded his head.

"Well, thank you. It's a pleasure to meet you, ma'am."

"None of that ma'am horse shit. You call me Ruth or get the fuck out of my house!" She let out an infectious laugh. Nathan could tell that Sadie's mount rubbed off on her, or was it the other way around? "I got the information you wanted. You wanna hear about it now or after the zucchini bread is done?"

Sadie looks at Nathan, but before she can speak, he does.

"We aren't in a hurry, we can wait. How do you and Sadie know each other?"

Ruth smiles and holds up a finger, "Sadie can tell you our history. Have a seat at the table. I'm going to grab the tea, and I'll be right back.

They have a seat at the kitchen table as Ruth turns and takes the kettle from the stove. As she sets down the cups and plates, Sadie smiles, her eyes lighting up. "Ruth reached out to me after she discovered my podcast. She was a huge fan and offered some insights into local mysteries."

Ruth looked up, nodding. "Mhmm. I found Sadie's podcast while searching for content on unsolved cases. Her passion for storytelling was infectious. I loved how she tackled tough subjects with such authenticity."

Nathan raised an eyebrow, intrigued. "You're a fan of her work?"

"Absolutely," Ruth replied, a warm smile spreading across her face. "Sadie has this incredible way of bringing forgotten stories to life. I reached out to her, sharing some of my findings on cold cases, particularly the one about Lisa. It felt like we were kindred spirits in this quest for truth."

Sadie chuckled. "It turned into a great friendship. Ruth's like a mentor to me. I greatly rely on her expertise, especially when digging up information."

Nathan nodded thoughtfully. "That's a powerful connection. It's great to have someone with experience on your side, especially dealing with something as serious as murder."

Ruth added, "And it's nice to have someone as passionate as Sadie around. After losing my husband, I needed that spark of energy in my life again. It's a reminder of what matters—seeking justice and keeping these stories alive."

"I'm sorry to hear about your husband." Nathan offers his condolences. "May I ask what happened? If you don't want to talk about it, that's understandable."

"Oh no, it's okay. When I think of Ronnie, I'm flooded with memories that are both beautiful and heartbreaking. He was my everything—my partner, my best friend, and a dedicated homicide detective in Atlanta. Ronnie had an incredible passion for his work; he believed in justice for the victims he served. Every evening, he'd come home and share stories from the precinct; his eyes lighting up as he talked about the complexities of the cases he worked on. I admired him but often felt a nagging worry deep in my gut.

One fateful evening, Ronnie received a tip about a suspect's location related to a string of violent murders. He was determined to follow up on it immediately, even though I begged him to wait for backup. "It's just a lead, Ruth," he said, flashing that reassuring smile. "I'll be fine. I promise."

But I couldn't shake the feeling that something was wrong. Hours later, while I was waiting for him to come home, my anxiety grew unbearable. I was in the kitchen preparing dinner, constantly checking my phone for news. Just as I began to lose hope, the call came from the precinct.

"Ruth, I'm so sorry. Ronnie has been shot. He's at the hospital."

Time froze. I remember screaming and my heart pounding in my chest as I rushed to the hospital. When I arrived, they were still working on him, but deep down, I could feel it—this was the moment my life would change forever. Despite the doctors' best efforts, Ronnie succumbed to his injuries. My world shattered in an instant, and I was left standing in the sterile hospital hallway, numb and lost.

In the months that followed, I wandered through life in a fog of grief. Once a city filled with laughter and love, Atlanta felt like a prison of memories. Every corner held reminders of Ronnie —his laughter echoing in the hallways, the scent of his cologne lingering in the air. I couldn't bear it.

After what felt like an eternity of mourning, I realized I needed a fresh start. I had always dreamed of living somewhere quieter and surrounded by nature, where I could breathe again. After some soul-searching, I decided on Cedar Point.

So, I packed up my life and left behind the ghosts of Atlanta. The move was both liberating and terrifying, but it was what I needed. In Cedar Point, I threw myself into my passion for sleuthing, channeling my grief into something productive. I started investigating cold cases and seeking out stories that had long been forgotten. It felt like a way to honor Ronnie's memory, to continue the work he loved in my own way.

As I immersed myself in research, I began to heal. I found solace in unraveling the mysteries surrounding me. Meeting Sadie was a turning point. Her passion for storytelling reignited my spark, reminding me that hope could flourish even in the darkest times.

Nathan noticed that Sadie held Ruth's hand as she spoke, softly chewing her lower lip. He glanced between them, sensing the depth of their bond. "Well, your husband sounds like he was one hell of a good man, and I wish I could have known him. It also sounds like you two make a good team."

"Thanks," Sadie said, her expression resolute.

Ruth nodded, her determination matching Sadie's. The Oven buzzer went off, and she stood and took out the Zucchini bread from the oven. She flipped it onto the cooling rack and sliced a few pieces for Sadie and Nathan. As she sat down, she asked, "So, are y'all ready to learn what I found?"

"Yes, let's do it." Sadie nods.

"When Lisa was murdered, sheriff Dalton was just a teenager then, but... he was different. He vanished right after."

Sadie leaned forward, her curiosity piqued. "What do you mean, 'vanished'?"

"He was sent to military school," Ruth explained, her voice lowering as if the name alone could conjure dark spirits. "Right after the murder. Four years later, he returned, and everything seemed fine... until another girl went missing. It was like something had changed in him. The town was still reeling, and he was suddenly back—older, more serious, and with a certain darkness about him."

Sadie exchanged a glance with Nathan, both sensing the gravity of Ruth's words. "And after that?" Nathan asked, his voice low.

"Two years later, he joined the police force. His father, George, was the sheriff before him, and when he retired, Jim took

215

over. Since then, there have been multiple disappearances. Girls just vanishing without a trace," Ruth said, her voice trembling slightly as she recounted the grim history.

Sadie felt a chill creep up her spine. "Do you think there's a connection between the murders and the disappearances?"

"I don't know," Ruth admitted, her eyes glistening with the weight of memories long buried. "But it's hard to ignore the pattern. Dalton's always been a bit... off. Like he's hiding something. I've heard whispers, but no one dares to confront him."

Sadie felt a surge of determination. "Thank you, Ruth. You've never let me down."

As they left Ruth's house, the sun dipped lower in the sky, casting long shadows across the yard. The heaviness of their conversation lingered in the air, but now there was a fire inside both Sadie and Nathan. They were on the cusp of something big —something that could shake the foundations of their town and unveil a web of secrets.

"Dalton's hiding something," Nathan said as they reached the car, his voice steady yet intense. "And we need to figure out how far his secrets go."

"Agreed," Sadie replied, her spirit unyielding. "Let's find a way to connect the dots. If he was involved in the past, maybe he's still pulling strings today."

As they drove away from Ruth's house, Sadie couldn't shake the feeling that the truth was closer than ever, hidden beneath layers of silence and fear.

"Do you think we should go to the Library?" Nathan suggested, his mind already racing ahead. "We could dig up old police reports, anything connected to Lisa and the other missing girls."

"Absolutely," Sadie replied, her enthusiasm rising. "If we can find a connection between Dalton's past and the cases, we might uncover something big."

They decided to head to the local library which was known for its small but thorough archives. As they arrived, the setting sun cast an orange hue over the building, transforming it into a fortress of knowledge. Sadie felt a rush of adrenaline as they stepped inside.

The librarian, an elderly woman with a sharp gaze, looked up from behind the counter. "What can I help you with today?" she asked, her tone wary.

"We need access to old police reports and newspaper articles, specifically about the murders and disappearances in the last few decades," Sadie said, trying to project confidence.

The librarian raised an eyebrow, but she nodded after a moment's hesitation. "We have a dedicated section for local history. Just follow me."

They followed her to a back room filled with dusty shelves and rows of filing cabinets. The air was thick with the scent of aged paper and forgotten stories. Sadie's heart raced as they began to sift through the files, searching for anything that might link the past to the present.

Hours passed, and they combed through articles detailing the shock of Lisa's murder, the community's grief, and the unsettling pattern of disappearances. Nathan noted the eerie coincidences; a web of connections forming in his mind.

"Look at this," Nathan said, pointing to an article dated two years after Lisa's death. "A girl named Hannah went missing under similar circumstances. And there's another one from a few years later. It's like the same story repeating itself."

Sadie leaned over scanning the article. "And Dalton was already on the force by then. What was he doing while all of this was happening? How does this relate to Lisa's murder? Maybe she was the first, and whomever Dalton is covering for learned not to even leave a body for the police to find?"

As they dug deeper, they uncovered a chilling truth: sheriff Dalton's rise to power coincided with the town's increasing list of unsolved disappearances. Each case seemed to lead back to him, casting a dark shadow over his impeccable career.

CHAPTER 30

"I Fought the Law"

Sadie pushed through the library's heavy double doors as the cold autumn air bit against her skin. She shivered as goosebumps lined her arms. Nathan followed closely behind, his jaw tight, his steps purposeful. He looked every bit the man who had lived through too much and seen more than most people could stomach. Sadie glanced over her shoulder at him, her stomach twisting. They'd uncovered a lot of dirt on sheriff Dalton, but the question remained—what would they do with it?

"We can't just sit on this," Sadie said, her breath puffing. She tucked her hands into her jacket pockets. "We have to talk to him. Confront him."

Nathan's eyes flickered with something dark—maybe doubt, maybe fear. His voice was steady, but there was an edge to it. "You think he's going to admit to anything? The man's been covering his tracks for decades."

"Yeah, but—" Sadie stopped, feeling frustrated. "We can't just following fuckin breadcrumbs, catching pedophiles, and running in circles like a fuckin goat with its head chopped off. He's the common link. We need answers."

Nathan chuckled. "You mean chicken?"

Sadie stopped, obviously flustered. "Chicken? What fuckin chicken?"

"Nevermind." Nathan chuckled and shook his head. They reached Nathan's truck, and he paused with his hand on the door handle, staring at her. The weight of the situation pressed down on them both. "It'll be dangerous," he said after a moment. "He's not just a suspect. He's the sheriff. And if he's been killing all these years—if he killed Lisa—then he's more dangerous than we realize."

Sadie swallowed, her throat dry. The enormity of it hit her again. The man who was supposed to protect this town, to serve justice, could very well be its darkest monster. "We don't have a choice, Nathan," she said quietly. "Let's nail this cocksucker."

Nathan let out a long breath, then nodded. "Alright. But we don't go in blind. We need to be smart about this."

They climbed into the truck and the silence between them was heavy with unspoken fear. Nathan started the engine, and they drove through the small town in silence, noticing the streets almost eerily empty. The night was falling fast, and the fading light cast long shadows across the road.

Sadie stared out the window with her thoughts tangled. She thought of Lisa, and all the other girls who had met a wretched end in this quaint quiet town.

The library research had only confirmed what Ruth had suspected: sheriff Dalton had left town under strange circumstances right after Lisa's murder, spent four years in military school, and came back like nothing had happened. And now, with every year that passed, more women went missing, more bodies were found, and no one seemed to make the connection. No one but them.

"What's our move?" Sadie asked after a long stretch of silence. Her fingers drummed against her knee, restless, anxious.

"We need leverage," Nathan said, his voice low. "Something solid to back up our suspicions."

"You think what Ruth found isn't enough?"

"It's circumstantial at best. People like Dalton—he's been in power too long. He knows how to manipulate, how to make people doubt what they know."

Sadie bit her lip, followed by a wince, forgetting that she had it split open by Deena. "So, what then? We break into his office? Find something incriminating? Maybe he's got kiddie porn like Kenny."

Nathan glanced at her, eyebrow raised. "Break into the police station? You know how crazy that sounds?*

"No, not the police station," she shot back. "We break into his fucking house. That's where he'll keep any souvenirs or whatever."

"Ok, you are nuts." Nathan rubs his face with his hand and slowly shakes head.

"If we're going to do this, we need to commit. Dalton's not going to hand himself over. He's smart. If we confront him with what we have now, he'll either shut us down or worse—disappear us."

Nathan's hand gripped the steering wheel. He was silent for a beat, then he said, "You're right. He's not going to make this easy." He paused, considering. "Let's do it."

Sadie slaps the dashboard with two hands and exclaims, "Fuck yeah! Let's go baby!"

The quiet hum of the truck's engine faded as Nathan killed the ignition. Sheriff Dalton lived in a large house down near the park where Lisa was murdered. It was an old style three story house with a wrap around porch. It was past midnight, and the house was as lifeless as the rest of the small town. No one would suspect anything at this hour—not here, in this quiet little place where nothing was supposed to happen.

Sadie glanced nervously at the house, which seemed large and imposing. The windows were dark, and the driveway was empty. They parked down the road on a small gravel area. Sadie slid out of the truck and tugged her jacket tighter around her, her mind buzzing with questions. What if Dalton came home early? What if someone else was inside?

"Ok, Maybe we shouldn't be doing this," she whispered, even though she knew there was no turning back. "Breaking into the sheriff's house isn't exactly the smartest move."

Nathan opened the truck door and stepped out without hesitation. "You said it yourself, Sadie. We need to stop playing it safe. If we're going to get anything solid on Dalton, this is our best shot."

Sadie took a deep breath and followed him, her stomach tight with nerves. Nathan had been calm the entire time, but she could see the tension in his shoulders and the way his eyes scanned the surroundings. They both knew how dangerous this was. If they were caught, especially by Dalton himself... well, she didn't want to think about that.

Nathan led the way around the side of the house, while trying to stay low in order to avoid any cameras. His years of experience as a Private Investigator showed in the way he moved—calculated and quiet. Sadie stuck close to him, her heart pounding louder than her footsteps.

When they reached the back door, Nathan produced a set of tools from his pocket. Sadie glanced around nervously as she could hear her pulse racing in her ears. Dalton's house wasn't exactly Fort Knox, but this still felt reckless, like they were crossing a line they couldn't come back from.

Nathan worked the lock with careful precision, his eyes focused. It took a little bit longer than normal, with his arm being confined to a sling. Eventually, the click of the door unlocking sent a chill down Sadie's spine.

"We're in," he whispered, pushing the door open just enough for them to slip through.

They walked through the back down into the kitchen, which was dark and eerily silent. The smell of old coffee and disinfectant hung in the air. Sadie hesitated in the doorway, feeling a strange sense of trespassing, but Nathan was already moving, his steps quiet as he headed down a hallway towards a set of stairs leading into the basement.

"Come on," he urged.

Sadie followed, her heartbeat thudding in her chest. Every creak of the floor seemed amplified in the silence, but there was no turning back now. They had to know. They had to see if there was something—anything—that could tie Dalton to Lisa's murder and the string of disappearances that had haunted the town for years.

The basement was dark and Nathan looked for a light. Sadie pulled a string from the ceiling and a faint light flickered on, casting long shadows across the basement. There was a large table with an elaborate model train set constructed on it. Off against the wall was a large wooden desk.

Nathan moved to the desk, rifling through papers with the efficiency of a man used to searching for things hidden in plain sight. Sadie stayed close, her eyes darting to the stairs every few seconds, expecting Dalton to come bursting down at any moment.

"We need something solid," Nathan muttered, pulling open drawers. "Something that proves he's connected to all of this."

Nathan opened a large drawer and felt around inside of it. He removed a few notebooks and a bottle of whiskey, then hit the bottom with a closed first. A false bottom gave way. Inside were old case files, thick and yellowed with age. He flipped through them quickly—missing person reports, unsolved homicides—all young women. Sadie moved in close beside him to see.

"What is it?"

Nathan moved beside to allow her to see, her eyes scanning the files with a grim expression. "Jesus..." he muttered. "They're all here. Every single one."

Sadie pulled out a file, her hands trembling. Lisa's name was on it. Her heart twisted painfully. She opened the folder, her eyes skimming over the details, the familiar notes about Lisa's death. But there were other things—things that hadn't been in the public reports. At the bottom were three words that made the air grow cold. The signature of his Father, sheriff George Dalton.

"He knew," Sadie whispered. "His father knew."

Nathan's face hardened. "This isn't enough, we need more."

Before Sadie could respond , a sound echoed through the basement. Footsteps.

Both Sadie and Nathan froze, their eyes snapping toward the stairs.

Nathan's hand went instinctively to his side, but they had no weapons. Sadie's heart raced, her throat tightening. The footsteps were slow, deliberate, and getting closer.

"Nathan—" she started, but her voice was cut off by the unmistakable creak of the door being pushed open followed by a series of thuds as boots hit the stairs.

Sheriff Dalton stood at the bottom of the stairs, his silhouette dark and imposing against the faint light from the hallway. His gaze swept over the room, landing on them, and the expression on his face sent a chill down Sadie's spine. His eyes were cold and hard, like a predator who had just cornered his prey.

"Well, well," Dalton said, his voice low and dangerous. "What do we have here?"

Sadie's blood ran cold. They were trapped. "What did you do to Lisa?"

Sheriff Dalton smiles and puts his hands on his service belt. "You two just don't know when to leave well enough alone, do ya?"

"No, Jim, we don't. So cut the shit. We know that you killed Lisa, and we know that you killed all these girls!" Nathan slams a few folders down on the sheriff's desk. "So just tell us what the fuck happened?"

"Oh, you wanna hear what happened, huh?" He rolled the toothpick in the corner of his mouth and drew his service pistol, motioning them away from the desk as he moved and sat on the big leather chair behind his desk. "I'll tell ya what happened."

CHAPTER 31

"The Night He Came Home"

October 30th, 1977. The sky over Cedar Point was a fading bruise of purples and grays, the last traces of daylight slipping beneath the horizon. The wind whispered through the trees, their barren branches clawing at the sky like skeletal fingers. The air was sharp, the kind of cold that gnawed at your skin, but Lisa barely noticed. She was too focused on what was ahead, the small playground just beyond the trees, where Johnny had asked her to meet.

She could see the swings swaying lightly in the breeze, their chains creaking softly, and the old metal slide looming like a forgotten relic of her childhood. She and Johnny had spent so many afternoons here, talking about everything and nothing, their laughter echoing through the park. It had been their place. But tonight, something felt wrong. Her stomach twisted in knots, and the hairs on the back of her neck stood up.

It was probably the curfew. Every year on Devil's Night, kids ran amok across Cedar Point. The sheriff had set a strict 9 p.m. curfew for Halloween weekend, a decision no one questioned. Cedar Point was the kind of town where you followed the rules and you didn't ask too many questions.

Lisa glanced at her watch. 8:15. She had time, but the pressure of the curfew hung over her like a ticking clock, adding weight to her already anxious heart. She pulled her jacket tighter around her body as she stepped into the playground.

Johnny was already there sitting on one of the swings with his head down and his hands buried deep in his jacket pockets. He looked different—distant, as if he was somewhere far away, even though he was right in front of her. His dark hair, which usually fell in playful curls, was mussed, and his whole posture seemed weighed down by something unseen.

Lisa felt her heart skip a beat as she approached him. "Johnny?" she called softly, her breath visible in the cold air.

He didn't respond immediately; he just kept staring at the ground. Finally, he looked up, but there was no warmth in his eyes, no recognition of the girl he had once promised to love forever. The cold in his gaze was worse than the wind biting at her cheeks.

"Hey," he mumbled, his voice low, almost apologetic.

Lisa stopped in front of him, her brows knitting together. Something was very wrong. "What's going on? You sounded weird on the phone."

Johnny shifted on the swing and ran a hand through his hair in a gesture she had seen a thousand times but now seemed unfamiliar and foreign. "We need to talk, Lisa."

Those words sent a jolt of dread through her. Her pulse quickened. "About what?"

He stood up then, towering over her. His hands were shoved into his jacket pockets, and his breath came out in foggy puffs. "About next year. You know I'm leaving, right? I'm going into the service. I already enlisted."

She nodded slowly. She had known for months. Johnny has talked about how much he wanted to leave Cedar Point once he graduated, but she had never let herself think about what that meant for them. For their future.

Johnny's voice dropped, and he looked away, his jaw tightening. "I don't want to do this anymore, Lisa. I don't want to drag it out."

Her throat tightened. "What are you saying?"

"I'm saying... it's over." His words were blunt, cutting through the cold night air like a knife. "I don't want to make things harder when I leave. You'll be here. I'll be gone. It's not fair to you to pretend we're going to make this work when we both know we won't."

Lisa stared at him, disbelief flashing across her face. "Johnny, we have time. You're not leaving until next year. We can make it work—long-distance, something." Her voice cracked, the desperation she had been trying to hold back spilling out. "We've been together for too long. You don't just throw that away. I'll wait for you."

He finally looked at her, and for a moment, she thought she saw something—guilt, maybe pain—but it was quickly replaced by the same cold indifference. "It's better this way," he said flatly. "For both of us."

Lisa felt like the ground was falling out from under her. Her chest tightened, her breath coming in shallow gasps. "So you're just leaving me?" She couldn't stop the tears now, hot streaks down her cold cheeks. "Just like that?"

Before she knew what she was doing her hand reached out and slapped him across the face. Johnny didn't react, nor did he answer. Instead, he took a step back, shoving his hands deeper into his pockets. "I'm sorry," he muttered, but it sounded hollow, rehearsed. "I've got to go."

And just like that, he turned and walked away, his figure disappearing into the shadows of the trees. Lisa watched him go, her tears blurring her vision, her heart breaking with every step he took.

She didn't follow him. She couldn't. Her legs felt like they were made of lead, her chest tight with the weight of his words. She sank down onto the swing he had just vacated, the cold metal digging into her skin as she buried her face in her hands and sobbed.

In the darkness beyond the playground, Jim Dalton watched. He had been watching for a while, hidden just beyond the circle of light cast by the streetlamp. His breath came in shallow, excited bursts as he observed Lisa now alone on the swing, her body trembling with sobs.

This was it.

He had seen her with Johnny before—see the way she smiled at him, the way she touched his arm, and laughed at his jokes. It made Jim's skin crawl. Johnny didn't deserve her. None of those boys did. But Jim had been patient. He had waited for his moment, and now, it had finally come.

His hand slipped into his jacket, fingers closing around the cold, heavy blade of the hunting knife he had stolen from his father's garage. The weight of it felt right like it belonged in his hand.

He stepped forward, careful not to make a sound, as his boots crunched softly on the gravel. Lisa didn't notice him at first, too wrapped up in her own despair. But when he was close enough that she could feel the change in the air, she looked up.

Her tear-streaked face, lit by the dim street lamp, showed confusion first, then recognition. "Jim?" she asked, her voice trembling but not yet scared.

He didn't answer. He just kept walking toward her, his eyes locked on hers. There was something in them—something dark, something unrecognizable.

Lisa stood up slowly, taking a cautious step back. "What are you doing here?"

Still, Jim said nothing. His hand tightened around the knife hidden in his jacket, his pulse quickening with each step.

"Jim, are you okay?" Her voice quivered now, a flicker of fear in her eyes as she backed away, her feet crunching on the gravel path.

Without warning, he lunged.

The knife flashed in the dim light as it left his jacket, a quick, brutal arc that Lisa barely had time to process. Her scream was sharp, but it was cut off as Jim's hand clamped over her mouth, muffling the sound. The blade found its mark, plunging into her chest with a sickening thud.

Lisa gasped, her body jerking as the pain hit her like a freight train. Her wide eyes locked on Jim's, pleading, confused, but he was lost in a frenzy now. His hand was slick with blood as he pulled the knife out and plunged it in again, the hot, sticky warmth soaking through his fingers.

She tried to fight, her hands pushing at him weakly, but her strength was fading fast. Blood poured from the wounds, pooling on the ground beneath her, the dark red almost black in the dim light. Jim's breathing was ragged, his movements erratic as he stabbed her again and again, each strike more savage than the last.

The world around them seemed to shrink. The only sound to be heard was the wet sickening noise of the blade penetrating the soft flesh along with the faint rustle of the wind and Jim's frenzied gasps.

Lisa's struggles grew weaker with her body slumping against him as life drained from her. Her eyes, once full of terror, began to dull, her breath coming in shallow desperate gasps.

And then, it was over.

Lisa's body went limp in his arms, her blood-soaked dress clinging to her skin, her face pale and lifeless. Jim stood over her, his chest heaving, the knife still clutched in his hand. For a moment, he felt a strange sense of calm wash over him as if everything had fallen into place.

But as he stared down at her lifeless form, the reality of what he had done began to sink in. The playground, once filled with innocent memories, was now a crime scene, the blood-soaked ground a silent witness to his violence.

Jim wiped the blade on his jeans, his hands shaking as he shoved it back into his jacket. He took a step back, his breath coming in short, sharp bursts.

The night had swallowed them both.

The playground was deathly silent now save for the faint whisper of the wind through the trees. Lisa's body lay crumpled in the dirt where Jim had left her, the blood still warm as it soaked into the earth. But Jim wasn't finished.

A strange calm had settled over him after the frenzy, a stillness that seemed to hollow him out inside. He felt nothing as he dragged Lisa's lifeless body toward the slide, her blood leaving a slick, dark trail behind them. The metallic taste of the night air filled his lungs as he worked, mechanical, methodical.

He ran his fingers over her blood-soaked dress, tracing the lines of her body, his touch disturbingly tender. The knife was still in his hand as he hovered it above her chest for a moment before pressing the tip against her skin. The power, the control—it surged through him like electricity. He slid the knife down her body removing her clothes and discarded them aside.

He dragged her limp body over and lifted it onto the slide, arranging her almost carefully as her arms flop unnaturally to the sides. The metal was cold beneath her skin. Her eyes still open staring blankly at the stars above, their light dim and distant. Jim stood back, his breath fogging in the night air, as he admired his work.

Something shifted in him as he looked at her. There was no remorse, no regret—only a dark fascination. He stared at her pale mutilated and now naked form glowing in the moonlight. A thought entered his sick, demented head.

A pair of headlights cut through the darkness, flooding the playground in harsh white light just as Jim's body tightened with sexual release, and his head fell back with a long, satisfied moan. After the shivers ended, he opened his eyes and blinked against the sudden brightness. The cruiser pulled to a stop at the edge of the park, and a door creaked open.

"Jim?"

The voice was low, wary, and unmistakable. sheriff George Dalton stepped out of his patrol car, his boots crunching on the gravel as he took in the scene before him. His heart, already heavy with the weariness of a long shift, plummeted when he saw his son standing over the body.

"Jim!" George's voice was harsher now, almost a bark as if he could will away what he was seeing.

But Jim didn't flinch. He pulled up his pants and turned slowly to face his father, his expression blank, devoid of the fear or panic that should have been there. The knife was still in his hand, slick with blood. His eyes, dull and lifeless, locked with George's.

Sheriff Dalton stopped dead in his tracks, his breath catching in his throat as the full horror of the scene settled in. Lisa. He recognized her immediately, her blonde hair matted with blood, her face pale and lifeless as it lay stripped naked and bare against the cold metal of the slide. She had been the girl Johnny dated, the one who had always smiled when she saw him around town.

Now, she was just another body.

For a moment, George couldn't move. His legs felt rooted to the ground as the enormity of what his son had done washed over him. His stomach churned violently and bile rose in his throat. He wanted to scream, to rage, to demand answers, but all he could do was stand there, staring at the grotesque scene before him.

"Jesus Christ..." he whispered, his voice barely audible over the wind.

But Jim said nothing. He simply stood there, his eyes empty and his face a mask of indifference. He held the knife loosely at his side as if it were an ordinary object, not the tool he had just used to end a life. There was no fear, no guilt—nothing.

George's mind raced. This couldn't be happening. Not his son. Not Jim. But there was no denying what lay before him. He took a tentative step forward, his boots crunching on the blood-soaked gravel. "Jim..." His voice wavered. "What the hell have you done?"

Jim blinked as if the question didn't quite register. "She was crying," he said flatly, as though it were the most mundane explanation in the world. "She was alone. So I killed her."

The words were spoken without emotion, without hesitation. George felt his knees threaten to buckle. His son—his own flesh and blood—had just confessed to murder, and not just murder. This was something darker, more twisted. He could see it in the way Jim looked at Lisa's body, the way he hovered over her like a predator who had claimed his prize.

George took a deep breath, his mind was racing through the options. Panic gripped him, but he shoved it down. He was the sheriff. He had dealt with crime scenes before. He knew how to handle this. But this—this was different. This wasn't just another body. This was his son's doing.

If anyone found out, Jim's life would be over. Their family would be destroyed. He couldn't let that happen. Not to his boy. Not to his Jim.

He took another step toward his son, his voice steadying, though his insides churned with revulsion. "Give me the knife, Jim."

Jim stared at him for a long moment, his head was tilted slightly as if he didn't understand the request. But then, slowly, almost reluctantly, he extended the bloodied blade toward his father.

George snatched it from his hand, gripping it so tightly his knuckles turned white. The handle was slick with blood, warm and sticky, and the metallic scent filled his nostrils. He swallowed the bile rising in his throat as he tucked the knife into his jacket pocket.

"Get in the car," George ordered, his voice low and hard.

Jim didn't argue. He moved past his father without a word, his footsteps were slow and deliberate as he made his way to the patrol car. He slid into the passenger seat with his face still blank and emotionless, as if none of this mattered to him at all.

George stood there for a long moment, his heart pounding in his chest. He looked down at Lisa's body, her pale face frozen in death, and the reality of what he was about to do settled over him like a weight he knew he would never escape.

He stared at his son seated in the passenger seat of the cruiser, searching for some sign of emotion, some flicker of remorse, but there was nothing. Just that dead-eyed stare, that same eerie calm that made George's skin crawl.

For a moment, George's vision blurred with rage. The logical reactions like a father's instinct to scream or to shake his son and demand answers play on a loop as if to make sense of this nightmare. But he knew, deep down, that there would be no answers. No explanation would ever make this right.

His heart hammered in his chest, his thoughts continued racing. He had to think. Had to act. Not as a father, but as a sheriff—no, as someone who had to protect his son at all costs.

He could fix this. He had to fix this.

"Stay in the car," George ordered his voice hard. He moved toward the slide, his boots crunched on the gravel beneath him as he approached Lisa's body.

She was so still with her face pale in the dim light and her wide eyes staring blankly at the night sky. Blood had begun pooling beneath her, dripping from the edge of the slide. It was everywhere—on the ground, her clothes and on the cold metal. George's throat tightened. He pushed the emotion down and buried it deep inside. He couldn't afford to feel anything right now. He had a job to do.

He pulled off his jacket with his hands trembling as he used it to wipe down the slide, erasing any traces of Jim's presence. The blood smeared under the fabric, dark and wet, but George scrubbed harder trying to ignore the sickening feeling of the warm sticky mess under his fingers. He wiped down the slide's edges, the handrails, and anywhere Jim might have touched. He wasn't just removing fingerprints—he was removing his son from the scene; erasing him as if he had never been there.

Every trace had to go.

Once the slide was clean, George turned his attention to the ground around it. His sharp eyes scanned the dirt and gravel for anything that could tie Jim to the crime—footprints, a dropped object or anything that could implicate his son. He kicked dirt over the bloodstains to scuff the ground to blur the prints and make it look like it had never been disturbed.

All the while, Lisa's body remained exactly where it was. George knew he couldn't move her. To do so would risk leaving evidence

—hair, prints, something that might connect Jim to her even after she was gone. No, it was better to leave her here as gruesome as that was. Her death would be a mystery, a tragedy even, but not one that would lead back to his boy.

When the area was as clean as it could be, George stepped back, his breath coming in ragged gasps. His jacket was soaked in blood, his hands trembling as he shoved it into the cruiser's trunk, out of sight. He wiped his hands on his pants, but the blood seemed to cling to his skin, a sick reminder of what had just happened.

George climbed into the driver's seat and his hands gripped the wheel tightly as Jim slid into the passenger seat beside him. He glanced at the slide one last time, at Lisa's body lying there, bathed in the pale glow of the streetlamp.

As he started the engine, the reality of what he had done began to sink in. He had just covered up a murder—his son's murder. He had erased every trace of Jim's involvement and wiped away the evidence as if it had never existed. Now, he would have to live with that for the rest of his life.

"Dad," Jim said quietly, breaking the silence. "Are you mad at me?"

George's grip on the steering wheel tightened causing his knuckles to turn white. His throat tightened as he forced out a response, his voice barely a whisper.

"No, Jim," he lied with his chest aching with the weight of the words. "You didn't know any better, but now you do, don't you?"

Jim nodded, staring out the window as the dark shapes of Cedar Point blurred past.

CHAPTER 32

"Dredd."

sheriff Jim Dalton leaned back in his chair, the faint creak of the old leather barely audible over the pounding in Sadie's ears. The basement was dimly lit by a single bulb hanging from the ceiling, casting long, sinister shadows that seemed to dance along the walls. His face was unreadable, but there was a cold satisfaction in his eyes as he finished the last haunting sentence of his story.

"And that's how Lisa Fields died," he said, his voice low and deliberate. "She was alone, she was weak, and she didn't stand a chance."

Sadie's stomach twisted into knots. The room felt like it was closing in around her, the air thickened with the weight of his confession. She knew the sheriff was a prick, and most likely corrupt, but to hear this from his own lips, to hear the way he so casually admitted to murdering a 16-year-old girl all those years ago—it was too much.

Nathan stood beside her, his fists clenched so tightly that his knuckles were white, and his arm pulled from his sling. His eyes were locked on sheriff Dalton, filled with barely controlled fury. Every muscle in his body was tensed, ready to spring.

The sheriff leaned forward slightly, resting his elbows on the desk. His gaze moved between them, assessing, calculating, the pistol dancing between the two of them. "As you started sniffing around Lisa's murder, I thought maybe I'd let you get close enough to understand how things really work around here. Thought you would be smart enough to let sleeping dogs lie. Turns out you're dumber than ya look."

Sadie swallowed hard, trying to steady her breathing. Her heart raced, the full horror of what Dalton had done—and continued to do—crashing down on her. This wasn't just about Lisa. This was about all the other girls. The disappearances. The rumors that had plagued Cedar Point for decades.

"You think you're so clever," Dalton said, his voice almost amused. "Running around town asking questions, stirring up bullshit. Catching the Coach diddling a little boy. Big fucking deal. Then you break into my office like you're some kind of detective, but you're not! You're a goddamn low-budget podcaster. You talk into a goddamn microphone. And you're a low-life Private Investigator who'd rather get drunk and pass out on his porch than participate in reality. What you fail to understand is that this town—this place– it has always been mine. Always."

Sadie forced herself to speak, though her voice trembled with barely contained rage. "How many, sheriff?" She spat that title with venom. "How many girls have you killed since Lisa?"

Dalton's lips curled into a thin smile, and he leaned back in his chair, a chilling calmness in his posture. "You make it sound so dramatic. Like I'm some kind of monster." His eyes darkened. "But those girls... They were weak. They were like Lisa. They were... nothing. And they had to leave this town."

Nathan exploded. "You killed them because you could, you sick bastard!" He took a step forward, but Sadie grabbed his arm, holding him back. They couldn't lose control now. Not yet.

Dalton's smile didn't falter. "You're missing the point. I 'had' to. It was... necessary. Cedar Point—it feeds on weakness. Always has.

My father knew it. His father knew it. The town would rot from the inside if we didn't keep order."

"Order?" Sadie's voice cracked. "You think 'murdering' girls is keeping order?"

Dalton's eyes, sharp and deadly, flicked toward her. "I think surviving is keeping order. I thought I killed Lisa because there was something wrong with me. My daddy set me straight with that Military Academy. They taught me that I had to do what I had to do to survive. And my father taught me that I had to do what I had to do to keep this town together."

Sadie couldn't hold back her disgust. "Your father was just as twisted as you. You've been hiding behind your badge for years, covering up what you've done. Every girl who went missing, every life you destroyed—it's all on you."

Dalton's calm demeanor faltered for a brief moment with a flicker of something—guilt? fear?—crossing his face. But then it was gone, replaced by cold indifference.

"They were just girls," he said softly, his voice devoid of emotion. "Like Lisa. Alone. Weak."

Sadie's anger boiled over. "Lisa wasn't weak! She was a child who trusted this town, who thought it was safe! You butchered her because you're a coward who couldn't handle seeing someone else vulnerable!"

Dalton's eyes narrowed as he tapped his pistol lightly on his desk, "Careful now, girl."

Nathan moved, stepping in front of Sadie, his voice low and threatening. "You can't intimidate us, Dalton. We know the truth now. You're going down for this."

Dalton smirked, but there was a hint of something else behind it—uncertainty. "And what's your plan? Do you think anyone's going to believe you? I *am* the law in Cedar Point."

"Not anymore," Sadie said. "We're not the only ones who know about Lisa. We've talked to people. We've found records. We've connected all the dots. You might have gotten away with this for years, but it's over now. People are going to know what you did."

Dalton's smirk faltered for a second, but then he stood up from behind his desk. He was tall, imposing and the basement suddenly felt even smaller as his shadow loomed over them.

"And what do you think happens now?" he asked quietly, his voice deadly. "You think you can just walk out of here and tell people? You think I'll let you?"

Sadie's breath hitched, but she stood her ground.

"You're not walking out of here," Dalton said softly, stepping closer. His eyes were dark and predatory. "You're going to disappear, just like the rest of them. People will wonder, but they'll forget. Just like they always do."

"It doesn't matter what happens to us because the world already knows that you're a chicken shit little dick douchebag who probably jerks off to Polaroids of his mommy!" Sadie held up her cell phone, which showed that she was currently live-streaming her podcast. It currently had over fifty thousand listeners which was growing rapidly as Jim's eyes focused. His face twisted with rage as he raised his pistol.

Nathan moved fast—faster than Sadie had expected. He lunged at Dalton, catching the sheriff off guard. The two men collided with a thud, crashing into the desk. Papers and objects scattered to the floor, the lamp toppling and casting wild shadows across the room. Nathan knocked the gun from the sheriff's hand and it slid under the desk.

Dalton fought back, throwing a punch that connected with Nathan's jaw sending him stumbling. Sadie's heart pounded as she rushed forward grabbing the first thing her hand could find

—the whiskey bottle that Nathan had pulled from the drawer. Without thinking she swung it at Dalton hitting him squarely on the side of his head.

Dalton grunted in pain, his body recoiling as he clutched the side of his head. Blood trickled down his temple, but the blow hadn't been enough to take him down. He lunged at Sadie with rage blazing in his eyes.

Nathan was there again, wrapping his good arm around the sheriff's neck and trying to choke the life out of him. Dalton slammed Nathan repeatedly back against the cinder block wall. In spite of the pain ripping through his shoulder and the breath that was slammed out of him, Nathan held on with all his strength.

"Sadie, the handcuffs!" Nathan barked, his voice strained.

Sadie scrambled to the desk with her hands shaking as she grabbed the handcuffs Dalton had left there. She rushed over, her heart hammering in her chest, and together, she snapped one cuff on Dalton's wrist before he kneed her in the gut and flipped Nathan over his shoulder.

She landed on the hardwood floor with a sickening thud, the air had been expelled from her lungs and her head began ringing as it bounced off the floor. Her eyes came into focus just fast enough to move out of the way as Nathan was slammed onto the ground by Dalton. She tried to force herself onto her hands and knees only to have her head yanked back by the sheriff, who stuck the barrel of the gun so deep into her throat that she started to gag.

"You nosey fucking bitch couldn't leave well enough alone! I'm gonna have fun with you. After I put a bullet in the head of your stupid boyfriend, I'm going to take you home. I'm not gonna kill you like the others, oh no. I'm gonna keep you as my little toy. I have such... sights... to show you..."

He leaned down and slowly ran his tongue up her cheek and across her forehead. Her stomach turned as she gagged again on the barrel of the gun.

"I'm not her fucking boyfriend, asshole!" Nathan hollered as he grabbed the sheriff's head and pulled down on it just as he brought his knee up into his face. Blood instead exploded from Dalton's nose and mouth as he fell backward. Nathan could feel his teeth break off on top of his kneecap. Before the sheriff could come to Nathan, he flipped him over onto his back, twisted his arm, and connected the two handcuffs together. He finally came to rest with his sore knee resting in the small of the sheriff's back.

Dalton snarled and tried thrashing in their grip, but he was caught. His eyes burned with fury, but there was something else there now—panic... Fear.

"It's over, Jim," Nathan said, his voice ragged. "You're done."

Dalton's breath came in ragged gasps as he glared up at them, his face twisted with rage. He could barely talk with his nose smashed across the side of his face and most of his teeth missing. As he gurgled on blood, he mumbled, "You ink iss is over?" he chuckled. "Iss isn't over. Iss is not over..."

Sadie stared down at him, her chest tight with anger with relief. "No, pussy mouth, you're wrong. This is over."

As the distant sound of sirens grew louder, Sadie felt a wave of exhaustion wash over her. It was over. Finally, after all the lies, all the secrets, all the years of suffering—justice had come for Lisa Fields.

The door burst open upstairs. Deputies announced their presence as they worked to clear the first floor. Nathan hollered up to them.

"Down here, in the basement. We are unarmed!"

The Deputies rushed down the stairs single file and their guns drawn. But when they saw who it was on the ground, handcuffed and bloodied, they froze.

"It's sheriff Dalton," Nathan said grimly. You can place him under arrest for the murders of Lisa Fields and all the girls who disappeared after her."

"We know. We had about three thousand people call in from listening to your livestream." One of the deputies said. He motioned to the other deputies, who lifted the sheriff up and transported him out of the office.

Sadie and Nathan stepped out of the house, onto the porch, and stood side by side, not speaking. The night air was cool on their skin, the stars overhead bright and indifferent. Slowly they turned to face each other and their fingers entwined. Sadie smiles.

"You hungry?"

"I could eat." Nathan smiles back.

CHAPTER 33

"Silver Shamrock"

The off-tune melodies of a karaoke machine hit Sadie and Nathan in the face as they push the doors open out of the cold autumn air and into the warm, dark embrace of Shamrocks Bar and Grill. They glance to their right as they enter. The pool table was pushed aside so that a group of middle-aged women could sway arm and arm howling the words to the song "Girls Just Want to Have Fun." They turned to the left and headed over to the extended, slender bar area to have a seat to watch the entertainment and get the bartender's attention quickly. The bar was mostly empty except for the group of women singing, their middle-aged husbands cheering them on, and a few random couples that could care less about the music.

They had stopped back at the hotel to feed the dogs and give them a potty break. They changed out of their clothes into something more bar-appropriate. Sadie threw on a black hoodie with a death metal logo so complex that Nathan couldn't read it. Underneath, she wore a black tank top, black leggings, and black Converse. Nathan wore blue jeans, a black T-shirt, and a gray work coat.

The flannel-wearing, bearded bartender spotted them sitting at the bar. He finished washing the glass in his hand and headed over to take their order. When he stopped, he looked at Nathan. Sadie thought he was just taken off guard by their injuries until she saw the man's face start to grow red and point at Nathan.

"I told you to stay the hell out of here!"

Nathan holds up his hands in surrender, wincing as he attempts to lift his bad arm.

"Easy, buddy, that was a long long time ago. I paid my fines, served my community service, and have grown greatly since then! I can assure you, there will be no trouble here."

"I don't give a shit about any of that. You destroyed my bar last time you were in here! Your girlfriend can stay, but you have to go!" The bartender throws his dish rag at Nathan who doesn't try to deflect it. It softly lands on the counter in front of him.

"Wait, wait, wait! Hold on now!" Sadie holds her hands up to prevent Nathan and the bartender from going at each other, even though neither man has moved. On the T.V. behind the bar was a special news report announcing the arrest of the sheriff. Sadie jumps up to stand on the foot rail below the bar and points at the screen.

"Hey! That's us! We just brought down a pedophile high school coach and the serial killing sheriff! How are you going to deny us service after we did all that? Especially Nathan. None of this would have been possible without this guy here." She flashes that wide, warm, comforting smile as she shakes Nathan's good shoulder. The bartender turns and looks at the T.V. just as it shows Nathan and Sadie talking to some Deputies outside Dalton's house. The next shot is a photo of Jim Dalton's mugshot. His nose is heavily bandaged and already swollen and black. He is snarling at the camera, showing dark red gums and black holes where teeth used to be. The bartender looks back at them and shrugs in defeat.

"I guess you're right. But I swear to God, if you so much as spill your beer, I'll personally throw your skinny ass out of here! Now, what'll it be?"

Sadie lets out a cheer and claps her hands as she sits. "Alright now! That's what I wanted to hear. Let's start with two shots of Jameson, and I'll take a Vodka and Redbull, no ice."

"Thank you. I promise, best behavior. Although you might want to watch her after that sixth Vodka and Redbull." Nathan smiles and tosses the dish rag back to the bartender. "I'll just have a beer. Whatever dark beer you have on tap is fine with me."

The bartender catches the dishrag before he turns to start fixing Sadie's drink. He pours a long liberal pour of Vodka until almost half of it is full before squeezing the can of Red Bull into the glass. He pours Nathan's beer and sets it in front of him carelessly, which causes the foam to spill onto the bar. He plops down two shot glasses and splashes them full of Jameson before asking, "Anything else?"

"Yes, two menus, please." Sadie sips her drink and lets out a sigh of pleasure. "Ahhhh. That hits the spot."

Nathan lifts the shot glass in a toast.

"Here's to cold cases being closed."

Sadie smiles and holds up her shot glass as well.

"Here's to that. And to questions being answered."

"And to us." He smiles and clicks his shot glass to hers before downing it.

"To us." Her smile flashed back at him before her shot was also down the hatch. "So what was that all about with the bartender?"

Nathan shrugs and smiles, "Well, I came here a decade ago when I first moved into town. I got a little trashed and kind of, well, smashed the place up."

Sadie almost chokes on her drink as she laughs, "No fucking way.

What do you mean by 'smashed the place up'?"

"Well," Nathan takes another mouthful of beer before slowly swallowing, purposely taking his time for dramatic effect. "I got really, really drunk, by myself, and smashed the place up. I forget how it all started, to be honest. That was probably 30,000 hangovers ago. Maybe he cut me off, maybe someone said something to me that set me off. Maybe someone glanced at me, and I took exception to it and started throwing glasses across the room; I threw stools through the bottles behind the bar and into the mirror. I kicked a hole through the wall into the men's bathroom and pissed through it. Um...." He stops and chuckles when he notices Sadie staring at him, mouth wide open in surprise.

"Ho...ly.... Shit, man. You were a fucking wild one, weren't you?" She shakes her head playfully then turns to the makeshift stage and claps her hands as a man finishes singing Elvis Presley's rendition of "My Way." Nathan claps along, then picks up a menu the bartender had dropped off for them. Sadie grabs hers and scans it thoughtfully. "You've been here before, what's good?"

"I don't remember, I was drunk, remember?" He chuckles. The bartender approaches them with a small green pad of paper.

"Do either of you know what you want? Or do you need more time?

She slams the menu closed and nods her head. "A Fuckin bacon cheeseburger and waffle fries."

"Sounds great. I'll have the same with a side of Mayo." Nathan slides the menu to him. "Waffle fries are the best."

"They really are!" Sadie follows suit and slides the menu as well. "And I'll take another drink and another brown beer for the naughty boy next to me."

The bartender places the menus aside before preparing the two beverages.

"So tell me about Tango and Cash! They are such good boys. How long have you had them?"

"About six years now."

"Tell me their story. You obviously trained them well or did you adopt them already trained?"

Nathan finishes his beer. "I didn't adopt them; I rescued them. I don't mean I found a dog being fostered because its original owner got a puppy for Christmas for his kid, and the kid couldn't take care of it, so they gave it up. No, I mean I physically rescued them."

"Rescued them from what? Or rather, from who?"

"Before I moved into the cabin, I lived in a run-down house on the south side of town by all that farmland. I used to get drunk and wander along the rows of cornfields. One night, I must have wandered too far because I came upon a farmhouse. I staggered around and played with the cows for a bit before I went and tried to catch a chicken like I was fucking Rocky or something." He chuckles, takes a sip from his beer, and continues.

"I went into this old barn and was almost knocked over by the smell. It stunk like death and shit, all rolled up into one terrible stink. It was like an old horse stable, but it looked empty. That is until I started looking inside the stalls. There were dead dogs in most of them, or dogs that wouldn't survive the night. When I got to the last two stalls, I looked inside and saw two scrawny Rottweilers. They couldn't have weighed more than 20 lbs each and were too weak to walk."

Sadie covers her mouth with her hand in shock and sadness. He can already see her eyes starting to glisten.

"I carried them out of there but they were feral. They kept trying to bite me, but they were too weak. Those dogs would have eaten me on the spot if they could have eaten me., but just didn't have the fight in them anymore. Both were beaten and starved almost to death. It took months and months of bottle-feeding, then hand-feeding, and slowly teaching them to walk again. It was a long, hard process, but they were finally healthy again after a year. It wasn't tough to train them after I spent a year raising them from death's door. We had gained a bond that some people will never have. I earned their trust so completely that they eagerly awaited my commands. I was their everything, and they were my everything." Nathan looks down, feeling his own eyes start to moisten.

"These last four years with them have been some of the best years of my life. Although I was utterly alone, with no friends or family or hardly any human interaction, I wasn't alone. They are my best friends. They are my family. They love me in a way no human could love me, and I, in turn, love them unconditionally."

Sadie wipes a tear away and laughs to suppress the tears. "Oh my God, that was really heart-wrenching. That was so sad, and yet, at the same time, it was so happy that you saved them, and they saved you. I don't know if I want to cry or drag you into the bathroom and fuck you in the stall!" She laughs and finishes her second drink before holding it up to the bartender to single another. Nathan chuckles and finishes his beer.

"Now, if you could cry while you bang me in a stall, that would be hot."

Sadie laughs with a snort. "That would be hot? Oh my Lord, are you Paris Hilton? What decade is this? And is that what you are into? Chicks crying during sex?"

"Hey now, I didn't say that! I'm just open to ideas. I'm not a prude like you!" He holds up his hands playfully.

"A prude?! I'll show you a prude!" She goes to wrestle with him playfully but pulls out of it as the small crowd starts clapping.

She didn't even realize that a young couple who probably snuck in with fake I.D.s had just finished singing Gangster's Paradise by Coolie. She claps along emphatically. "So what happened to the farmers? Did you call the cops?"

Nathan chuckles, "No, I did not call the cops. Back then, I was still fighting the world and angry with God. After I got the boys home and made sure they would make it, I grabbed my 9mm pistol and loaded the clip. I got all the way back to the farm before I had a moment of better judgment. I left the pistol in the glove box, and I'm damn glad I did. If I had brought it with me, I would still be in jail for murder."

"Well, I'm definitely glad you aren't in jail." She places a warm hand on his forearm.

"I walked right up to the farmhouse door and knocked. An older balding man with a week's worth of facial hair and a giant stomach contained by a wife beater opened the door. He asked me what the hell I wanted. He asked if I was the one messing around his bar. As usual, I snapped. He was pretty strong for an older guy, and I was still pretty young and untrained. He had that farm boy strength you get from a lifetime of throwing bales of hay. We wrestled through his entire house, smashing everything in the process. His wife kept trying to hit me with a broom, but her aim was piss poor because she kept hitting the farmer."

"No way!" Sadie laughs.

"Yes, way. Eventually, I choked him out and turned on her. I didn't hit her or anything, but I pinned her to the wall by her throat. I explained I would return when she least expected it. I told her that she and her dipshit husband were going to sell their remaining animals. That if they ever had another dog or any animals on this farm again, that I would see to it that their bodies would never be found."

"Holy shit, you sounded like Batman when you said that."

"Hey, it worked. A month or so later, I went for a drunken walk through the cornfield and checked out the property. All the stalls and animal pens were empty."

"Good!" She turns to the bar and raises her hand. "Hey bartender! Two more shots over here!"

The door closes just as another song starts up. Nathan glances over and sees Johnny walk into the bar with his hood over his head. Gaze fixed to the floor, he sits at the bar a few stools away from them. He lifts his head to look for the bartender to place an order, and that's when he spots Sadie and Nathan. He doesn't speak.

The bartender makes his way over and nods. "Hey Johnny, the usual?"

Johnny nods slowly and goes to grab his wallet.

"Put it on our tab!" Sadie calls out, quickly lifting her hand. The bartender nods and fixes Johnny a vodka on the rocks. Sadie motions Johnny over. Her voice started to slur a little bit. "Come here, Johnny, come talk."

Johnny slides his drink down two stools and sits beside Sadie. "Thanks for the drink, but what do you want? I already told you everything I know."

"Oh, Johnny, it isn't like that. We already know everything. I think we know something that you don't know." She pokes a finger lightly on his shoulder. Nathan could see that she was starting to get a little drunk, so he placed an arm on her shoulder to draw her back slightly."

"I think what Sadie is trying to say is. Have you not seen that news, Johnny?"

"News? What news? All that is ever on the news is shootings in

Portland, riots in Minnesota, or more lies from the White House. It's all depressing, and I have enough sadness in my life!" Johnny takes a large drink from his glass.

"Sheriff Dalton was arrested for the murder of Lisa," Nathan says solemnly, giving Johnny time to digest what he said. "When Doves Cry" by Prince hums to an end, and the crowd claps again. Neither of the three of them clapped; they just let the words hang in the air.

"How?" Johnny asks.

"Well, it was a big fight! I think Nathan finally got him with the Whiskey bottle." Sadie jokes, obviously drunk by now. Nathan interjects.

"We did some digging. Turns out that after the murder, he got shipped out to Military School. When he came back and joined the police force, we noticed that some of the more low-income women around town had started to disappear. We kind of broke into his house and found evidence. He caught us, and we had to subdue him until law enforcement arrived to arrest him."

Sadie leans back against Nathan and lifts an arm up around his neck as she smiles at Johnny. "Isn't he so procedural and exact? Sexy, I know."

Johnny ignores her, having dealt with many drinks in his life. Hell, he was a drunk himself, so who was he to judge? He looks at Nathan. "Why did he kill Lisa? How did he get away with it all these years?"

"From what we can tell and from what Jim told us, his father covered it up for him. He just couldn't punish his son or give him up. He must have thought that Military School would whip him into shape and sort out his behavior, but all it did was help him hone his skills to fit in. Blend in as a strict, normal individual. Meanwhile, he silently stalked his prey and used his position of authority to wash all evidence down the drain. As far as why he killed Lisa, I think it was just a crime of opportunity. She was alone and vulnerable. Honestly, it would have been anyone that night. He was out hunting, looking for a victim that night. If Lisa had left you sitting alone on the swing, it could have been you who was murdered."

Johnny stares at his glass softly swirling the melting ice cubes around hypnotically.

"So all these years... all these crosses I've nailed myself to... all this guilt and pain I've suffered through..."

"Was unnecessary. It wasn't your fault, Johnny." Sadie momentarily sobers up and interjects. Her face turned serious. "The only one who is to blame is that Daddy's boy bitch faced Dalton. Nothing you did that night was your fault. You weren't wrong to break up with Lisa and try to do what you thought was best. It's been long enough you can stop torturing yourself. I can assure you that Lisa wouldn't want you to wallow. Clean yourself up because it's not too late to start a new life. You can be happy now, John. Be happy."

Johnny tried to take a long, deep breath but it caught in the back of his throat. His hands quickly cover his face as sobs slip out, casually blending into the music. His sobs grow into wails. Sadie rubs her hand up and down his back in a soothing manner. Nathan quietly watched on. After a few moments, he wipes his hands down his face, then runs his shirt sleeve along his eyes to dry any remaining tears. He turns to Sadie and Nathan and smiles.

"Thank you for everything. For finding her killer. For what you just said. For everything."

Sadie just bows her head softly and smiles. "Of course."

Johnny pushes his drink away and throws some cash down on the bar as he stands. "I don't think I'll be finishing that. Don't reckon I need it anymore."

"That a boy Johnny!" Sadie starts clapping, and a few patrons look at her oddly since an older woman is currently singing a sad rendition of some Taylor Swift song. She notices, shrinks down, and laughs at herself. Nathan stands and offers his hand to Johnny.

"Take care of yourself. Your time of penance is finished. If you need anything, anything at all, just give me a call. You still have my card?"

Johnny shook Nathan's hand and nodded. "I agree, it's time to move past the past. I have your card at home. I doubt I will, but if I need something, I'll call you. Thanks again."

Nathan nods. Sadie jumps up and hugs Johnny. "Hang in there, John-boy."

Johnny awkwardly gives a half hug back to Sadie before turning and heading out the door and into the dark of the night.

"You think he'll be ok?" Sadie asks softly.

"Hard to say. Once you get that monkey stuck on your back, it's hard to rip it off. Those claws don't want to let go. Hopefully, he can kick it and move on with his life."

"Agreed." Responds Sadie.

"So where do we go from here?"

"I'm not sure. I'll check out of that shit-bag hotel in the morning and head back to my condo in Portland, I guess. Record an update for the podcast explaining to the listeners what happened. After that, I'll probably do one more episode as a wrap-up and see where the road takes me. Maybe I'll find another case? Who knows? What about you?"

Nathan shrugs. "I'm not sure. The cabin is a complete loss, but the land is still worth money. I'm not sure I even want to be a Private Investigator anymore. Maybe I'll change jobs and try selling cars or something."

"Shut the front door, Nathan! You couldn't water to a guy in the middle of the fuckin Sahara Desert! You're too honest of a person to sell anything. I'm sure there are plenty of P.I. cases in Portland you could work."

Nathan nods in agreement. "True. But there are too many people for my taste. Plus, there isn't a lot of open land in the city where Tango and Cash can run free. I'd have to sleep in my truck or shell out big bucks for a tiny studio apartment. Can you imagine me or my dogs in an apartment?"

Sadie smiles softly, about to offer to let him stay at her condo until they figure things out, only to have her eyes shoot wide open as she hears the Karaoke D.J. announce her name.

"Up next is Sadie and Nathan!" The D.J. starts clapping, signaling the crowd to follow his lead.

"What the fuck did you do?" She slaps his leg. "Did you sign us up? Oh my God, I thought you hated karaoke!"

"I do!" Nathan laughs and stands, offering his hand to her. "But I know a song that I can dedicate to you and one of the things I love most about you."

Sadie takes his hand and gushes as he leads her to the microphone.

"Oh, you're going to sing to me?? About what you like about me? Oh my!"

Nathan smirks as he takes a microphone.

"Yeah, I dedicate this song to one of your best features."

Sadie's facial expression changes from drunken love and aww to realization of the joke. She pokes him in the side with a huge smile as she mouths the world's "You are a punk." The song starts with the most Caucasian-sounding girl with the most recognized Southern California accent.

"Oh.. my... God.. Becky, look at her butt..."

CHAPTER 34

"From the Heart"

Sadie slowly inhales a large breath and holds the air in her lungs before gently letting it out. She wets her lips with her tongue and opens her eyes. She moves the cursor on her computer over to the record icon and clicks on it. The icon turns red as the computer begins to record. She leans in a few inches from the microphone and begins to speak.

"Welcome to the Growing Cold Podcast, I'm your host, Sadie Loop.

When I first started this podcast, I never thought it would have taken the path that it did. I was just looking for a passion project, a fun hobby that maybe could do some good in the world. I started small, and I started local. I initially received a lot of pushback from people, which is understandable. The world has become so jaded that it's hard for some people to understand there are good people left out there with honest motives.

I didn't set out to become rich, famous, or anything like that. I simply wanted to take something I enjoyed, doing research and investigations, and try to develop those skills so that I could tell my children one day that their Mother did something to help people.

I have helped people. I have helped bring names to faces that the world abandoned. I have uncovered clues to help bring closure to decades-old cold cases. I never took credit and I never asked for credit. I just asked questions, looked for answers and reported on what I found. Unlike some people, I never tooted my own horn. I always accepted help and never wanted to be in the spotlight.

Lisa's case was special to me. It hit so close to home in more ways than one. I'm very proud that I was able to help bring down sheriff Dalton and bring justice for Lisa and all the other girls he slaughtered. But I couldn't have done it alone.

Nathan Taylor was a gift from God. I honestly would be dead without him. I owe my life to him, and he'll never know exactly how grateful I am, mostly because he doesn't listen to podcasts, so he'll never hear this."

Sadie laughs, breaking her concentration for a moment.

"But in all seriousness, he didn't have to help me. He could have just stayed on his porch alone, and I could have kept investigating alone. Maybe I could have found more clues by myself. Could I have solved this without him? Absolutely not. I also couldn't have done it without my dear friend, whose name I will take to the grave. She doesn't want her name out there, and I don't blame her. When people know you, the crazies can come out. So, thank you for all your research, my friend; you know who you are.

So, what lessons have I learned working this case?

For one, if you see something say something. If you are a kid and someone is making you feel uncomfortable. If they are saying or doing things that you don't feel are right, or if you see someone doing something suspicious, then tell someone. If the person you tell doesn't believe you or do anything, tell someone else. There are people like Kenny in the world, and they can only be stopped by being exposed. If you are being groomed like he did to those boys, just know that the groomer doesn't love you. That's not what it is. If you are missing love from your parents or lack friends, these perverts might seem like they are the only person in your life who cares for you. That is the furthest thing from the truth. If they cared for you, they wouldn't hurt or take advantage of you.

Also, you must realize that sometimes things are just outside your control. Like Johnny, sometimes, the outcome is inevitable no matter what you do or how you try to prevent things. Someone was going to be murdered that night, and it was not Johnny's fault. It wasn't Lisa's fault. The only person responsible was the coward Jim Dalton. I suppose his father, George Dalton, shares some blame as well.

Who knows what happened in Jim's childhood that brought him to the point of murder. Maybe he had a traumatic brain injury as a young boy. Maybe he was just born evil. George might have missed all the signs leading up to it or just ignored them all. If he was anything like his son, he couldn't let himself believe that there was anything wrong with his boy because that would reflect on him. He couldn't admit that he failed as a father or that his son was a monster.

He figured he could just send him off and let others raise him properly. Let the military teachers turn his psycho son into a normal human. When was the last time the military turned a violent man peaceful? That's not what the military does. It creates war. It turns children into machines.

I'm not bashing the military or the military school that Jim attended. However, I have uncovered some shocking details regarding the school and some of its instructors.

The school was so overcrowded that kids had to sleep on cots in the hallway. Three other military academies across the country have been closed down, and the one here in Oregon was the last one to open. So, already fully booked with 406 kids, they brought another 350 from the other School. Luckily, many of the kids that originally went to the now closed schools did not sign in to go to the Oregon location. They told their parents of the horrors they were enduring, and their parents actually listened.

Unfortunately, the rest of the kids either felt like their parents wouldn't believe them, or they did tell their parents, who refused to believe them. There was psychological abuse, physical abuse, and sexual abuse.

I believe that Jim Dalton thrived there and he probably felt right at home. He rose through the ranks quickly and was accepted by the staff as someone who would snitch on the other students. As he embedded himself with the abusers, he was soon able to inflict punishments on the other kids.

Can you imagine a teenager who had just committed his first murder? His dad is the sheriff, the most trusted person in town. Now he's at a military academy that is corrupted as shit, and he's in a position of authority over all these victimized and outcast kids? It one hundred percent sent him down his murderous path.

This brings me back to the entire nature vs. nurture debate. I do feel that in spite of how evil Jim may have been naturally, if he had just had the right person in his life, if he had the proper direction, he might have been able to adjust. I don't feel that anyone is lost until they are actually lost.

If you feel there is something off about your child, first off, do not blame yourself. Did you fuck up as a parent? Probably. But all parents fuck up. It's part of being a parent. Second, as soon as you notice something about your kid, do something. If you don't feel like you are equipped to handle it, then seek professional help.

I'm not saying dump them off at a Boarding School or Military Academy, but reach out to a therapist. Get them professional mental health help. Every child can be saved if they are given a chance.

I'm not sure where exactly I wanted to go with this episode since

I've kind of wandered all over the place. I just wanted to wrap everything up and get all my feelings out. I don't know where to go from here because I don't have any cases lined up. Honestly, I'm not sure I want to do this any more. I've been doing this for a long time now and I almost just died. I was in a car that did a dozen cartwheels through a farm field. I had guns in my mouth, pistols smashed across my face and serial killer tongues on my face. It's all fucking horrific.

What I'm saying is that I'm not sure if I'll be back with another episode. If I'm not, I want to thank every single person who listened to my podcast. Thank you from the bottom of my heart. It honestly means so much to me anytime someone reaches out and says I'm doing a good job or thanks me for what I've done. That's all I ever wanted: to do something good. Well, I did something good. Mission accomplished.

What now? Maybe I'll get a nursing degree or start selling fake nails or something stupid and kind of shady. Who knows. All I know is that I have a wonderful man asleep in my bed right now and two Rottweilers staring at me wondering why I'm talking to nobody instead of giving them a good long walk.

Anyway, you've been listening to the Growing Cold Podcast. The case is solved, so there's no need to send in your tips. You don't need to leave a review because I'm not sure I'll still be doing this. But as always, thank you for listening."

Sadie clicks the record icon and the recording stops. She moves the cursor to the save button, names the file, and saves it with a sigh. She takes a sip from her cup of coffee and drags the file over to be uploaded to her podcast feed.

Leaning back in her chair with her mug of coffee held between her hands, her eyes gaze out the window. The sun is starting to rise off in the distance over Mount Hood. The view from her 14th-floor condo is spectacular. A condo that she could barely afford before and now feels cramped and small compared to the freedom she felt when she was in Nathan's cabin. However, the condo felt a little more like home, with Nathan snoring from the next room.

Her eyes blink as an idea pops into her head—a memory of something Nathan had told her. Just like any good idea, it slowly begins to grow. Her mind races with thoughts as she feels her stomach start to growl. She turns off her computer monitor, heads to the kitchen and opens the coffee machine to make a second pot.

CHAPTER 35

"Home Sweet Home"

Nathan sits up suddenly in bed gasping for air. The sheets soaked with sweat cling to his nude torso. He's forced awake from a dead sleep by the same nightmare that's haunted him for years now. One that has tortured him almost every single day. It seems that the only way to keep the night terrors away is to drink enough that he passes out outside on the porch of his cabin. But he didn't drink at all last night. He hasn't drank since he and Sadie did karaoke at Shamrocks two days ago. Sadie had finally gotten over her hangover yesterday.

Nathan lets his head drop back onto the pillow and grimaces, forgetting about his arm being secured to a sling. He looks down and sees a little blood seeping through the bandage over his collarbone. He closes his eyes and is surprised by how big and plush the pillow is. The entire bed feels like he's floating on a cloud. He feels weightless underneath the mound of blankets, duvets, and Egyptian cotton sheets.

He looks down at the foot of the bed and sees Tango and Cash both splayed out beside him with their tongues hanging out and snoring. The two of them take up most of the other half of the king-size bed that he's lying in. He glances around the room and takes in the scenery. The dresser is slightly askew with a few drawers half open and a lace bra hanging out of one of them. On top are a few framed photos and a jewelry box. The walls are mostly empty except for a few pieces of art. He scratches Tango's butt since it's closest to him, and then shoves the covers off of him and onto the dogs. They don't even budge, considering how much more comfortable this bed is than the one they are used to sleeping on.

Nathan stands and stretches wearing only a pair of black briefs. He grabs a pair of gray sweatpants from the floor on the side of the bed and slips them on, and heads out of the bedroom. The aroma of coffee and bacon with a small smell of smoke guides him down the hallway to the kitchen. He wonders if the smoke smell is actually there or if it's just ingrained into his psyche; permanently embedded in that moment he ran up to his cabin, fearing that his dogs were trapped inside the flaming structure.

As he enters the kitchen, he finds the source of the smoke. Beside the antique-looking toaster lay two blackened pieces of burnt toast. On the table are two plates, each adorned with scrambled eggs, corn beef hash, and crisp bacon

Sadie is standing by the cabinets beside the stove. Her shoulder-length brown hair is a mess as if she had rolled out of bed and gone straight into the kitchen. She's wearing Nathan's gray long-sleeve Henley, which explains why he only finds sweatpants beside the bed. As she reaches up to grab a couple of coffee mugs from the top shelf, the shirt rides up her athletic form, and her toned cheeks peek out from beneath her pastel pink laced panties. He can see large bruises on her hips and legs from the car accident. She turns and catches his eyes. Even with her bandaged eyebrow, split lip, and bruised face, she still seems perfect to him. She smiles at him, holding up the two coffee mugs.

"Coffee?"

"Sure. Thank you." he returned the smile. He thinks to himself that he could get used to this. It might take a while but something about Sadie makes him feel at home, wherever he is.

"How long have you been up? You didn't have to do all this." Nathan take's a mug and takes a sip before putting the mug back on the table.

"Well, you did save my life so I figured the least I could do was make you breakfast. The last thing I wanted was to be that asshole sheriff's fuck doll until he got fed up and killed me. So yeah, I burnt the toast because my toaster is 300 years old, and it was my last two pieces, so we are all out. Unless you eat the end pieces, in which case you can get the fuck out of my apartment." she gives him a smile.

"Well you bailed me out of jail and you let me crash here for the past few days, so I guess I'll be making you dinner tonight."

He places his hands on her hips and pulls her towards him with her hazel eyes sparkling up into his cold steel eyes. He leans his head down and places a soft kiss on her bottom lip; careful of the split in it. She smiles and rests her cheek against his bare chest.

"Sounds like a good deal to me. "

He kisses the top of her head slowly to let the smell of her hair linger in his nostrils as they hug each other tightly. After a moment, they move to the table to eat. Nathan washes down a strip of bacon with his coffee.

"How'd you sleep?"

"I didn't." She covers her mouth as she chuckles, trying to quickly finish chewing and swallow her mouthful of eggs.

"What? Not at all? How are you even functioning after everything you went through yesterday?"

"Oh, this is actually the second pot of coffee I've brewed." She holds her mug up and then takes a drink. "I had to record the ending of the podcast, and then of course after I posted it I had a bazillion more thoughts which prompted me to record one more episode. This one is a little more from the heart. I posted them both about an hour ago, and they have already received a quarter of a million downloads each. A quarter fuckin million! I bet I'm gonna get the People's Choice Award. No, I fuckin better get that award. I almost died making this podcast."

"I don't know shit about podcasts, but you deserve every award they have."

"Do they have Private Investigator awards? Cuz you deserve one of those!" She laughs at herself, obviously a little sleep-deprived.

"Just being here with you, and Tango and Cash, is enough for me." He smiles at her. She smiles back and then notices the two Rottweilers sitting in the doorway like bookends with drool running down their chest as they beg from a safe distance. She tosses each of them a strip of bacon.

"So I've been thinking.." she trails off, letting the words hang in the air. Nathan takes a sip of coffee and leans back against the back of the chair and waits for her to continue.

"I've been thinking about your sister."

Nathan raises an eyebrow.

"Nellie? Why have you been thinking about her?"

"Ok, this might sound crazy and it probably is, but hear me out."

"Alright? Let's hear it."

"So you said that your sister's murder has never been solved. Well, I was thinking. So.." she takes a sip of coffee and collects her thoughts. "By myself, I never could have solved Lisa's murder. And you, by yourself, if someone else had hired you to solve it, you wouldn't have done it yourself either. But us working together as a team, we were able to solve an almost 50-year-old cold case that the goddamn sheriff committed when he was a teenager and his sheriff asshole daddy covered it up for him! We just solved almost half a dozen murders TOGETHER!"

She really emphasizes that last word, together. She runs her hands up into her hair, then lets it fall back onto her shoulders. She crosses her muscular bar legs and continues.

"I want to record a podcast about your sister and I thought we could work together. We could go back to your home town, Investigate and I could record as we go. Maybe I could meet your parents?" she bats her eyelashes at that last statement with a coy little smile.

Nathan smiles and shakes his head slowly as he looks down at the table, trying to take in everything she just said. It had been over two years since he spoke to his parents and longer than that since he's been back in his hometown. His silence begins to make her nervous.

"I mean, it was just an idea. However, I thought it was a good idea."

"You really wanna go to Minnesota with me? Investigate an unsolved murder in negative 20-degree snow storms? And then you wanna go to the state prison to meet my parents?" he leans back and folds his arms against his chest.

"Fuck, why couldn't you have grown up in California or someplace warm." she quietly mutters to herself as she looks at her now empty mug. She feels like she's crossed a line now and starts to fill with dread and regret. Her eyes glisten as she looks up at him sheepishly.

"Yes, of course, I'll burden the cold and the snow with you. Why are your parents in prison? Did it have anything to do with your sister's murder?"

"They shot Kennedy," he states matter-of-factly.

"Wait, What? Who? Who's Kennedy?"

"The President. You know, JFK."

She doesn't respond; she just stares at him with a look of confusion. He watches her for a moment almost able to hear the gears turning in her head as she processes what he just said. Finally, unable to keep it in anymore, he bursts into laughter.

"I'm fucking with you. My parents still live at home, and I grew up in Arizona, not Minnesota."

"You're such a cock!" she throws her napkin at him and laughs. "Well, thank fuckin God because I am so sick of cold weather! Bring on the desert! I knew you were lying cuz you don't sound like you're from Fargo."

"Fargo is actually North Dakota," he corrected her.

"Same difference." She laughs as she gets up and moves over to him. Sitting sideways across his lap and wrapping her arms loosely around his bare shoulders, careful of the injury.

"So is that a yes, then? Do you want to do a podcast with me and solve your sister's murder?"

"Sure. As long as I don't have to talk."

"That's literally the entire point of a podcast, ya goof! "she rolls her eyes at him in an overdramatic fashion. He smiles and wraps his arms loosely around her waist.

"I suppose so. So when do you want to leave?"

She shifts herself and swings a leg to his side so that she's straddling him. She smiles down into his eyes.

"Maybe in a couple days?"

His hands move down to her bare thighs, his rough hands running up her soft, smooth skin, over her lace underwear, and up her silky sides to her muscular back.

"Couple days sounds good."

She squirms seductively on his lap.

"Think your parents are gonna like me?"

Blood rushes through his body as his fingertips knead onto her back muscles. Her warm body makes him forget all about the horrors that await him back in his hometown.

"They're gonna love you."

The End

———————————

Made in the USA
Monee, IL
09 December 2024

71080750R00156